THE GRAVITY OF SHOOTING STARS

ASH KNIGHT

For anyone who has ever felt lost
and was found.

1

———

Hawken's arm was on fire. The burning quickly spread to her hand until she couldn't feel her fingers. *Only three more flights of stairs to go until I walk into the mouth of death*, she thought. *Thirty-six more stairs.* Yes, the elevator would have been a wise option on a typical day, but there were at least ten other people in line, and if she dropped any of her boxes or bags that would be the end of it. She figured she may as well endure the pain now and get it over with. *Once everything goes numb, it won't hurt anymore, right?*

Once she reached the gunmetal grey door labeled "Four," she peered through the small, square window, her eyes comically magnified in-between glass diamonds of reinforced metal links. She felt as though she was looking out from a prison cell. *Okay*, she thought. *You only get one chance to make a first impression, so slap on your Cheshire cat smile and knock 'em dead.* Even she rolled her eyes at this.

"Eff," she said as she turned the metal handle towards the floor. The box of clothes balancing on her forearms was sliding down against the door. And one-point-six seconds later, everything was sprawled out on the floor and rolling down the echoing metal stairwell. "Son of a motherless goat," she mumbled, her voice muffled by the stack of clothes now smothering her.

"I'm so sorry. I wasn't paying attention and pulled the door open. Here, let me help you." Out of nowhere appeared a hand. One with very warm, large fingers that wrapped themselves around hers and gently pulled her to standing. Hawken looked up and saw a boy grinning at her like he'd never seen a girl before. "I'm really sorry. Here," he said, handing her the stack of clothes. "Let me just grab all of this that rolled down the stairs. My name is Jason. I'm in 520. And you are?" he asked, looking up at her from six stairs down.

"I'm Hawken. I'm in 415. You don't have to worry about that stuff. I can get it."

"What kind of hero would I be if I left a damsel in distress —in distress? Nah. It's the least I can do," he said, smiling as he threw her books back into the overturned box. "I'll follow you with this. Lead the way, Hawken."

She glanced through the window again, then pushed down on the handle and freed the door. Looking both ways, she turned left and headed down the dark hall. There was blue indoor/outdoor carpet with red and green flecks covering the floors and climbing about a foot up the walls. Fluorescent lighting poured down over her head. A group of girls passed by her, headed in the opposite direction, nodding and smiling. They had to walk single file to slip past each other. Each of the girls raised a hand and said, "Hey," to Hawken and Jason. Hawken thought they all looked like they'd been in the ring with Muhammad Ali. *Got to love overhead fluorescent lighting*, she said to herself.

After passing a couple of doors she found one labeled "415." "This is me. Thank you so much. You can just set that down here," she said, trying to smile at Jason, nodding to the floor by the door. She hated awkward moments more than a root canal.

"I can bring it in for you. It's actually pretty heavy. Do you have more? I can help you with the rest. It's no problem. I'm already done unloading and unpacking my stuff." He was grinning at her again and she felt like an idiot.

Jason was nice. *Don't be an idiot, Hawken*, she thought to herself. "Actually, that would be amazing. Let me just throw this stuff in the room and I'll be right back out." She didn't want to meet her new roommate with him grinning maniacally behind her. This whole situation was difficult enough without a third party.

Hawken already felt like she was slowly drowning. She was walking into a situation in which there were too many variables and it was rapidly becoming overwhelming. She spent the last seven hours driving to Southern California University worrying about meeting the person she'd be living with for the next nine months. Her parents couldn't understand why she was so hesitant to live with a roommate and took every opportunity over the summer to consistently drive her crazy asking about it.

"Hawken, do you want to go to a movie with us?" her parents had asked.

"Sure," she responded.

"When you have a roommate, you'll have someone to go to the movies with."

"I hate you," she retorted.

Or:

One time her dad said, "You seem like something is on your mind. Do you want to talk about it?"

"Actually, no."

"You realize, when you have a roommate you will always have someone to talk to, right?"

"Seriously, Dad? Maybe I shouldn't go to college."

And eventually:

"Hey, Hawken. How was your day?"

"When I have a roommate, every day will be a dream."

Or:

"Hawken, can you take out the garbage?"

"When I have a roommate, I'll never have to take out the trash again."

The concept of having a roommate wasn't what was eating away at Hawken. From what she had envisioned, it would probably be nice to have someone to eat meals with and talk to. She had been hoping that her roommate would be someone who valued personal space. Hawken enjoyed being with people in theory, but in the past few years had been hesitant to really open up to anyone. After 'the Incident' the summer after ninth grade, she'd concentrated most on mastering the art of invisibility.

HAWKEN PULLED her key out of her jeans pocket and pushed it in the doorknob, then took a deep breath. The room was empty. Exhale. Everything was so symmetrical she could have believed there was a mirror in the center of the room. Both side walls consisted of a dresser, a bed and a desk. The far wall was three feet high and the rest of the vertical space was windows meeting at the ceiling. Hawken walked in and set her clothes down on the bed, then turned and looked out the window. A wonderful view of the parking lot, she thought. Taking a moment to glance at her room, she noticed that there were a couple of dresses hanging up in her roommate's closet. Weird. The only other proof of a roommate was a small lamp on the desk and an alarm clock.

"Okay if I just set this here?" Jason asked.

She'd already forgotten that he was standing there with a heavy box. "Oh, sorry. Yes. Thank you so much. There are just a couple more suitcases," she said, looking at him wearily. "You really don't have to help me. I can manage," she smiled. In reality, she wasn't sure what she wanted. If he helped her, she would be moved in quicker, but she wasn't sure that she could hold her tears in much longer. She'd already felt the dam crack open when she opened her cell door.

"I'm happy to help. And, it's nice to have a hot friend in the building," he said on his way out to the hall.

And there it was. Just the kind of attention that Hawken didn't want. She was flattered, of course. She just didn't have much experience with boys. Other than the Incident, she had none. She had virtually banned and shunned all boys for the last three years. This was supposed to be the year that she broke that ban. The year that she was finally going to put the Incident behind her and move on. So what was she waiting for? Being nice to Jason wasn't an engagement ring. *I just have to remember what normal feels like,* she thought.

AFTER TWO EXHAUSTING trips from the car to her new room, Jason sat down on her roommate's bed and stretched his legs out. The room was so small his feet were touching Hawken's metal bed frame. She was sitting on her desk chair deciding where she should put her book collection. She had brought over fifty books with her and was now reconsidering. There was no way she could have parted with them.

"I CAN'T BELIEVE you actually still have books. Don't you have a tablet or something to read e-books with? I could help you buy one if you want."

She looked over at Jason and smiled. He seemed to be one of those guys that you wanted on your team. The kind of guy that you could call in an emergency and know that he would drop everything to help you. Maybe it was serendipitous that she literally crashed into him today. He was looking at his phone now and she took a minute to steal a sizing up glance at him. He had long sandy blond hair and brown eyes that were large and round and framed in a sea of freckles. He was long, lean, tan, and she could see part of a tattoo running under the sleeve of his "Kiss Me, I'm Not Irish" t-shirt. He turned his head to look at her and pulled his hand up to his eyes. The sun was shining directly into her window and was making the room glow orange.

"Hey, are you hungry? I was going to find the cafeteria with Alex, my roommate, but I kind of wanted to leave campus to grab something. Our last night before school starts and everything, you know? I'm not sure how much I'll actually be leaving campus after that. What do you think?" He put his hands behind his head, pulling his long hair back and grinning at her again.

Her cheeks flamed pink and ignited.

"Why not? It looks like I don't have a roommate yet anyway. Do you know where anything is? I can use The Oracle for directions."

Jason raised an eyebrow. "The Oracle? You mean, like, the Bible?"

Hawken laughed. "No. I mean, like, Google."

"Oh. Gotcha. Okay, well, what sounds good? I am not picky. Just no rabbit food."

Hawken nodded while looking down at her phone. "Well, there's Taco Bell, McDonald's, Burger King, Chipotle, oh, hey—there's something called Salad Farm. Sounds perfect," she teased.

"Ha ha," he said, smiling back. "Any of those is fine with me. Let's just get out of here for a while before we have so much homework and studying to do that we can't even think about the world of 'off campus.'"

THEY SAT at a booth in the back of McDonald's. Hawken had momentarily forgotten about her anxiety over meeting her roommate, starting school the next day, and basically the last three years of her life. This was the longest conversation that she'd had with anyone that wasn't a blood relative since the Incident. It felt like breathing after holding her breath too long. Like she'd finally come up for air and found land. Not just land, but an entire inhabited continent where no one knew her past. She could start a new life. Wasn't that why she left home for college in the first place? To finally start fresh and begin to really live again. She wanted to have all of the experiences that she'd seen everyone else having. No one was going to know what she'd been through. She felt like she'd finally arrived. *Welcome to the first day of the rest of your life.*

"So, where are you from, Hawken? And how did you get that name?" Jason asked, his mouth full of Big Mac.

She swallowed her french fry and took a sip of her Diet Coke. It was a story she'd memorized over the years, moving around constantly. "Most recently, I'm from Phoenix, Arizona. My dad is in the Air Force and so I've moved around quite a lot. Every three years or so. His family is originally from Scandinavia and he always liked the name Hawk, but surprise, 'It's a girl', so, Hawken it was." She smiled before she knew what she was doing. "What about you? Where are you from?"

Jason picked up a napkin from the half inch stack on the table and wiped his mouth. After crumpling the napkin, he grabbed his Fanta Orange and sat back against the booth. "I am from Sacramento. Lived there my whole life. In the same house, in fact. I decided it was time for something new, so here I am," he said. He took a gulp from the side of his cup and squeezed out of the booth. "Refill. You need?" he asked, pointing to her cup.

"No, I'm good. Thank you," she said, watching him walk away, quickly turning her head back to her food. She was actually enjoying herself, which seemed like such a childish school of thought. But. It had been so long and it felt nice to be out with people again. Jason was friendly, helpful, and extremely cute. She hadn't really noticed before, but he had a dimple on his chin that made her want to reach out and touch it with her thumb. Instead, when he returned to the table, she asked him what his major was.

"I haven't really decided yet. I'm thinking Physical Therapy. It is a lot of science and math, which I'm pretty good at, but it is also a lot of school. We'll see what happens." He took a handful of fries and smashed them together, then took a bite. "What about you?" Hawken watched him chew, and watched his dimple bob up and down.

"Architecture. Lots of math and science, too. Maybe we'll have some classes together," she said, smiling down at her tray.

When they had both finished eating and Jason refilled his drink again, they decided to go back to their dorm and get ready for the Big Day. Jason walked her back to her room, quietly fumbling with his phone and asked her for her number. After adding it to his contact list on his phone he held up a fist, bumped hers and said. "See ya, Hawken. Have a great first day," then turned on his heel and made the trek down the hall to the elevator.

Hawken pulled her key out once again and unlocked her door. The room was completely dark. After feeling around the wall, she finally found the switch and turned the light on. One overhead light. The room seemed even smaller now in the darkened shadows, if that was possible. Letting out a long sigh, she walked over to the bed and lay down. The watch on her wrist said eight thirty-three. Her first class of the day was at ten and was Physics. She tried to ignore the pain in her stomach, like swirls of darkness consuming her. She had promised herself that she wouldn't cry on her first night. What a cliché. First night away from home and she's a disaster. And it wasn't even that she was homesick. She'd love to be homesick. Maybe her insides wouldn't be boiling right now if she were simply homesick. No, she was scared. Scared of the future, scared of who she was going to be. She had spent the last few years stagnant. Waiting. *Waiting for what?* she thought. *For my life to start? Here I am. Almost nineteen. It's started, idiot. Go live it. Just jump. No one cares enough to push you. Just freaking jump already.*

After about fifteen minutes of silently tormenting herself, she stood up and walked over to her desk. Tomorrow she would buy herself a bookcase. Tonight, she would unpack her clothes and go to bed. Alone.

Where the hell was her roommate? Wasn't the whole point of having a roommate so that you wouldn't spend scary nights in new places alone? And to take out the garbage. And to go to movies with. She decided to unpack her iPhone dock first and put it on the shelf above her desk. Blink 182 blasted through the room without even a worry over her neighbors coming over to complain. The last thing she needed was quiet right now.

At ten-fifteen she had changed into her pajamas and stood in line in the bathroom with her basket of toiletries like a little kid waiting for the ice cream truck. There were eighteen rooms on the floor and one bathroom in the center of the two long hallways, complete with three toilet stalls, four sinks and two showers. *How is this ever going to work?* she thought to herself.

Standing in front of the mirror brushing her teeth, she looked over at the petite girl at the sink next to her. It was physically painful not to laugh at this little girl, standing on a pink plastic stool, attempting to pluck her eyebrows in the horrendous bathroom lighting. She looked like a miniature Barbie doll with her blond hair in a high ponytail and pink flannel pajamas. Hawken finished and turned to walk out of the bathroom, crashing her basket into another girls' basket. "Oh, I'm sorry. I keep doing that today," she said.

The girl was smiling, toothbrush in her mouth, hair wrapped up in a towel. "Hey, don't worry about it. I hope it isn't this crowded in here all day every day. This is cray-cray." She pushed past the line and spit in the sink that Barbie was using. Barbie said nothing, but pushed her stool over six inches and continued plucking. Hawken had never felt so superfluous.

She made it back to her room in one piece, plugged in her night light from home and listened to music until she fell asleep, dreaming of locked doors, broken pencils, and faceless people.

2
_____

Sleeping in a strange place always came with its nuances, leaving Hawken waking up disoriented and tired. After seeing every hour pass on the clock all night, the time had come to give in and start the day. At six o'clock, she left her cell for a jog around campus. Feeling insecure and unsure of herself, she ran along Jefferson Blvd in a straight line for twenty minutes, then retraced her steps back home. *Home.*

After sliding out of her running shoes and socks, she slipped on her shower flip-flops and picked up her basket, heading towards the bathroom. Earlier in the morning it seemed like rush hour in the halls. She couldn't remember seeing so many girls in towels and slippers in her life. She thought, *I bet this could be a scene for a porn flick. And I'm living in it.* She would try to remember not to leave her room until after seven if she could help it.

"Looks like we are the lucky ones. The mob scene has died down. I think most girls have eight o'clock classes." The words hung in the air in front of a girl in a hot pink bathrobe, holding out her hand. "I'm Elise." Hawken shook it and introduced herself.

"I'm Hawken. I'm in 415," she said as she parted the shower curtain and walked in. She was not here to make friends. She didn't want friends, did she? She wanted to be able to go to class, study, and not have to deal with the anxiety of girls and their emotions. Making friends was always work. It almost felt as exhausting and time consuming as dating had seemed. Friends always had to know where you were at all times, and who you were with. Like a dog on a leash. It should have been easy by now, what with moving every few years her entire life, but she still got that pit in her stomach around new people. She could feel the stinging in her eyes during the barrage of personal questions that she despised answering. Hawken always got by with one or two people in her life that she ate lunch with at school, and shared homework with. They would trade funny stories about accidentally bumping into their school crush or go to the movies together on Saturday nights, but Hawken was never close enough to any of them to share her feelings. She never shared what happened to her that summer with anyone. Well, none of her 'friends' anyway. Only one person knew that secret and they couldn't tell anyone now anyway.

"WELCOME TO PHYSICS ONE-TWENTY-FIVE. I'm Professor Burke. You'll find syllabi stacked on the ends of each row. Please take one and pass it down," said a plump, red faced man with a small circle of orange hair crowning his head. He was standing behind a wooden podium on a small stage, waving his small hands in a circular motion when he spoke. Hawken feared he might actually take flight at some point during the lecture.

Hawken had been fifteen minutes early to her first class of the day, along with the rest of campus it seemed. After pushing her way through the fray outside to get into the SLH building, relief hit her as she noticed it seemed to be quite empty. When she walked in, clutching the straps of her backpack like it was a parachute, she stepped aside in the lobby to catch her breath. Her heart was pounding out of her chest and she was sweating.

Like the architect she hoped to become, she surveyed the building and noticed a lounge area with couches right inside the door, connected to an open space with tables and chairs set up for studying. The main lecture hall was set beyond and hallways paralleled the room like bookends. She made a mental note that this would probably be a good place to study and do homework.

Hawken walked over to the lecture hall and opened the wooden double doors. She stepped into the back of the auditorium and walked halfway down a flight of stairs lined with brown carpet. The space smelled like aftershave and dust. Turning around she was overwhelmed by the size of the room and the sea of red velvet lined seats. She picked a seat, three in from the aisle, and sat down, closing her eyes. *Okay*, she thought. *First day, first class, first everything.* She was officially a freshman in college now. This was the start of the first semester and, so far, it wasn't as terrible as she had imagined it would be. But, it was still early in the day.

After class dismissed, Hawken had taken a moment to sit and gather her thoughts. She ran over her notes from the lecture and stuffed the syllabus into her folder. As she leaned over to zip her backpack a shadow fell over her.

"Hawken. Hey. I thought that was you." She looked up to see Jason grinning at her. *Was that his default face? A perpetual grin?*

"Jason. Hi. Are you in this class?" she asked, feeling like an idiot. She stood up and stepped back quickly, realizing that she was only inches away from him.

"Oui," he said, pushing his hair out of his face. Leaning back, he turned his head and pointed to a guy with jet black hair cut short against his head. "This," he said, "is my roommate, Alex. Alex, this is Hawken. She lives in our building on the fourth floor."

Alex held out a hand and she shook it before he quickly pulled his back. He looked like he didn't belong and was looking for an exit strategy.

"It's nice to meet you, Alex," she said.

He nodded curtly in response.

"So, where are you headed next? We are on our way to English Lit. I believe it's somewhere across campus so we'd better jet." He looked back at Alex and then said, "It was nice to see you again. I hope you have a good day," then quickly squeezed her shoulder before turning away. She watched them climbing the stairs two at a time from her row before heading out.

Her next class didn't start for an hour, so she pulled out a campus map and sat back down, looking for somewhere to eat. McDonald's was the last thing she'd eaten since the night before with Jason and she was starving. Now over her initial nerves of the day, she could feel her stomach twisting out of hunger instead of anxiety.

The sunlight that warmed her face as she ducked through the double doors and out onto the concrete walkway was radiant. Why were all the buildings on campus so dark? The hallways in her dorm room were something out of a horror movie. She could picture the twins from The Shining standing at the end of the hall every time she crept to the bathroom.

Finding a good cup of coffee was remarkably easy on campus. Everywhere you turned there was a coffee cart or Starbucks. After grabbing a cup, she sat down on a wood and concrete bench, leaning back to stretch her neck so that her face was in the sun. It felt good to be outside with the rays of the sun pouring down on her. Like a cat, she was stretched out, unmoving, listening to the snippets of conversation around her, trying to block them out. After a few minutes, she had no choice but to return to the real world. A muted voice brought her back to reality.

"Hey," the voice said. "Do you mind if I sit here?"

Hawken brought her hand to her forehead in a salute, abating the sun from her eyes. "Of course," she responded, adjusting to a more conversational posture. She looked over at the girl who was untangling her long brown hair from her messenger bag strap.

"I hate my hair. Seriously. Hate it," she grimaced. "I've decided this instant that I'm cutting it all off. Like yours," she said, reaching over to stroke Hawken's hair. Hawken tensed, a statue. The girl drew her hand back to her own head and smiled. "I'm Katherine. With a 'K'. Kat, actually. What's your name and your story, sunshine girl?"

"I'm Hawken. Not much of a story. This is my first day. What about you?" Did everyone have to be so nice and sociable? Maybe she needed to rethink this. What was the worst that could happen if she made a friend?

Kat was leaning in. "I'm a freshman, too, but I started summer quarter, so this is my second semester. It gets easier. More familiar. I pretty much know where all of my classes are this time," she said, a smile forming on her lips. "Don't think me nutty, but I think we are going to be good friends, Hawken." This time she held out her fist for Hawken to bump, which she reluctantly returned.

"What are you studying?" Hawken asked, trying to change the subject. If she was going to have a friend, this girl seemed like a good choice. She was pretty and sweet, and seemed to dress nicely. Kat was definitely more outgoing and outspoken than herself, but maybe that would make a good balance.

"Architecture." She looked at Hawken's expression and read

it wrong. "I know, most girls aren't interested in math and science but that is where I excel."

"No, that is awesome. Architecture is my major, too!" Hawken beamed.

The rest of the morning and afternoon went off without a hitch. Like a Venn diagram, it seemed like Hawken's old life and her new and improved life were going to be compatible in at least a few overlapping areas.

Returning to her building, Hawken was joyful. Not only had she conquered her first day of school, she'd effectively forged a friendship with Kat, who seemed as enthusiastic about Hawken. Today she was winning. Kat had been in her Physics lecture that morning, was also in her Physics lab on Fridays, and her Critical Writing class three days a week.

Reeling from the success of the day, she plugged her key into the round doorknob and turned.

"OMG. You are finally home! I'm Allison. I've been dying to meet you all day," said the Victoria's Secret supermodel in jeans and a sweater set. She cat-walked over and wrapped her two, pink cashmere draped arms around Hawken. "We are going to have the best year ever. I'm sorry I wasn't here last night, but I'm a local," she explained, still not giving Hawken a chance to respond or move out of the doorway, or even breathe. "My parents live twenty minutes away, so I'll be splitting my time between here and home like a child of divorce!" She was smiling so wide that Hawken could see all her bright white veneers back to her molars. Seriously, who was this?

After she finally extracted herself from Allison's death grip, Hawken set her backpack on her bed and turned towards the door. Allison was still talking about what it must be like to live in two separate houses when your parents are divorced, even though her parents were still very much together.

"Like a man without a country, right? Hawken? OMG. Where are you going?"

OMG is right, she thought. "I just need to go wash my hands. I'll be right back," she said as she backed out of the room like she was trying not to wake The Beast. What had she gotten herself into? Once in the bathroom, she locked one of the stall doors and took a breath. *Holy Crap.* The smell of Allison's perfume had penetrated every one of her pores. She smelled like she had spent all day at a Chanel counter. How was she ever going to survive with Allison as her roommate? Two minutes with her and Hawken was overwhelmed, breathless, noxious and on the verge of tears. She could feel the wave of emotion beating against the backs of her eyes. Or maybe that was from the fumes in the room. It was impossible to tell.

You can't spend the next nine months in the bathroom like a maniac. Don't let her have the upper hand. You live there, too. Boundaries, Hawken thought. *Set the boundaries.*

Splashing her face with warm water was what she needed. Now only the scent of her clothes and hair repulsed her. She walked back down the hall and paused at the door. Taking a breath, she entered, wearing a suit of armor.

"Sorry about that. I just needed a minute," she said, walking over to her desk. The tension in the air had dissipated, but the fragrance still lingered. "So, you are only spending half of your time here, then?" she inquired, head tilted.

"I have early classes on Tuesdays and Thursdays so I will be here on Monday and Wednesday nights. The rest of the week I'll live at home. My parents and I came to an agreement that this would serve me the best. I can still meet new people and have exciting, new experiences, but also have the security of my own room in my own home. The best of both worlds!" She almost squealed out the 'worlds' part.

Hawken nodded and opened her laptop. Fumbling with the plug, she bent over the desk and noticed her roommates bedding. Her jaw fell open like a cartoon character seeing a delicious plate of food. She must have been so overtaken by the smells in the room and the overgrown personality that she missed the red satin sheets and pillowcase that accompanied the yellow lace trimmed duvet on her bed.

"Good Lord. What is wrong with cotton?" she asked, under her breath.

"Nothing. Unless you've been to the other side and felt the finer things in life. Then there's no turning back." Allison responded, completely and utterly serious.

"How can my life be this divided?" Hawken muttered under her breath.

3

Hawken settled into a routine in the next few weeks that started out with a run, shower, getting dressed, and leaving for school. On the days she was in classes with Kat, they met for coffee by the science building before they parted ways and met again later for their other shared class. Kat had become the core and foundation of her survival. Most of the anxiety Hawken felt was diluted by Kat's awareness of the locations of buildings and eateries on campus. She'd shown her places that she used to study, including the science lecture hall lounge. Kat also warned her about where the congested zones were and at what times of day to avoid them.

"I'm glad that I can help a fellow newbie out so that you don't get lost on the way to class and end up in an Interpretive Dance class, like I did," she relayed to Hawken while standing in line for coffee. "I'll never forget that. I walked into the back of the room and there was a guy on stage in tights feeling his way out of his mother's womb. I kid you not." They both laughed while simultaneously blowing into their brown paper coffee cups. Kat reached up and worried her earring. "Hey, let's stay after class in the science lounge and work on our writing assignment before lab today, okay?"

"Sure. I'm so glad that I don't have to work on this alone. I don't even know where to start. I know nothing about arguing aesthetics. I might as well be dividing by zero."

"I'M ALREADY TIRED of this class," said Kat, slamming her notebook closed, "and it's only the first couple of weeks. Maybe I should drop it and add something else. Like pottery. Or badminton."

Hawken laughed. "You'll just have to retake it later. And then the last couple of weeks would have been for naught." Hawken said, reopening the notebook. "It's almost time for lab and we're making progress here. Come on. Fifteen more minutes and then we can pack it in. Okay?"

Kat pulled her elastic out of her hair and ran her fingers through the long, wavy strands. "Okay, but if I ace this class, I'll totally hate you for it." She collected all her hair in her fist and retied it in a ponytail. "Holy shit, Hawken. Don't look over, but there is a stone-cold fox sitting at my three o'clock. I'll bet you two coffee's he's studying nuclear physics or waiting for his Jennifer Lopez-type girlfriend to finish class." Kat was flushed and practically panting. Hawken laughed at her, rolling her eyes.

"You should close your mouth before you start drooling. And I'm sure you are probably too smart for a guy like that anyway." Hawken flicked Kat's pen with her finger. "Seriously. If he's that hot, just go over and say hello."

"Oh, sure. I'll just trip over my own feet six times between here and there and he'll look up and ask me what mental hospital I've just escaped from. It will be quite the meet-cute."

Hawken rolled her eyes so hard they stung, but she was

laughing. Kat was crazy. She never merely walked into a room. She glided, like she was on ice skates. She was beautiful. With gorgeous, long, brown, wavy hair that never looked crimped when she took it out of the elastic. Her heart shaped face was perfectly balanced with huge, amber eyes and full lips. She was thin and curvy at the same time. All hips and lips. Hawken was never comfortable with her appearance. She'd cut off her blond hair three years ago after the Incident and had kept it shoulder length or less since then. She was taller than Kat, though, which made her shape look stretched when they were side by side. The one feature that she did like about herself was that she looked athletic. She wasn't bony and she wasn't ripped, but she had muscular arms and shoulders. She knew she could rock a tank top.

"Just shut up and let's finish this," Hawken said, pointing to her notes. "Hey, what about Alex? When I introduced you guys in class, I thought I saw you checking each other out." She was leaning back on her chair, balancing on the back legs. "Anything there, you think?"

"I don't know. He's not really my type, but there could be something, I guess," Kat said, shifting her eyes back to the fox. "Shit, shit, shit. Don't look. He's totally looking over here. He caught me red handed." She was half covering her face with her papers. Hawken was cracking up. "Eff all. How embarrassing." Her face had momentarily drained of color, then was overrun with crimson.

"I'm totally going to have to check this guy out," Hawken said, lifting her eyes from her paper to the opposite side of the room. "Okay, I don't see anyone looking over here. Which guy is it?"

"I'm afraid to look." Kat said, turning her head in slow motion. "He's not there. He was wearing a red shirt. Jesus. Do you think I've scared him away?"

Hawken laughed loudly at that.

"Shhhh. Now I'm going to have a complex." Kat whispered.

"Maybe he turned to salt. Like Lot's wife. He looked back at you and that was it. Death by crystallization. It probably wasn't painful." Hawken's face was hiding a smug smile.

"You are such a b—"

"Tony Hawk?" A male voice surprised them and they both started, turning their heads in unison towards the origin of the sound.

The Stone-Cold Fox. In a red shirt. Standing right there. Looking like a Stone-Cold Fox. Effing eff.

Kat kicked Hawken under the table.

Hawken stood up. Then sat down. Then stood up.

Fox's face morphed from Hot Guy to Super-Hot Guy to Super-Hot Guy Smiling a Perfectly Crooked Smile at Hawken.

"Wait," Kat said, breaking the silence and standing up. Now they were all standing on their own sides of the table. "Did you just say 'Tony Hawk'?" She looked over at Hawken and pushed her on the shoulder, knocking her back into the present. "Do you know him, Hawken?" Now she was looking back and forth between them like she was watching a ping pong tournament.

"Um. Yes?" Hawken answered, interrogatively. She immediately reached up and touched her hair, then rested her hand on her neck. After shaking her head once, as if to bring herself back to reality, she said, "Henry Lewis, right? Wow. It has been a while." She held out her hand and he took it. He squeezed it not letting go right away. He just stood there, like the statue of a god with a groundbreaking smile. The ground might have actually shifted and/or cracked beneath them.

Seconds went by. Maybe more. Telling time in a vacuum is difficult.

Kat tried to karate chop the air of weirdness by unclasping their hands and offering her own in substitution. "I'm Kat," she directed to Henry, then turned to Hawken to finish with, "How the hell do you know each other?"

Henry answered first. "We went to high school together in Germany for a few months." His smile never faded, and he never turned away from Hawken.

Then Hawken said, "We were both on the cross-country team, too," finally looking away from Henry to Kat.

"I can't believe you go to school here. Wait, are you a freshman?" he asked, still not looking away from Hawken.

"Yes," she answered, then pointed at Kat and said, "and this is my new friend, Kat. Kat, this is Henry."

"Well, Henry. It's nice to meet you. I've got to ask—is there a reason you called her Tony Hawk?" Kat was now eyeing Hawken suspiciously.

"Yeah, but I'll let her tell you that one. I don't want to get in trouble for anything." He answered then made a fist and knocked it softly against Hawken's shoulder.

"So, what brings you to the science building to study? Do you have a class here?" Henry asked, finally letting the corners of his lips fall into line with the rest of his mouth. Kat was starting to wonder if his smile was a permanent fixture.

"We actually have a few classes here," Kat answered. "We are both Architecture majors. What about you, Henry? Are you studying to be an astrophysicist?" It was now Hawken's turn to kick Kat under the table.

"No, I'm an Electrical Engineering major, so I pretty much live in this lounge and in the lecture hall. I also TA for a Chemistry professor in the building." The smile returned. "So, I guess I'll probably see more of you here, then?" The timbre of his voice elevated on the 'then'.

"Yes. Sounds like a plan. It was nice to see you again, Henry." Hawken was barely controlling her voice now that it felt like she'd swallowed a bomb that was about to explode. She was starting to sweat, and her ears were ringing.

"It is actually really, really great to see *you* again. You look so...different." Henry paused and tilted his head slightly. "Better." Henry was now shifting his weight and ran his hand through his chestnut hair. Hawken noticed a small scar beneath his left eye. "Sorry, is that terrible? I've spoken to you for less than two minutes and I'm already making an ass of myself. I've surprised myself by recognizing you, I think." His smile returned, making Hawken look over his shoulder. *Never stare directly into the sun.* "You aren't so incognito these days it seems."

"No, I suppose not. I guess I figured it was finally time to make an appearance. I'm not the same girl you knew in high school." Hawken looked to Kat for help but found her staring directly at the sun.

"Yes. Well. Well done, you.'" Henry flashed another brilliant smile and Hawken turned fifty shades of red. He turned to Kat for the first time and said, "Nice to meet you, Kat." Then, he looked into Hawken's eyes and said, "See you later, then, Tony Hawk." Turning on his heel, he walked away, but not without turning back and winking. *Oh.Dear.God.*

One. Two. Three. Annnndddddd, here it comes...

"OMG. Are you kidding me? We are dropping all of our classes and you are telling me *everything*, Tony Hawk." Kat whisper-yelled while simultaneously punching Hawken's arm and darting her eyes around the room like she'd just entered in the secret nuclear missile launch codes.

"Shut up. And don't call me that." Hawken was quickly throwing her notebook and pen into her backpack. "Let's get out of here," she said standing up, pulling Kat's hand.

"Geez. Okay, I got it." Kat was stumbling behind her, clamping her free hand on her mouth to dampen her laughter. "Why are we running away? That was amaze balls."

Once they broke out into the crush of the student body, they headed towards the science building where they had their lab. Before Hawken could pull the door open, Kat grabbed her forearm, pulling her back.

"What is wrong with you? A super-hot, nice guy that you seem to know flirts with you, and you are acting like your grandmother just took her pants off in front of the Village Inn."

Hawken turned and tore her arm free from Kat's grip. "It's a long story and we don't have time." She looked down at her watch and said, "Okay?"

Kat narrowed her eyes and said, "Fine. But you will spill after class. Deal?" She shoved her hand in the space between their bodies.

Hawken sighed. "Deal." She ignored the hand and opened the door. *Well, I lasted a few weeks. What a life,* she thought to herself.

4

"I can't believe you were so emo, Hawken. I'd love to have seen that." Kat laughed, then snorted, which made Hawken break her serious face open and crack up.

"I wasn't emo. Geez. I just used to wear baggy clothes, hoodies, and hats, that's all. It's not like I wore a collar and a cape or something." Hawken threw her pizza crust at Kat. "Besides, if Henry recognized me, I couldn't have looked *that* different." Hawken had been dreading this conversation ever since seeing Henry.

"I don't know. Now I'm picturing you with black scruffy hair and a cape. It isn't a good look on you." Kat threw the pizza crust back. "Okay, so how do you feel about him after seeing him today? I mean, hell, he seems to like you. Right?"

THE SECOND THE BELL SOUNDED, alerting them that their Physics lab had ended. Kat immediately grabbed Hawken in a death grip and hadn't let go until they were sitting in Hawken's dorm room. Hawken spent the full class time going through the motions with her partners, who, fortuitously happened to be Kat, Jason and Alex. They'd been bugging her all afternoon to "just spill it already."

"Nothing happened. There's nothing to spill." Hawken was giving Kat the evil eye. "Are you happy now?"

Kat pulled her hair into a high ponytail and twisted it into a bun, then rolled her eyes. "I don't understand what the big secret is. So, you knew this ridiculously hot guy in high school and now he's here and he thinks you are hot. What's the problem?" she asked, hip checking Hawken.

That perked up Jason and Alex, who were supposed to be learning about the Vernier Caliper. "Wait. What?" one of them said, both turning around to look at Hawken's now strawberry colored face. Jason set the glorified ruler on the black lab table and put his hand on Alex's shoulder. "What do you mean, 'he thinks you are hot?' Did he say that?" Alex was now looking at Hawken from her Vans to her blond hair.

Hawken smacked him in the bicep. "Stop that. You guys are ridiculous. He was just being nice," she said, very unconvincingly. She walked around Alex and Jason to the lab table and picked up a round dial attached to a triangular shaped piece with three pointed ends. "What is this one?" They were supposed to get acquainted with measuring devices from ancient times as their lab assignment.

Jason reached over her shoulder and grabbed it out of her hand. "It's a spherometer," he said, quickly setting it down. He pulled Hawken by the shoulder, turning her around so that she was facing them, her back to the table. "So, if nothing happened, then why are we still talking about it?" He ran his hand through his long hair, then looked over at Kat.

"We are still talking about it because Hawken looked like she'd seen the Ghost of Christmas Past up close and personal."

Kat was flailing her arms as she described the entire conversation. Being the good friend that Hawken hoped she would be,
she failed to mention him calling her Tony Hawk.

The first time Hawken spoke to Henry directly was three
years before. She had moved to Germany the summer before
her sophomore year of high school. The Incident just
happened, and she had taken to being a loner. She started
running and joined the cross-country team. She would spend
hours during the day out running in the fields around the
house that they had rented off base. It gave her time to think
and deal with her thoughts and anxieties. She felt like she
could take some control back from her life by focusing on her
breathing and her pumping her arms and lengthening her
stride. She would time herself and try to beat her previous day's
best.

She found herself running behind an outdoor skate park by
a local German high school. The first time she saw those kids
doing ollies and grinding, she was hooked. She forced her mom
to take her to the skate shop downtown and bought her first
short board deck. She spent the entire summer at the skate
park learning everything she could about skateboarding.

After school started, she spent most of her time on base at
school, then at cross-country practice every day after school.
After practice, she would walk over to the base hospital where
her father worked and waited for him to drive her home. It was
while she waited for her dad one day in the hallway of the
hospital, by the nurse's station, she met a woman who quickly
became her best friend.

Anna sat down next to Hawken, handed her a candy bar
and said, "Tell me your secrets. You can trust me. You don't have
to hide. Not from me." She smiled so wide Hawken thought her

face would crack in half. Then she picked up Hawken's hand. "Sweet girl. Whatever it is, I'll help you through it." It took Hawken a while to trust her fully, but the relationship grew on friendship and trust. Anna had shown Hawken a park on base behind the elementary school in the trees that housed an old half pipe. The place looked like a cemetery for pine trees. They were everywhere, most of them half dead, some leaning on others. The half pipe was usable, and it seemed like it was Hawken's own space in the world, left for her by some heavenly being.

She was skating there one afternoon, waiting for her dad, when she heard the crunching of branches and pine needles brushing against the earth. It was almost dark, the time of day that is the most spectacular, where the remnants of the sun cast an orange glow on everything in its path. Everything seemed to dance in the light, as if on fire. She ignored the sound, figuring whoever it was would follow the path down to the school, but the sound suddenly halted. Hawken stopped and listened. She dropped her board on the cement and walked towards the tree line. Out from behind a tree stepped Henry, his backpack bouncing on his back. A blue baseball hat was crowning his head and his brown hair curled around the edges of it above his ears. He had seen enough to know that she was skating there, so she walked over and introduced herself. He stayed just long enough to introduce himself and leave her with two words. "Tony Hawk."

"Now that Kat has given you the play by play, can we please finish this lab so that we can get out of here and start our weekend?" Hawken was leaning over the table trying to fill in her answer sheet. There were ten questions laid out about the inner workings of the three instruments on the table. She stared at them all and lost focus, trying to filter her feelings about seeing Henry again. Unexpectedly, he had brought up her past and she realized, in that moment, that it wasn't a puddle that she could step over and move on from. It was the ocean, and she'd have to swim through it. The realization of this was overwhelming and her heart started beating like it was trying to escape her chest. In an effort not to attract attention to herself, she turned to Jason and said, "I'm just going to get some water. I'll be right back," then turned and slowly made her way across the linoleum floor, counting each square as she made it out the door into the hall. Then, she booked it down to the bathroom, found an empty stall and locked the door. *Get a grip*, she thought. *People recover from trauma every day. You can. You will.* Acting like this in front of everyone was just making it worse. They would worry about her if they knew what was happening. *That's what friends are for. To care. To help and take care of you.*

By the time their lab was over, everything had returned to normal. Jason and Alex were copying Kat's drawings of the tools and Hawken's descriptions. Someone had finished thirty minutes before the end of lab, so the competitive juices were now flowing and the nervous energy to be the next to finish was so dense you could cut it with a nail file.

"Why don't we get pizza later? Kat, you can come over and hang out at our building." Alex had asked, looking directly at Kat, then the ground. There was something brewing there. She smiled back at him and nodded. Then everyone looked at Hawken, who was walking a foot behind them, stepping on all the cracks in the sidewalk.

"Sounds fun," she said to the cement, then looked at her watch. "Hey, can you give me a little while to Zoom with my parents first? I'll come up to your room, okay?" She picked up her pace and walked in line next to Kat.

"Yes. We'll wait for you, so don't take all night. Oh, and tell them only nice things about us!" Jason said, smirking.

Kat grabbed on to Hawken and said, "I'll just come with you and hang while you call them, K?" She flashed a look that Hawken didn't dare dismiss.

Hawken never did call her parents. Kat wanted to know why Hawken wasn't as excited as she should be to see Henry again.

"How long did you know him in high school?"

"Not long. He was a senior and I was a sophomore. He left a week or two after Thanksgiving break."

"Is that weird? To move during the semester and right after a holiday like that?" Kat asked, dropping down onto Allison's bed. "Oh, crap," she said, looking at the bedspread and the sheets. "This is too much for me to handle. What the hell is wrong with your roommate?" she asked, slipping off the satin bed onto Hawken's cotton comforter. She lay down and crossed her arms over her stomach. "There's something to this that you aren't talking about. I need to know. I'm your best friend," she said, looking at her watch. "I've been your best friend for weeks now. Don't you trust me?" Now she was mocking her.

Hawken laughed. "Yeah, okay. He moved mid semester because his mom died. Car accident. She was the one employed by the military, so there was no reason for them to stay. The funeral was going to be in the States, anyway. So, end of story." Hawken sat up and pulled down the cord to lower the blinds covering her window until they crashed onto the sill. She sat back down and said, "I didn't even know him. We sat on the same bus to our meets and said hello in the halls. That's really it." She sighed and sat down at her desk.

"So then why did you get so embarrassed when he remembered you? I would have been flattered. Even thrilled, you know?" She was twisting a piece of her hair around her finger and then sat up to look at Hawken. "Don't you like him? I don't get it."

"It's complicated."

"From what you just said, it isn't complicated at all. Either you aren't telling me everything or you are crazy. Which do you prefer?"

"How about a little of both?" She paused and looked down at her sweatshirt. "It's complicated because I knew his mom and he didn't know that I knew her. Okay?" Hawken started playing with the strings on her hoodie. "It is just weird for me because I was in a bad place when he knew me, and his mom was amazing to me. I am just now starting to feel like a real person again and seeing him today brought back a wave of memories that I thought I had locked away. That door opened today and now there are skeletons flailing about the room." Hawken looked over at Kat and smiled.

"Thanks for—"

The incessant banging at the door sent the mood swirling down the drain.

"Hey, let us in. We're freaking starving already." Alex and Jason were practically kicking down the door. Kat waited until they were both pressed against the door, making heavy breathing sounds into the jam, then swiftly pulled it open and jumped back, out of the way. Jason went down first, Alex landing on top of him.

Laughter from the girls, swearing from the guys echoed through the room.

"That was so not cool, Kat." Jason said, kicking Alex off his leg, then lunging for her, knocking her against the bed.

"Dude, get your nasty paws off of me!" Kat half-screamed, half-swallowed in a laugh. Then Alex jumped on top of them and Hawken pulled out her phone and snapped a picture.

"This is a good look for you guys," she said, laughing.

So, the four of them ordered pizza and Hawken set her phone on its dock and set the playlist to shuffle. They spent the next three hours eating and talking and dancing and laughing. Hawken had never felt so happy and free in her life. This was the most connected she ever felt to anyone since Henry's mom. She felt safe and whole. And at the end of the night Alex kissed Kat and Kat spent the night on Hawken's floor and they talked and laughed until they couldn't keep their eyes open any longer.

5

To most people, Mondays were typically the worst day of the week. Hawken always looked forward to Mondays. They signified the start of a new week. A fresh start. A blank page, but also it felt comforting to have a routine. Saturday and Sunday were play days. Days full of shopping and sleeping and laundry and reading. No schedules, no clocks, like your life was on holiday. Hawken preferred the structure of the weekday. There was always a specific place to be and a relief to know where that place was, and who would be there. Like sitting in the same seat, tenth row down, third seat in, at every Physics lecture. There was a pleasant satisfaction in knowing that, in space and time, there was a place for you, and you were in it. On the flipside, it also meant that you were a foregone conclusion and were easily found.

Kat, Alex and Jason all walked into the lecture hall looking like they belonged. Like 'The Beautiful People.' Hawken could sense them when the door creaked open and turned her head to confirm their presence. They looked like they were shooting a zit cream commercial. It wouldn't have been surprising in the least if a gust of wind started blowing their hair around their faces. The way they leaned into each other and unconsciously touched each other was incredible. They looked like they knew each other since grade school. Well, Alex and Jason had. They'd been best friends since Jason saved Alex's ass from getting kicked in seventh grade. But Kat was new. Hawken was almost envious at how easy they were around each other. Hawken thought back to Friday night. *If I was an outsider*, she thought, *I would assume that the four of us had known each other forever.* That thought put a cheesy grin on her face.

"Hey, Hawken. What has you so chipper this morning? Thinking of your boyfriend?" Kat knew just what to say to ruin a moment.

"No. Geez. It's just nice to see my friends." Hawken replied, tripping Kat as she stepped over her feet to squeeze into the seat next to her. She noticed that Kat was wearing her hair down today, which was a first. Alex stepped over the pair to sit next to Kat while Jason fell into the seat next to Hawken. She instinctively pulled her hand off the arm rest and laid it on her lap. Jason reached over and returned it to the wooden rest between them, smiling at her.

"You should have come out with us last night. The party was uber lame," he said, his eyes sparkling.

"Well, now I'm super sorry I missed it. I have a wild proclivity for all things lame," she responded, rolling her eyes at him.

"That's not what I meant," he said, looking at her mouth. Hawken looked down at her hand. "It would have been bearable if you had been there," he continued. He was still looking at her. When she didn't look up, he bent over and unzipped his backpack, extracting his notebook. She let her eyes drift over to his hair, noticing how it curled up and the ends in back, just over his collar. She also couldn't stop herself from noticing the line running down the back of his arm, accentuating his tricep muscle. He sat back and pulled a pencil from behind his ear.

Hawken turned to Kat. She was leaning over, whispering something to Alex, looking to the world like they had been together since birth. They were both shifted in their seats so that their knees pointed to each other, their feet almost touching, hands interlocked over the arm rest between them, and Hawken felt like she could get sick just sitting next to them. She elbowed Kat in the ribs and Kat whipped her head around so fast Hawken braced to catch it.

"What?" she asked, loudly enough that everyone in the five rows nearest turned and gaped.

Hawken whispered, red faced, "Nothing. Just—when did you two get so affectionate?" Jutting her chin up at 'you two', pointing it at Alex.

"Seriously? We're holding hands. I've been holding hands with guys since second grade." She rolled her eyes and turned back to Alex.

Hawken was instantly the outsider again. How did this happen? How did everyone else become a grown up and she was still an awkward dork-wad roaming the streets? It was as if she had gone to sleep one night and woken, finding that everyone had magically coupled off and knew where and how to interact together, leaving her holding her books and skateboard.

After the most agonizing lecture in the history of the world of Physics, Kat and Hawken scrambled across the quad to the science lecture hall. They were racing across lawns and weaving through pedestrians like they were racing against time to find a bomb in the lounge of the science building, which they kind of were. Kat was sprinting across campus to get there and see if Henry was there. She was hoping to find him and see how much she could torment Hawken in his presence. Hawken was racing to stop Kat from making fools of them both. Hawken reached the door first, having practiced for this for the last three years. Kat stumbled in front of the door and sat down on the top step, winded. She was more frustrating than a mosquito in your car.

"You are so frustrating, Hawken. I don't understand you at all. It's like you've never been around boys before." She controlled her panting and looked up at Hawken. Pulling her hair back in an elastic, she asked, "Is that it? Have you even had a boyfriend?" Hawken could see the pity in her eyes and hear the pathetic sound in her sigh.

"I've never had an actual boyfriend, no." Hawken sat down on the brick step next to Kat. "It's complicated. I've been around guys. I've kissed a guy. Then, I became invisible for a couple of years. Now I'm back in the real world and I'm realizing that it has progressed without me. Loserville, ticket for one." She sighed and picked at the blade of grass peeking up through the grout line.

Kat bumped her shoulder with her own and said, "You aren't a loser. I don't get it, but whatever. There's nothing wrong with you. At least you have your looks. Guys are into you for some reason," she said, cocking her head slightly. "I don't know if it's the cute blond hair or the sad clothes, but you get attention, so just relax and be yourself. That's a great start, psycho." She stood up and pushed Hawken's head forward for balance.

"Hey, Kat?" Hawken stood up and grabbed Kat's shoulder, turning her so that they were face to face. "Thanks," she said and smiled.

"Don't thank me. I haven't done anything." She started pulling the door open and turned back to Hawken and smiled. "If he's in there, you are going to talk to him." She pulled the door shut behind her.

The room was empty save two girls who looked like they witnessed the sun fall from the sky.

∽

ALLISON WAS BACK and in rare form. "Hey, roomie! I've missed you! Come have a seat and tell me all about your day!" She was sitting cross-legged on her bed and was bouncing like Tigger after six cups of coffee. Hawken tried not to look at her. Her constant motion felt like she was spinning the room.

"What is going on with you? Can't you sit still? You're giving me a headache." Hawken sat lightly on her bed and put her hands to her temples.

"Nothing is wrong. I'm in a great mood!" She was still springing up and down. "I just finished my homework and I don't have anything else to do tonight. Let's bond, roomie!" She stood up pulling Hawken's hands away from her face.

"Stop! Get off me," Hawken shrieked. "I have a headache and a lot of work to do. I just stopped by to get a sweatshirt," she said as she jumped up and slid open her closet door. She pulled out a pink hoodie and slid the door shut. When she turned around, she saw Allison sitting at her desk, legs crossed, bouncing. *She's got to be off her meds*, Hawken thought. Grabbing her backpack and sweatshirt, she yelled, "See you later," then ran out the door.

Now what? Going to Jason and Alex's room was out. She didn't feel like partying tonight, and their room was always full of people. She felt like finishing her homework and reading. Quietly. Hawken headed down the stairwell, the echoes of laughter from above pulsing in her ears.

After grabbing a coffee from Starbucks, she made her way over to the science lecture hall. The perfect place to sit and study in peace. Standing in front of the glass door, she looked at the reflection of the sky, the sun just starting to set. It was casting a pink glow on the building that made it look like something from a cartoon. She stepped through the doors and set her backpack on the nearest table, pulled out the wooden chair and collapsed into it. Pulling her phone out of her pocket, she grabbed her earbuds from her backpack and turned on her study playlist. Then she pulled out her Calculus book and started in.

Twenty minutes in, she was hung up. *Explain why f is continuous on the given interval:*

$F(x)=-pix4 + x10; (-inf, inf)$

Seriously. The brain can only take so much in at a time. And what was the deal with Allison? She had to be on medication, right? Anyone that off the rails had to be, didn't they? Should she tell someone? Do her parents know?

Without warning her earbuds were ripped from her ears.

"You look burned out. Need a break?"

Hawken turned and was face to waist with Henry's green gingham shirt. She looked up and saw white teeth and big, green eyes glaring at her. He pulled the chair out adjacent to hers and settled in, leaning back, hands behind his head making his elbows stick out like wings. He had that rugged look —cuffs rolled halfway up his forearm.

"Is it that obvious? I can't remember the last twenty minutes, but I'm positive I'll remember that equation I was staring at for the next ten years." Looking directly at Henry's face was difficult. She was positive that he could read her mind if she let her eyes settle on his. She mostly stared at his ears or his mouth. He had perfect teeth except for the canine tooth on the left was twisted ever so slightly. *Just enough edge,* Hawken thought. She eventually realized that she was staring at his mouth and looked down at her watch. Seven fifteen. An hour had gone by and she didn't even notice.

"Are you almost done for the night?" he asked, pulling her back out of a haze. He had put his arms on his chair and was leaning in towards the table.

"What? Oh, I suppose. Hopefully, osmosis works with calculus because nothing was flowing from my pencil to my paper. What are you doing here this late? Do you have class?" Hawken's stomach was full of butterflies that seemed to be trying to break their way out. This was why she never spoke to people. Her body was not adjusted to life outside of Planet Hawken. The first step was always the most arduous. *One small step for man, one giant leap for Hawken.*

"I was actually upstairs working on Professor Randall's slides for his Chem 105 class tomorrow. I came down here to raid the vending machines for dinner. I just love vacuum sealed sandwiches in those triangle packages. Can't get enough," he said and let out a short laugh. "I was, uh, walking by and saw you sitting here, alone." He looked around. "Where's your friend? Kat, was it?" A stray section of hair fell over his eye and he wiped it away with his right hand.

"Yes, Kat. She's with her boyfriend. He lives in my building and his room resembles a fraternity daily. My roommate is home and she has decided not to take her medication, which turned her into positively charged ion. Literally bouncing around the room. So, here I am. Cast out. Banished to the science lounge." Hawken was unable to just shut up. She was concentrating on smiling whenever he smiled, which seemed to be continually. His smile was an infinite loop.

"Well, I have to finish work, but I should be done by eight. I could forgo the aforementioned egg salad sandwich and we could get a burger or something." He tilted his head slightly, looked directly at her and said, "Will you wait for me?"

As soon as Henry left, Hawken felt a wave of nausea that rivaled Hokusai's. She stood up and quickly raced to the bathroom. Staring at the mirror she saw nothing of consequence. Boring, short blond hair, which wasn't completely uncooperative today. A retouch to her makeup would have been ideal, but impossible. Chap Stick was her one consistent accessory. It would have to do. Jeans and a band t-shirt, her standard issue wardrobe. It wasn't glamorous, but it could be worse. Better than what he'd seen her wearing in previous years.

After calling her parents, she was pacing the sidewalk outside, under the light of the moon. Determined to make herself believe that this was nothing of importance, just catching up, Hawken's breathing became more stable and unnoticeable. The fear was that she would scare him away with the bass drum of her heart beating, its deafening sound leaving no room in the air for anything else.

Ten minutes after eight, Hawken tried not to notice as Henry strolled down the hallway, his full attention directly focused on her. It was too much. Once he saw her, he pulled a crazy wide grin out of his back pocket and slapped it on for her. How could his face show so many emotions just employing his mouth and eyes?

"Sorry. It took longer than I had expected." He ran his hands through his hair and bent over to pick up her backpack. "Are you still hungry? We could go across the quad and get something to eat." He held her bag, intending on carrying it for her.

"Here. Let me. It's not heavy," she said, throwing it over her shoulders. "I'm hungry. I don't really know what there is, so you pick."

As Henry led the way, Hawken became very aware of her body parts. Suddenly, her autonomic system seemed to be breaking down. She had to remember to breathe, swing her arms, and silently prayed that her heart would keep pumping blood into her head so that she could use words and not just drool. The fear of tripping over her own feet and blood spilling from her mouth was now real and in the running of top thoughts on her mind.

When they made it to the café on campus, Henry stopped and turned to her. He said nothing, just smiled a slight smile, then turned and pulled the door open. The large room was packed with students, backpacks, and plastic food trays at tables full of books and newspapers. Her heart immediately dropped into her left knee and started to throb. It was so loud in there she may as well be sitting on a football field during marching band practice. Henry grabbed her arm and pulled her over to the end of the roped zig zag line.

"They have pretty much everything. Sandwiches, salads, hamburgers, tacos. What sounds good?" He was leaning down, talking into her ear. She couldn't think. He smelled like soap and boy.

"I don't care. Anything is fine. I just really need a Coke." She was getting dizzy breathing in his scent.

The line went quickly, and Hawken stood behind him while he ordered. It was so loud in there that she couldn't hear what he was saying. He pulled money out of his pocket and handed it to the guy behind the counter wearing all black, with a black apron. Hawken started unzipping her backpack and pulled out her wallet when Henry reached over and touched her hand. She felt a lightning bolt shoot through her arm and down into the recesses of her stomach. When she looked up at him, he shook his head, not letting her pay. As she pulled her bag back over her shoulder, she felt her hand slowly gain back feeling.

After waiting a couple of minutes, Goth Guy handed Henry two bags of food and two large drinks. She eyed the bags. Henry looked at her and responded with a nudge to the shoulder, directing her to the door.

"It's too crowded and loud in there." He looked up at the sky. "It seems rather cold out here, though." Hawken opened her mouth to formulate words, but Henry got there first. "Hey, we can go sit in my car and eat. I can turn the heat on. It's just right around the corner in the lot. Yes?" He already started walking towards the street.

Hawken took one of the drinks and tried to keep pace. His long strides made it difficult to keep up with Henry. As soon as he noticed, he slowed down. "Sorry," he told her, realizing she was behind.

"I got you a turkey sandwich with cheese and mustard," he said once they were sitting in his car. It was a silver BMW with dark leather seats. He had reached over and slid her seat back so that she had room for her legs and bag before she climbed in.

"Sounds good. Thank you. What did you get?" She pulled her sandwich free of the foil it was wrapped in.

"Same thing. They make amazing hot sandwiches there. The turkey is my favorite." He unwrapped his and took a bite. As he chewed, he turned his body so that his knees were under the steering wheel column and pointed towards the center console. There was enough light from the overhead lighting in the parking lot that they could see each other, but not enough to determine eye color or if either of them had lettuce in their teeth.

"Tell me something silly." He had swallowed and taken a sip of his drink.

"Ha. I forgot about your questions," she said, cheeks turning pink as she covered her mouth with her hand.

"How could you forget that? That was basically the only time we ever spoke to each other in high school." He answered, wiping his mouth with a napkin.

"True. Do you drive your friends batty asking them 'tell me something' questions all of the time?"

"No." He stopped and took a deep breath. "You are the only one that I've ever asked questions to, actually." Another deep breath. "I used to ask my mom 'tell me something' questions all of the time. It was like our game. My dad hated it. She always answered each with total honesty. Like you." He smiled a crooked smile at her.

"Wow." She took a breath. "Okay. Something silly." She wiped a smear of mustard from her lip and paused to think.

"The world's largest cucumber is over thirty-six inches long," she said, matter-of-factly, then smiled.

"It's official," he laughed. "You never disappoint." It was an amazing sound. It made Hawken swallow wrong, forcing her to take a gulp of her drink. A piece of her hair fell free and Henry reached over to tuck it back behind her ear. Hawken flinched.

"Sorry," Henry said, wincing.

"No, I'm sorry." Hawken set her sandwich onto the foil in her lap. His expression told her that he didn't understand.

"Really, Henry. I'm just not used to being touched." He looked at her like she'd told him she was joining the circus. "That sounded weird, but it's true. My parents have never been highly affectionate, and my little brother has Autism Spectrum Disorder and won't let anybody touch him but me." She looked up at his temple. "I'm really not good at this. At one-on-one stuff." The car was barely big enough to fit all her baggage.

Henry laughed and sighed. "Touching someone is my way of connecting with them. I'm not able to help it. It's reflex. You will just have to get used to it." He slowly raised his hand and put his thumb on her left eyebrow and traced it over her eye, then traced down her jaw and rested his thumb in the hollow under her lip. He smiled and pulled his hand away. "No flinching. See? It's easy."

Hawken sucked in a deep breath and swallowed. *Sure, easy.*

Henry sat back in his seat, his back against the door. "What kind of music do you listen to?"

"A wide variety, actually. My dad is really into music and so I started liking some of his older stuff like Simon and Garfunkel—"

"My roommate," Henry interrupted, "was obsessed with them for a while. I think I've heard every album of theirs, hundreds of times. What else?" He looked at her with anticipation.

"Okay, well, I mostly listen to independent punk and alternative like 30 Seconds to Mars, 21 Pilots, and AJR. Like I said, a wide variety. What about you?"

"It seems that we share the same taste in music. I don't like country and I don't like rap, but I pretty much like everything else."

They both sat in a comfortable silence for a while, finishing their food. Then Henry leaned in and said, "Are you tired? It's getting late."

"Yeah, okay," Hawken said in an almost whisper as her hand reached out for the door handle.

Henry's stopped her hand and he said, "Don't be silly. I'm going to drive you. Which building?"

"I'm in Pardee Tower. It's not far, I can walk."

"No way. It's late and dark. And we're already in my car." He turned and smiled at her while the car roared to life. Two minutes later, they pulled up in front of her building. Henry jumped out and walked around to open her door as Hawken quickly collected her bag and trash and stepped out.

"Thanks for dinner and the ride, Henry. It was nice to see you again." The space between them was awkward and Hawken was awkward anyway, making this a scene from a What Not to Do at The End of an Evening bloopers fest.

Henry was standing mere inches from her and she felt her insides flip as he disarmed her with a glance. "Hawken. I'd like to call you sometime. Can I have your number?" For a moment he looked shy, which was a definite rarity on Henry.

"Of course," she said, once again turning red. He pulled out his phone and typed in the digits, smiling (of course) as he slipped it back into his pocket.

"Thanks for waiting for me tonight. I'll see you later."

Hawken didn't wait for him to get back into his car and drive away. She opened the door to her building and saw a group of girls standing around, talking to two guys that looked like they were drunk and high. Instead of waiting for the elevator, she raced up the stairs to the fourth floor, silently praying that Allison had disintegrated in the last couple of hours. No such luck. She was asleep in her bed, and she had early classes on Tuesdays and Thursdays, so Hawken wouldn't have to see her at all again until Wednesday night.

She grabbed her basket and walked down the hall to the bathroom. After brushing her teeth and washing her face, she hurried back to her room and jumped into bed, still in her clothes. After a few minutes had passed, her phone chimed a text alert from an unknown number.

Good night, Tony Hawk.

6

Tuesday and Wednesday went by quickly. College really can take up most of your life, whether sitting in class, studying, or doing homework. So, after classes on Wednesday, Hawken went home to type her paper that she had finished working on with Kat that morning. Two pages in, her cell phone rang.

"Hello?"

"Hi. It's Henry."

"Hi, Henry." *Holy. Moses.*

"What are you doing right now?"

"Nothing." *Dying. I'm dying.*

"I don't think it is physically possible to be doing nothing. What you are doing?"

"Okay. I'm typing up a paper for English. What are you doing?" *I'm smiling like an idiot.*

"Where are you?"

"Sitting at the top of a lighthouse on Nantucket. Hang on, a ship is docking and I've got to turn on the spotlight."

Henry laughed. *Henry laughed.*

"I'm in my cinderblock cell, four floors above civilization." Hawken answered seriously this time.

"I may be a hero, then. I've been at school since eight." Hawken looked at her watch. Two-forty-nine. "I need a break before my class at four. Do you want to escape with me?"

Hawken's heart started beating out of her chest. "Sure. Where are you?"

"Right outside your cell block. Come down. I'm driving the getaway car."

He hung up.

By Thursday, Hawken had a list a mile long of things she needed from the bookstore. She had decided after class that she would stop by on her way home, so she didn't have to be burdened with carrying everything around all day. Walking through campus, she replayed the day in her mind. It had been full of stress and she was now feeling it in her bones. Somehow, she had been late to her first class, thinking it was Wednesday and showing up at the wrong building. Then, she left her notebook in her architecture class and didn't notice until after her next class, which was on the opposite side of campus. By the time she retraced her steps and made it back, there was a new wave of students, heads bobbing along with the animated professor at the podium. She found herself slumped over, almost crawling between the seats to get her notebook back.

The school day was finally over, and she made it to the bookstore unscathed. *Knock on wood.* She grabbed a hand basket and started filling it with graph paper and pencils and erasers. She needed a protractor and a compass. While she was looking for a T-square someone pulled on her backpack. She turned to see Henry, leaning against the ruler display. And, he was excellent in the leaning department.

"Are you stalking me?" He teased her, eyes more green than blue today.

"No." His smile dropped infinitesimally, but just enough to give Hawken the courage to say, "Do you want me to be stalking you?"

"It wouldn't be the worst thing in the world." He was looking directly into her eyes, which consistently threw her off balance.

"What **would** be the worst thing in the world?" she retorted, more to his collar than his face.

A pause. She looked up at his face. "You not standing here right now, with me."

Hawken looked at her shoes. "Geez."

He stepped towards her and said, "Are you mad at me for saying that?" His hand found its way across space and time and rested on her arm. She did flinch again, but he ignored it. Well, not completely. He smirked.

"No. How could I be mad? It just makes me uncomfortable. Like I should look behind me to see who you're actually talking to." She looked up but couldn't hold it. Her eyes drifted back down to her shoes, then to his hand on her arm.

"Hawken. I'm sorry if I make you uncomfortable. I just can't help myself." He spun on his heel and starting walking away, then turned and added, "And you don't have to look around. I'm always only talking to you."

FRIDAY WAS MIND NUMBING. Foam core and an X-ACTO knife were the new pencil and paper for an architecture student, and Hawken's hands were full of callouses and band aids. She already decimated her three sheets of foam core and still needed a roof on her building before turning it in on Monday. Not having to fret over it all weekend sounded like a better idea.

A trip to the store was in order and she immediately thought of Henry. Should she call him to take a break and come with her? Would she be bothering him? Their relationship, if you could call it a relationship at this point (maybe a friendship?) had been one sided. Did making it binary change anything? Maybe she was overthinking this.

She picked up her phone and dialed.

"Hey, beeotch. What are you doing?" Kat picked up on the first ring.

"Kat, I have a question." Hawken was pacing the length of her bed, then stopped, worrying that she would wear out the carpet. Chewing on her fingernails seemed a better approach.

"Okay, hang on." The phone turned fuzzy, like she covered it with her hand, but she could hear Kat's muted voice saying something, probably to Alex. "Sorry. I'm with Alex and Jason and they're asking me if you've reconsidered hanging with us." A pause. "Have you?"

Hawken let out a sigh. "No. I'm working on my model, but I need to run to an arts supply store. That's why I'm calling." She sucked in a deep breath. "Should I ask Henry to come with me?"

She could have heard a pin drop, but then an ear-splitting high-pitched squealing commenced on the other end of the line. Hawken pulled the phone away and held it at arm's length until the screaming stopped.

"Hawken. Yes! I can't say this anymore emphatically. Yes! This may be the best decision of your life, my friend. Do it. Promise?" She could hear Kat jumping up and down on the other end of the line.

"Yeah, okay. Thanks." Crap. If Kat had been this ecstatic, she better think again.

After a few more minutes of hyper-focusing, she decided on a text. The lesser of evils.

To Henry: What are you doing? @4:17pm

To Hawken: Flying an F-15 Fighter over San Francisco Bay @4:21pm

To Henry: Hope you remembered your G suit from the cleaners @4:23pm

To Hawken: Clever girl. What r u doing? @4.24pm

To Henry: Going out for arch supplies. U need a break? @4:24pm

To Hawken: Yes. U have a car or need a ride? @4:25pm

To Henry: I have a car. I'll pick u up. Where r u? Now? @4:26pm

To Hawken: In 5. science bldg. @4:26pm

To Henry: Red Honda @4:28pm

NOW THAT HE SAID YES, Hawken realized she was quite possibly in over her head with this. She stood up and ran to the bathroom. Standing in front of the mirror was a bad idea. She sprinted through the narrow corridor back to her room and hastily applied eyeliner and ran a brush through her hair. There was no time for anything else. As she descended the stairs, she looked down at her t-shirt and jeans to discern the level of bizzaro she settled on when getting dressed today. Not too bad. An Alice in Wonderland t-shirt with jeans and her gray Vans. At least she hadn't worn something ridiculous.

Pulling up to the science building, Henry loped over to the curb. Everything about him was effortless. His hair, long on top, short on the sides and back, always looked casually disheveled. His clothes fell so easily over his body and he always looked perfectly relaxed. He seemed so uncomplicated. Seamless.

He reached for the door handle and already had an easy smile on his face. As he shoved his backpack into the backseat and crawled into the front he said, "Hey, Tony Hawk. I'm very glad that you texted me. All work and no play makes Henry a dull boy." He fastened his seat belt and looked at Hawken square in the face. "Where are we going?"

"There is an art supply store in Culver City, about twenty miles from here. That was the plan. What time do you have to be back?" She turned off campus on Exposition Blvd, heading west. She tried, and failed, to look straight ahead, but couldn't help herself. He caught her, his smile never wavering.

"I actually don't have to be back. Classes are done and I don't have to work tonight. I've been given a temporary reprieve. So, I'm all yours." He leaned forward slightly to look at her face, to gauge her reaction. "How do you feel about that?"

She could feel the crimson spread quickly and fully across her face and neck. "How do you want me to feel about that, Henry?" she asked, turning it back on him and giving herself a second to breathe.

He moved even closer to her now. She was reeling. And really trying to watch the road. Meanwhile, her insides were somehow suddenly swimming around in her Vans.

"Like you won the lottery and don't have to share it with anyone." His mega-watt smile was just inches from her.

She looked right at his face. No sign of sarcasm or teasing. "Are you serious?"

"Why not? That's how I'm feeling right now." He said this without fear or trepidation, his voice never wavering.

"Henry. Don't say things like that to me. It's too much." She put her left hand up through her hair, then back on the steering wheel. She couldn't risk a look at him.

"Okay. Why is it too much? I like you, Hawken. It doesn't mean that we are soul mates and we're running off to Vegas. It just means that at this specific moment in time, I am exactly where I want to be, with who I want to be with. And I'm feeling extremely grateful for that right now."

He was watching her, waiting for her response. Nothing

came. She opened her mouth and closed it again. What was there to say?

"Tell me something that would surprise me about you." Bless him for changing the subject.

"Give me a second to recover," she said, not caring how idiotic it sounded. A minute later she said, "Do you know the New Order song 'Temptation?'" She looked in his general direction.

"Yes." He was still looking at her, making her feel like a shiny, new toy with a bow on top.

"When I hear that song, I stop what I'm doing, turn up the volume, and concentrate on the words, even though I know every single one. Like time stops for that song. It almost makes me cry every time I hear it and I have no idea why. It's one of my many Achilles heels." She looked at his face, but he was silent. "Music is a huge part of my life. I can be floundering and hear an amazing song and it changes my whole outlook on life. Like therapy." She smiled to herself.

She had pulled into a parking space in front of Aaron's Brothers art supply and turned off the engine. Henry didn't move, so she turned to him. "Are you okay?"

He was obviously having a moment of remembrance of something major. "My mom loved that song. It was her favorite. She would do the same thing. Put it on and turn it up, and you could tell she was transported somewhere else. That's incredible." He ran his hands through his hair and opened his car door.

ONCE HAWKEN PURCHASED her art supplies, they both walked over to her car and hesitated. She pulled her keys out of her pocket and said, "Do you want to go somewhere else?" She was worrying the key with her thumb.

"I never asked you if you had anything else you had to do today." He was standing two feet away from her and was closing the distance.

Something about his closeness and words gave her the confidence to say, "Nope. I'm hoping to enjoy my lottery winnings, actually." She reached out and punched him in the chest. The smile that appeared on his face was more than she deserved. He caught her hand and held it in his.

"Okay. Now that that is settled, what do you want to do?" He positioned himself directly in front of her and picked up her other hand in his, so that he was holding both. Hawken smiled at the feeling in her body that radiated from her hands, like sparks in the night.

"Let's go bowling," she said, her face lighting up.

"You constantly surprise me, Hawken Larson," he said looking into her eyes. "Let's go bowling." He waited a second before she broke free of his hands.

She said, "Here. You drive." And threw the keys to him. "I don't know where anything is."

"Promise me something first." His voice grew serious.

Uh oh. "I can't guarantee anything at this point. What's the request?"

"Don't make fun of me if I need bumpers when I bowl?"

Hawken laughed deeply at that. "Henry Lewis. Are you telling me that there actually exists something that you aren't good at?"

THEY BOWLED two games and Hawken won both. Henry wasn't completely lacking in skill, he just couldn't seem to knock over any pins today. "I'm usually worse than this," he said. Hawken laughed at that admission.

Afterwards he drove her to Taco Bell, her choice. "Are you sure that you're okay with this?" he asked.

"I've been dreaming about a Taco Supreme for a while now. Don't you want to make my dreams reality, Henry?" She loved saying his name out loud and did so at any opportunity. And the flirting. She had no idea where it was coming from, but it seemed to make him laugh, so she went with it.

"I can't argue with that."

They ate and reminisced about high school and the people that they knew in common. Hawken steered the conversation away from herself as much as she could. She asked him about moving to California with his dad and where and what he was up to now.

"He lives about twenty minutes from school. He teaches Chemistry in a local high school and loves it. It's actually how I got my job as a teaching assistant. I was able to stump my Chem professor freshman year and he heard that I was looking for a job, so he took me in. My dad has two cats, which he named Darwin and Aristotle and he says he's happy. He lives a small life, though. He is alone a lot. Basically, he goes to work and comes home to his cats. I take him to dinner at least once a month, just to make sure he's okay. We were never very close. He always called himself an outsider because my mom and I were so similar. There was a bond there with my mom that I never had with him. I think it is difficult for him to be around me now because of that. We get along, though it is mostly superficial at this point. He has a group of kids at school that love him. They've kind of taken up the role of needy children for him." Henry looked somber now.

Hawken rested her hand over his on the table. He didn't look up, but he flipped his hand over so that their palms were touching, then intertwined his fingers with hers. Hawken had the feeling that something had changed in that moment. The friendship was no longer just a friendship. It was on the cusp of evolving into something else. Something that Hawken had never experienced or believed in. That afternoon when she was deciding whether to text him, she would have been okay if he had declined. Now, she couldn't be sure how she would feel if she were to be rebuffed by Henry. This feeling was alien. Another one of those moments that had previously passed her over. Now it was here. And she couldn't stand it. What if nothing had heightened for him tonight, in this moment? Could she survive that? Okay, of course she would survive. *Survive* is a strong word. Could she recover from that? Was it worth finding out now? Ripping off the band aid before it fully adhered?

She looked at him and said, "Henry," her voice wavering. "I need you to be honest with me." She looked at her crinkled napkin on the table, then back to him. "Is something happening here, between us?" She motioned her hand at the available space between them. "Or are you just being nice?" She could feel her face pale instantly as the words tumbled out, hanging in the air. The smell of refried beans wasn't conducive to settling her nerves. When he didn't answer instantly, Hawken turned her head and looked out the window at the black night. She wondered how long they had been sitting there. Feeling his hand tighten its grip on hers, she turned to the table and braced herself for his response.

"Look at me." He waited. She looked at his chin, then his forehead. "Hawken. Look at me." She did. "I want to say something to you, but I am hesitating because I'm worried about your reaction." His eyes tightened slightly.

Her heart was racing. "Its fine, Henry. I'm fine. Just say what you want to say." Her eyes arced back to the window.

He waited until she focused on him again. It was agony. "I was not expecting you." A smile and a pause. "Ever since I saw you again that Friday, I can't stop thinking about you." The words hung in the air, in suspended motion. Time stopped. Sound stopped. Henry stopped.

He stood up abruptly, letting go of her hand. Once he picked up the tray and walked it over to the garbage, he turned to her again, grabbed her hand tightly and pulled her out of her swivel chair. "Let's go outside," he said, pushing the door open. The shock of the cold air and the tension combined in her body causing her to shake. "Crap. Sorry. You must be freezing. Let's get in the car." Still holding her hand, he walked her over to the car, opening her door first, not letting go of her until he had to move his arm to shut the door. He walked around the front of the car this time, watching her through the glass of the windshield. Hawken's stomach was performing aerobatics that would have medaled at the Olympics.

He sat in the driver's seat and started the engine, turning on the heat. He reached over, laying his hands on either side of her face, not acknowledging her flinching. "Hawken. I feel... I feel different when I'm with you. It's inexpressible. We've spent such little time together, but you've captivated me. I'm not saying this right." He stopped talking, his face worried. "Will you say something?" He pulled his hands down from her face and brushed them through his hair.

"Henry. I'm so bad at this. You always have the right words. I just need to know that you feel something, too." Hawken was still shaking like a paint can stirrer even though her body was radiating heat.

"I feel something, too. I feel everything." His eyes were searching hers for something more.

"You're making me feel like I've robbed a bank and gotten away with it."

7

"I'm coming. Are you freaking kidding me?" Hawken yelled as she rolled out of bed, tripping on her sheet to answer the door. "Stop knocking already. Have mercy."

The door opened and Kat was standing in her workout clothes, shoes unlaced. "Do you know what time it is?" She pushed Hawken to the side and went to the window, pulling the blinds up in one quick motion. The sun flooded the room and Hawken threw her arm over her eyes.

"What the hell? I have no idea what time it is, but I'm getting back in bed. Feel free to leave, but please close the blinds first." Hawken crawled under the comforter and pulled it over her head.

"Okay, here's the deal. It's after ten. You are going to tell me everything about you and Henry, then you are going to get your lazy ass out of bed, and we are going running." She sat down on the foot of the bed, crushing Hawken's foot in the process.

"Oww. What did I do to make you so nasty to me today?" Her voice muffled under the weight of the blankets.

"You left me all night wondering what happened. I had to assume that you called him. And, since you weren't here when I dropped by at nine last night, I assume you stayed out late with him. Hawken. Are we friends or not?"

"I'm not sure right now. Can I get back to you on that?" Hawken answered, as Kat pulled the covers back, exposing her face.

"Friends tell their friends everything. I understand that this whole thing is new to you, being an eighteen-year-old girl who's lived all over the world and has had many fantastic adventures, but I am here for you to gossip to and share your secrets with. Plus, I'm sure my life of partying upstairs in a ten-by-twelve room with the Hemsworth Brothers is marginally less satisfying than pole dancing with Hot Henry."

"OMG. You sound like I'm living on 'Lifestyles of the Rich and Famous.' What is wrong with you? And, I thought you really liked Alex."

"I DO, but it gets boring after a while. So, I came down here and you were gone. Missing. I had to *hope* that you were with Henry and hadn't been mauled by a lion, or worse yet, bludgeoned and eaten by your roommate."

"Well, thank you for caring." She smiled her Oscar winning fake smile at Kat. "Now get off of me and I'll get my running shoes on, jackass."

An hour later, Hawken was back in her room, music on, getting ready for a shower. Kat was crazy and a little off, but she really had been a good friend to her. She called her out when Hawken was acting like a lost, shaking kitten. She held the mirror to her face and forced her to look into it. That was the kind of friend Hawken needed, and finally found.

She had forty-five minutes before she was meeting Kat and Tweedle Dee and Tweedle Dum on campus to work on Physics. Just enough time for an Impromptu Dance Party. She pulled out all the best songs and went for it. It was late enough on a

Saturday that everyone was mostly gone, either out having fun or out studying, so she turned her speakers up and danced.

Hawken's phone alerted her of an incoming text message from Henry.

To HAWKEN: *What are you thinking right now? @11:53am*
    To Henry: *I'm not thinking anything @11:54am*
    To Hawken: *Impossible again. Tell me. @11:54am*
    To Henry: *Not impossible. Impromptu dance party, no thinking @11:55am*
    To Hawken: *Seriously? @11:55am*
    To Henry: *Seri*

HAWKEN'S PHONE started ringing and lit up the name Henry Lewis across the screen. Hawken jumped up switched her music off, then answered.

"Hey."

"Who are you impromptu dancing with, Tony Hawk?" She could hear white noise in the background, like he was in his car.

"Me, myself and I. Why? Are you jealous, Henry?"

"Unequivocally. What are you dancing to?" he asked, the smile in his voice traveling the distance to her ear.

"No way. Some things are better left in the vault. Guilty pleasures and the like."

"Curiouser and curiouser. Now you really have to tell me."

"Nope."

He sighed loudly. His voice sounded weird, like his mouth was super close to the phone.

"I will spend the rest of my life in bone splitting agony believing that you were dancing to Careless Whisper by Wham."

She laughed at the picture of that in her mind. "Not just dancing, Henry. Singing. There was definitely singing."

"Now you're just being cruel. You seem to be fine with me spending the rest of my days in agony, Hawken."

"Well, Henry, I'm just not sure the truth will set you free in the end, that's all." She was laughing now.

There was a knock at her door. Hawken slowly stood up and walked over to answer it. Henry was quiet on the line. The door was quiet. Suddenly, she felt caught in the crosshairs. She smiled to herself and then she knocked back. She heard Henry laugh in stereo through the phone and through the two-inch thick wooden door.

Unable to contain her smile, she ripped open the door and pulled him inside by his hand. He was wearing a matching smile on his face. They stared at each other until the moment flew away, and then Hawken said, "Henry. What are you doing here in my cell on a Saturday?"

Still holding her hand, he walked over to her desk and looked around. Like he was on a mission. "Hoping to catch the tail end of a dance party."

"Better luck next time, my friend." She rolled her eyes at him, then blushed.

He looked at her, his eyes now turned serious. His hair was hanging down in the front into his face and his light blue plaid shirt made his eyes look like the ocean.

He pulled her softly towards himself with a hand and whispered, "Don't call me that. I think we're beyond that now, aren't we?" Then, "No flinching, okay?" he asked, pulling her into him and wrapping his arms around her. "I just really needed to come over here and hold you for a minute." He rested his face on her head. When Hawken realized that she was missing a moment, she reached her arms around his waist and held them there.

After a minute, Henry said, "You smell like strawberries."
She laughed.

She pulled away first, after asking Henry the time. "Why, do
you have a date?" he'd asked, half serious. He didn't let her go,
just pulled her back after checking his phone for the time.

"Study group at the science building. We have an assignment for Physics that is due on Monday. I'm supposed to be
there at twelve thirty."

"I'm actually on my way over there as well. I'm meeting my
roommate to do homework for a while. I was supposed to be
there at twelve, but was sidetracked on my way." He was smiling
and playing with Hawken's collar. She wore a shirt without
graphics on it today. "What are you doing after?"

"I don't know. We were talking about getting something to
eat after. Why? What are you doing?" She could always get out
of pizza with Kat, Alex and Jason. They wouldn't care. She was
the superfluous member of the group now anyway.

"Hoping to win the lottery again, actually. What do you
think my chances are?"

She put her head on his chest and squeezed her hands
around his waist.

"I'd say you should double down, Henry Lewis."

Henry was parked in a red zone outside her building, so they
jumped into his car and drove over to the science building. As
they walked through the doors together, Hawken looked
around at the occupied tables and spotted Kat sitting at one
across the room alone. She thought how foreign this was, to see
the lounge so full on a Saturday afternoon. She felt Henry grab
her hand and pull her in the opposite direction.

"I want to introduce you to someone. Is that okay?" he asked
as he was leading her over to a table with a dark-haired rock

star flipping a mechanical pencil around his fingers with one hand. He was long and lanky and had amazing curly black hair that was gelled to perfection. He was wearing an AC/DC t-shirt and black jelly bracelets on one wrist, a leather band hung loose on the other. Weren't engineering nerds supposed to fit some profile of pale and unattractive? Hawken seemed to have found the jackpot.

"Hey, Sam. Sorry I'm late, man. I got caught up on my way over. It just couldn't be helped." A mind-blowing smile emerged on his face as he glanced sideways at Hawken.

Sam looked up at Henry and then dropped his pencil when he saw Hawken, having expected a solo Henry. Sam stood up and held out his hand as Henry introduced them. "Sam, I'd like for you to meet Hawken. Hawken, this is my roommate, Sam."

"It's really nice to meet you Sam," Hawken said, meaning it.

"Wow. You, too," Sam chuckled and looked at Henry, then back to Hawken and said, "I was starting to wonder if Henry had invented you. He can't stop talking about you. It's nice to finally meet you." As he sat back down in his seat, he added, "I hope to see more of you around, Hawken."

She nodded, then turned to Henry. "Kat's over there waiting for me. I'd better go. What time later?"

Henry glanced at Sam and winced, then said to Hawken, "I'll be done around five, and then I need to go home first. Can I pick you up at six?"

"See you at six, Henry." She drew her hand up to her face and saluted him as she walked away, smiling.

"So, what happened? I just left your room an hour ago to get coffee, and now you show up with Henry. Spill." Kat was nearly bouncing out of her seat.

Hawken set her bag on the floor and sunk into a chair she pulled close to Kat, then leaned towards her so she could whisper, "He just showed up at my door. He was on his way here to study, too, so we just came together. Oh, I can't meet for pizza tonight. We are doing something. Is that okay?"

"It's fine with me. I get it. I'd rather hang out with his face than mine any day of the week." She was craning her head to look at Henry on the opposite side of the room, tipping her chair back and almost falling over in the process.

A minute later Jason and Alex walked in slapping each other and laughing. Everyone in the room turned to see who the two morons were. Wonderful. Attention seekers be warned, you've met your match.

"Hello, ladies. Did you miss us?" Jason asked, sliding out the chair next to Hawken and falling into it as loudly as was humanly possible.

How is it that he and Alex were so amalgamated that they even spoke in plural pronouns when describing themselves?

Alex sat in the only available chair left, next to Kat, of course. They kissed each other when he sat down, long enough that Hawken kicked Kat under the table to break them apart.

"Let's just get this over with, okay, kids?" Kat said, leering at Hawken. "Okay, question number one. If an object weighs 35 N on Earth, what would its weight be on the moon?"

Hawken pulled her book out of her backpack and Jason responded, "Probably a lot less, right?"

"I'm not sure that is the answer we're looking for, brainiac." Kat threw her pencil at him.

"Oh, thanks. I forgot mine." Jason retorted, as he caught the pencil in the air and smiled.

"What were you guys going on about when you walked in here anyway?" Kat asked, directing the question at Alex.

"Oh. We had this amazing idea that we would only talk in clichés for the day. Wouldn't that be epic?" They literally high-fived each other, right there at the table. *When did they turn into twelve-year-old boys?* Hawken thought to herself.

"So, if m equals thirty-five over nine point eight, then if the mass of the object would be three point five-seven kg. Multiply that by the acceleration of the moon, which is one point six and we get five point seven one N." Hawken said, as she was writing the equations into her notebook. She looked up to see Kat following along, but Alex and Jason were staring at each other and making faces.

"All in a day's work." Jason's contribution.

Alex smiled and said, "All that glitters is not gold."

"Okay, guys, really? Grow the eff up." Kat slammed her fist on the table.

Hawken turned red and looked over to see if Henry heard it. He hadn't turned his head. She watched him for a minute, sitting across the room hunched over his table with his pencil resting between his lips. Kat cleared her throat and Hawken turned to see Jason and Alex gawking in Henry's direction.

"Hawken," Jason said, "don't bite off more than you can chew."

She turned to him and threw him a shocked look. "What the hell is that supposed to mean, Jason?"

"Between a rock and a hard place?" he replied, looking to Alex for assistance. "Birds of a feather flock together, Hawken." He was grinning, which made Hawken even more upset.

"Can you please say what you are saying in plain English so that I can make sure you aren't acting like a total jerk before I kick your ass unnecessarily?"

Kat chimed in with, "Jason. Are you saying that the guy over there in the blue shirt is too hot for Hawken?" She frowned at him.

The entire table was throwing daggers at Jason. His hands shot up, making a 'T', signaling a time out from the clichés. He looked at Hawken and said, "Look, I think you are totally hot, but he is in another league. And he's older than us. He's probably twenty or twenty-one. I'm not trying to be mean, but I don't think that is ever going to happen. You'd be much better off setting your sights on someone you have more in common with. You know, like me." He tried to reach for her hand across the table, but she pulled it away.

"Are you kidding me? After highly insulting me, you're what? Asking me out?" She looked directly at him and he smiled. "You sure know how to make a girl feel good, Jason."

"Look," he said, nodding his head in Henry's direction. The entire table turned in unison, watching a tall, leggy blond in a jean skirt walk over to Henry's table. "I'll bet that's his girl-friend," he added, stealing a sideways glance at Hawken.

They watched, unmoving, unbreathing, as the blond touched Henry's shoulder, inciting him look up, which he did. It was as if Hawken was watching this through a tunnel, able to see only the girl and Henry. Everything else, including sound, was blurred, abstract. She watched as the girl spoke to him, bending slightly in the process. Henry then smiled at her, but it was a smile in which Hawken hadn't ever seen before. Forced. Hollow. She felt herself release a breath she didn't realize she was holding. Henry said something back and the girl stood up, smiled, then walked away. Hawken's heart was beating like a hummingbird. She whisper-yelled to the table, "Stop looking!" and they turned back to find Hawken beet red.

Hawken stood up and turned to Kat. "I'm going to the bath-room." Then she gave Kat a look, which translated into "Don't tell them about Henry." Kat nodded.

An hour later, they were only on question number three out of ten. At the rate they were going they would still be there Monday morning, just in time to turn it in. Hawken set her pencil down and pushed her palms into her eye sockets and sighed. Her phone buzzed on the table. She picked it up and saw a new text from Henry. She glanced in his direction. He was looking down. She couldn't tell what he was doing.

. . .

To Hawken: I am almost ready to stab my pencil in my eye @2:03pm

    To Henry: What a waste of a perfect specimen. Please refrain @2:04pm

    To Hawken: Explain perfect specimen @2:04pm

    To Henry: Anybody would die for those beauties @2:06pm

    To Hawken: Ur making me blush @2:07pm

    To Henry: Aww. Ur turn and I'm missing it. No fair @2:08pm

    To Hawken: U can tell me again l8r and I'll blush for u @2:08pm

    To Henry: Deal @2:09pm

"Ahem." And then Kat cleared her throat.

"Hawken, are we working here or are we texting your parents?" Jason whined.

She turned to him and said, "What is wrong with you? Why are you being such a punk to me today?"

Kat said, "Hawken, let's go to get a drink, okay?" She looked at the guys and asked them if they wanted anything.

"Give Jason a break already, would you?" Kat said as they walked down the hall to the vending machines.

"Why on Earth would I do that? He's been so weird today."

Kat stopped walking and punched Hawken in the shoulder. "Oww. What was that for?"

"I thought it was obvious, but you seem to have issues with social situations, so I'll spell it out for you. Jason likes you. He's been upset all week because you turn down every opportunity to hang out with him, other than class or studying. Now he saw you staring at Henry and he's upset, okay?" She fed a couple of singles into the machine and pulled out three bottles of soda.

When Kat stood up, Hawken opened her mouth to speak but nothing came out. Then this. "Seriously? That's the problem?"

Kat nodded and turned to walk back down the hall.

"Kat, give me a second okay?" Hawken yelled after her.

"Sure," she said, waving her hand in the air while walking away.

Hawken pulled out her phone.

To HENRY: *Soda machine. thirsty? @2:17pm*

    To Hawken: Coke for me. Dr. Pepper for Sam? Hero! @2:18pm

HAWKEN WALKED down the hallway with three bottles of soda and leaned over to set hers on the table. "I'll be right back." She walked across the room as Kat, Jason and Alex watched her go. Halfway to Henry's table she turned and smiled at Jason.

She stepped next to Henry and placed one hand on his shoulder, setting the drinks on the table with the other hand. From across the room they could see her lips move, then his, then a huge smile on his face as he put his hand over hers. Hawken walked back towards them, also smiling. Kat shook her head and looked down at her paper.

Hawken sat down and looked at Jason. His face was incredulous. "That is Henry. We are sort of dating. I'm sorry, Jason. I knew him a few years ago and we just met again last week. I've been spending a lot of time with him. Please don't let this ruin our friendship, okay?"

He looked at her, wordless. She added, "I didn't know how you felt, okay? I'm sorry. I really like you when you're not being a total ass face, though."

He laughed. "Yeah. Sorry about that. Clean slate?" He held out his hand and she shook it.

An hour later they had two problems to solve. They could have been finished earlier, but they were making jokes and telling stories and every so often, one of them would let a cliché slip and hands would be slapped over the table in an unbearably juvenile fashion.

Hawken looked over at Henry. He was earnestly writing in his notebook. She felt her face turn down into a frown and quickly recovered. She wouldn't text him again. He looked busy and she didn't want to interrupt. Only she did. She did want to interrupt him. It was almost painful to see him across the room and not close the gap between them. She thought back to her high school self. There were plenty of times that they were separated by a short distance and she'd never once fought the urge to approach him. There wasn't an urge to fight. It was true that she was in a very different place now. A healthier place. Before, she rarely even noticed boys. They were the very last thought on her mind. Besides, the age difference was more apparent back then. And, he had a girlfriend. The lovely Amanda. Three years ago, it was inconceivable to think that she would have any kind of relationship with Henry. And today she is willing her phone to vibrate, because it means he is thinking of her.

And then it did.

She almost dropped it on the floor while trying to pick it up, like it was on fire. She flipped it over and her face fell. Not Henry. The display read 'Mom&Dad.' She clicked the icon to open the text.

We haven't heard from you for a while and hope you are ok. Call us sometime!

SHE SET the phone back on the table and took a deep breath. Her phone vibrated again. This time the display flashed 'Henry Lewis.'

TO HAWKEN: *Looked up. U look sad. R u ok? @3:47pm*

To Henry: Better now. U looked busy. @3:48pm

To Hawken: Yes. Another hour of torture @3:49pm

To Hawken: What song were you singing? Take pity on me @3:49pm

Hawken laughed out loud. She looked up and apologized to the table, then went back to her phone.

To Henry: U r still thinking about that? @3:51pm

To Hawken: In the fiery pits of hell. Help! @3:52pm

To Henry: U r building this up too much. Now it isn't worth it @3:53pm

To Henry: More than a Feeling-Boston @3:54pm

To Hawken: So much better than Careless Whisper AND no longer damned to an eternity in hell. Bravo @3:56pm

WHEN SHE CHUCKLED ALOUD, she looked up to see everyone at the table rolling their eyes in her general direction.

"I think we are done for the day," Kat managed. "We can finish the last problem on our own. Besides, I need to steal Hawken for a bit." She turned to Alex and said, "I'll come over in a little while, okay?" and then kissed him for longer than seemed appropriate to Hawken.

As her table became deserted, Hawken looked over at Henry, who was looking at her. She waved her hand at him as she stood up from her seat. He waved back and smiled, then continued with his work.

"What are you stealing me for?" Hawken pressed as she shoved her books and papers into her bag.

Kat pushed her chair in under the table and pulled her messenger bag over her head and shoulder in one fluid movement. "I assume you have nothing to wear tonight? Just a preemptive strike is all. Let's go."

Kat pulled Hawken through the room by her sleeve, kicking the back of her right foot the entire way out the door.

"Your closet looks like the inside of Hot Topic. Do you own anything other than jeans and t-shirts?" Kat was fiercely shoving hangers around and dropping t-shirts to the floor. She threw a disgusted look at Hawken and said, "This. This right here is why you are socially inept. Thank the Lord that I was sent here at this time to be your best friend."

"Hey," Hawken retorted, dodging a balled-up sweatshirt headed for her face. "I've never complained before. I've never cared before and you are making this quite an unforgettable experience. It never mattered to me what people thought of my clothes. I didn't want anyone noticing. But." She looked down. "Maybe now I do." She threw her sweatshirt back at Kat, who jumped to the side to dodge it. "Spare me the insults and help me."

"Okay, okay. We don't have enough time to set fire to this and completely start over, so..." Kat pulled a pair of jeans out from the darkest, furthest recesses of Hawken's dresser. "OMG. You have something here. Black skinny jeans? Don't get me wrong. I'm thrilled. I've got goosebumps. But...why?"

"My mom. She ordered them online for me not realizing they were skinny jeans. Hence, the un-broken-in look."

Kat shoved them into Hawken's hands and barked, "Put them on."

Hawken obeyed. The result was better than expected. She walked over to Allison's closet, pulled out the full-length mirror and rested it against the door.

"That girl is a nightmare, but at least she's vain enough to own a mirror. Turn around." Kat stood up and walked over, pulling Hawken's shirt up above the waist.

"Hey," she said, swatting at her hands.

"These are perfect," Kat said, then started rifling through her dresser drawers again. She unearthed a red tank top and flung it at Hawken. "Put this on. Don't worry, I have something that you can wear over it. I think this will be perfect."

They ran over to Kat's room in Marks Tower. While Kat searched her own closet, Hawken sat on Kat's bed and looked at all the pictures that she had stapled to her bulletin board. There must have been over fifty and every single shot had Kat with a different guy, his hand around her neck or looking at her face. "Who are all of these guys?" Hawken asked.

"What?" Kat peeked her head out from behind the sliding door. "Oh, just friends and boyfriends from high school. Why?"

"Nothing." Hawken sat back down on the bed and watched the closet door bow out and shake every time Kat bent over on the inside. "Tell me about you and Alex." She was feeling adolescent after seeing the epic wave of boys in Kat's past. Kat had figured out clothes, makeup, and hair years ago while Hawken was busy hiding under black, baggy clothing. She knew what to say to guys. She knew how to act and was obviously comfortable with the physical aspect of dating. She'd only known Alex for less than two weeks and they were making out publicly already. And shamelessly un-self-consciously at that.

"What about me and Alex?" she asked, her voice echoing through the door. Boots and bras were flying across the room.

"What do you guys do together? I mean, what do you talk about?" Hawken had no idea what she was getting at, but she was pretty sure their relationship was the exact opposite of hers and Henry's. Ozzy and Sharon versus Ozzie and Harriet.

"Uh, well." She paused, then pulled herself up from the floor and stepped out of the closet. "We talk about stuff. I don't know. Movies and music and Star Trek."

"Star Trek?" Hawken asked, laughing.

"Oh, he's totally into it. I can't stand it, but what can you do? We watch movies and TV a lot. There really isn't a ton of talking. Then we make out." She sat down next to Hawken on the bed and handed her a black silky see –through shirt. "Put this on top. It will be sensational. I promise."

After a second, Kat said, "What do you and Henry talk about?" She seemed genuinely interested.

"I don't know. People we knew. Things we like. Feelings." Hawken felt like this was a violation on her part. Wasn't this personal Henry information?

"Feelings? What does that mean?" Kat was gaping at her, like she'd never heard the word before.

"He's incessantly asking me what I'm thinking or what I like or don't like. I don't know. Feelings. Getting to know me, I suppose. Random thoughts." She turned to Kat. "Don't you and Alex ever talk seriously about things?"

"No." Kat responded, shaking her head. "We pretty much stick to topics akin to the weather and how many pumps of syrup I like in my Starbucks." She pulled a strand of hair that had fallen away from her arm and started to twist it. "I don't know that I've ever talked about more serious things with any guy, Hawken."

A FEW MINUTES AFTER SIX, Hawken was hyperventilating and dry heaving. Or at least she felt like it. Her organs were in knots and she was sweating out of every pore. Her hysteria was abruptly heightened, then crescendoed when there was a knock at the door. Suddenly she remembered Henry. *Henry.* This wasn't Some Guy that she was going out with. It was Henry. She took a deep breath and the panic released its hold on her organs. She swung open the door and was immediately blinded by the sun.

How was it possible for Henry's smile to outshine the largest ultraviolet star in the solar system?

He stood in the doorway wearing charcoal pants and a

Kelly-green gingham shirt, making his eyes the color of grass after a rain. The color of hope.

"Henry, you're gorgeous." It slipped out before Hawken realized the words were in her head. She instinctively put her hand to her mouth.

He laughed and raised an eyebrow at her. "You look amazing, Hawken. Truly." He stepped lightly to her and then stopped abruptly, peering down at something in his hand. Hawken hadn't noticed it when he walked in. "Here," he said, handing her a small ceramic pot containing a trio of cacti. "I thought it would remind you of Phoenix."

"Thank you, Henry. It's perfect." She set it down on her desk and grabbed her jacket.

"So, where are you taking me?" They were sitting in Henry's car headed west, but he hadn't said anything about what the plans were for the evening.

"I plan on dazzling you with my expansive knowledge of science this evening." He laughed at himself. "I just heard myself say that and even I want to slap me. Good grief."

"So, the nerd in you is finally breaking through the surface and coming up for air. I was wondering how long it would take." She looked out the windshield at the sun falling over the horizon. Again, her favorite time of day. There was just something so magical about the colors that rebounded from the sun onto every smooth surface.

Henry broke the silence with one of his questions. "Tell me something."

Hawken was waiting for the end of the sentence. There was always more to the question than that. When he didn't continue the thought, she said, "Something what?"

"Just something. Anything. What are you thinking about?"

He kept watching her, then looking back to the road. Hawken. The road. She couldn't help but smile wide.

"Hey, Henry? You said before that you never ask these questions to anyone else. Why me? I mean, didn't you ask questions like this to your girlfriends?" She had turned in her seat to face him and waited for an answer. Unsure what answer she wanted, she still felt safe in asking.

"I don't know." He put a hand through his hair. "Well, that's not completely true, I guess. Do you remember the first time I asked you to tell me about something?" This time his face was glowing pink from the sunset, making Hawken think of him blushing earlier.

She tried to think back to that first time Henry spoke to her. It took a minute. "We were on the bus going to a meet and I was sitting in the seat in front of you, listening to music and you pulled my hat off."

He was smiling. "Yes. And then you turned around and glared at me, like I'd taken a piece of your soul. I laughed and said, 'Tell me something that you are afraid of' and you said—"

"The beach. I remember. Why did you ask me that?" Hawken put her elbow on the armrest between them and rested her chin on her hand. She felt like she could watch him like this without feeling self-conscious. An opportunity to sneak peeks at him when he wasn't looking. She noticed then that he had just shaved.

"Every time I saw you, you looked like you were hiding from something. I wanted to know what it was." He took his eyes off the road and looked at her quickly. "I was intrigued by your answer, so I just kept asking you questions. You always said something unexpected. You still do. Now I'm addicted." He flashed a crooked smile at her.

"You never asked me what I was hiding from."

"I didn't think it was my business to ask you directly. I still don't, I guess."

Hawken was stunned. "You still think I'm hiding?" All this time she thought that she had been successful in participating in life. She had a best friend, people to help her study, and Henry.

"Yes." He put his hand on her leg and she jumped, not expecting the advance. He pulled his hand away and rested it back on the wheel. Hawken focused her gaze at his hand after that, unable to look away. She didn't want Henry to feel how much his comment hurt her, but she also understood that she had hurt him when she flinched. To a certain extent, he had to be right. She did still flinch. She had made progress, but this new world was still fresh. As she focused on his hand gripping the wheel, she thought about how much she wanted to get this right. How much she cared about Henry, even in the short time they had been hanging out. No one had ever been this close, this interested in her before. She didn't feel like she owed it to him to be less hidden, just that she wanted to be more real *for* him.

TWENTY MINUTES later they pulled up to a small brick building with a large circular turret at its peak. Henry turned off the engine and walked around the back of the car to open Hawken's door. She stepped out and found his hand with hers. She didn't look at his face but hoped that this gesture would make up for what happened in the car. Checking out the deserted parking lot, she was curious what they were doing there. They walked up a flight of stairs to the front door of the building, which was covered in white block letters.

"A planetarium? Awesome." She smiled genuinely at Henry and squeezed his hand.

"Have you been to one before?" he asked as he knocked on the door.

"Once." She'd gone on a field trip several years back to a planetarium with her class. She remembered because one of the kids was dizzy and tossed his lunch in the lap of the girl next to him.

"I don't think it is open, Henry." The interior of the building was completely dark, and the door was locked.

"Just give it a second," he said, raising his hand to smooth her hair down. "Patience, grasshopper." She laughed.

An older man with greying hair and a trimmed beard pulled the door open, smiled at Henry, then turned to Hawken and said, "Welcome. I'm Fred." He held out his hand to Hawken and she shook it.

"Fred, this is Hawken." Henry gestured to both with his free hand.

"It's nice to meet you, Fred." Hawken said.

He nodded and handed Henry a set of keys. "I have the room set up. You can switch the narration off if you want. You know where everything is. Just lock up and leave the keys in the usual spot. Have fun, kids." Fred nodded again and pulled open the door to leave. Hawken looked at Henry, who was smiling.

"How is it that it is a Saturday night and we are the only one's here, Henry?" Hawken turned, unable to see much of anything in the darkness. One short hallway had a red, glowing EXIT sign. The other longer hallway seemed infinite in the dark.

"They aren't open on Saturday nights. Come on." He led her down the longer, dark hallway to a large auditorium with a domed ceiling, reminiscent of a capitol building.

"How do you know Fred? And how many dates have you brought here, Casanova, that you have a 'usual spot' for the keys?" She asked, half teasing, the other half serious. She was on full alert. The darkness was creating an edginess that she hadn't expected.

"Fred is an old family friend of my dad's from college. Here, take a seat," he said, pointing to the right. "I'm going to get the show going." He left her at the end of a row of red velvet seats. She flipped the seat down and sat on it, leaning back. The room smelled dusty, like you would expect in a museum. She sat back up, glancing around the room and saw a window next to the door they had entered from. When her eyes adjusted to the darkness, she could make out Henry on the opposite side of the window in a small room, leaning over a sea of switches and knobs. He looked up at her and smiled, holding up an index finger, signaling he was almost finished playing Captain Kirk. The rest of the room had rows of seats, like hers, circling the room with a large empty space in the center.

Sitting back in her seat, Hawken closed her eyes. After a few seconds she felt Henry's presence in the room and opened her eyes to a room full of stars and Henry standing over her.

"Hey, Tony Hawk." Hawken felt like the world was spinning. Well, obviously it was spinning, but she felt like it was out of control. Like she was going to fly off if she didn't hold on tightly to something. So, she did. She picked Henry's hand to ground her, save her from the end of the world. "Come here with me."

He pulled her up and walked her to the middle of the room, sat down on the carpet, motioning for her to join him. "It's a completely different experience from down here. Trust me." His face was full of mirth.

Hawken tentatively looked around the room again, surveying the exits. She felt like a mobster checking a room before being able to relax. She sat down on Henry's right side. He pulled out a pillow that he must have gotten from the control room, set it behind him and lay back, resting his head on it. "Come here," he said and put his hand on her shoulder to pull her down. She shook her head at him, biting her bottom lip and he sat up. "What's wrong?" She needed him to answer her questions. She needed to know what this was before it went any further.

"How often do you do this, Henry?" she asked, waving her hands around in the air, stirring up all her emotions at once. She felt sad, scared, and nervous. In one minute the most romantic night had turned into disaster.

He put his hand on hers and she pulled back. "Hawken, I'm sorry." His face looked pained. "It's fine. Perfectly safe. I come here all of the time."

She inhaled hard and started shaking. He came here *all of the time.*

"Jesus, Hawken. What did I do? Do you want to leave? I'll take you home, but you need to tell me what is happening." He kneeled in front of her and, as if remembering her questions, said, "I've never brought anyone else here. I come here by myself to clear my head. I come here when I want to think about my mom. She used to bring me here all the time when I was a kid. It's the one place that I can still feel her near me." He looked at her face. "I'm sorry. Tell me what to do here."

She felt herself relax and started to cry. "I'm sorry Henry. I don't want to leave. Just give me a minute, okay? Please?" She reached out for his hand and he gave it to her.

She sat in the darkness under the millions of twinkling stars, crying. Henry sat and watched her, unsure of what to do. Hawken knew he didn't deserve this, but she couldn't pull herself together.

After another minute, Henry said, "I'm going to touch you. Is that okay?" He looked at her like she was a lost kitten, not a sobbing, freaked out dating disaster of epic proportions. She nodded.

He put his arm around her and wiped her tears away with his thumb. "Shhh," he whispered. It was so tender that Hawken couldn't take it anymore. She was ruining the evening. Henry didn't cause any of this. She could trust him. She knew she could, but the darkness and intimacy of the room brought back too many memories that came flooding back, like the dam had finally burst open, drowning her in memories. And at the worst time.

Poor Henry. She pulled his arm away and asked him for the bathroom. He helped her up off the floor and walked her out of the room. She had never been so grateful for dark hallways in all her life.

Stepping into the bathroom, Hawken flipped the light switch on and pulled a long stretch of toilet paper from the middle stall to blow her nose. Afraid to look in the mirror, she wiped under her eyes and cleaned the last of the tears away with the paper. Finally assessing the damage in her reflection, she saw what she'd expected. The scared, shaking, blotchy, red face of her fifteen-year-old self all over again.

8

W hen Hawken opened the door to the darkened hallway, Henry was sitting on the floor across the hall. He had his arms crossed over his knees and his head was resting on top. He looked up and blinked when the light from the bathroom hit his face. Jumping to his feet, he started to step towards her, then hesitated.

"I'm sorry, Hawken. I thought this would be special, but somewhere I must have miscalculated—"

Hawken walked over to him and picked up his hand. He tensed at first, then gave in to her. "Henry. I'm sorry. It had nothing to do with you. It's all my fault. I'm so sorry." She looked down at their hands, hanging like a bridge connecting their bodies together.

"How is it possible that this has nothing to do with me? Can you explain that to me, please, because I'm feeling oddly villainous here." He bent down to look at her downcast eyes.

"Yes." She looked down the hallway, then back at Henry. "Can we go back in there, but turn on a light or something?"

"Of course, but... Are you sure?" he asked, wavering. She could understand why he would hesitate to take her back in there. She turned into a circus act. The one-eyed woman who spits fire.

"Yes. I don't want to do this here, outside of the bathroom."

He walked her down the hall, one hand in hers, the other in his hair. He left her in the hallway while he stepped into the control room and flipped a couple of switches. There was enough light in the room that you could see, but not enough to be self-conscious about her puffy face. It suddenly dawned on her how quiet it was. Almost a complete absence of sound.

Henry walked back into the hallway and motioned for Hawken to enter the room. She went back to the center and sat on the carpet, akimbo. Henry turned to take a seat in the chair across from her, but she pulled on his pant leg and said, "Please sit with me here." Henry sat down and Hawken positioned herself so that she was directly across from him, knees touching. She reached over and took both of his hands in hers and rested them on their joined legs.

"Hawken, you are totally freaking me out here. I'm out of my element and I'm not sure what is happening." His eyes were searching her face.

"Sorry. I know. I just really need to tell you something and it's not easy for me." She looked up to the stars for strength but could barely make them out now with the light shining down into the room. She glanced at Henry again and took a breath.

"Henry. A couple of weeks before I moved to Germany—" She took a deep breath in and, in what felt like slow motion, said, "I was raped by a guy from my school at the beach." She exhaled and felt her entire body shudder. She let go of his hands and put hers to her face, rubbing her forehead with her fingertips. Her heart was beating out of her chest as she sweat profusely. Henry was still and she couldn't bear the thought of looking at him right now. After another deep breath, she closed her eyes. A few heartbeats later, his hands were on hers, pulling them down from her face. He pulled them close to his own face. She could feel his breath on them, then his lips. As she opened her eyes, he kissed her knuckles and then rubbed them over his lips. He looked up at her, moving only his eyes and lowering their hands to his knees.

"I don't know what to say. I'm so sorry." His eyes were mournful. "I'm furious and at the same time I feel overwhelming sadness."

"Are you mad at me?" she whispered, feeling unsure.

"No!" His face was angry, but then he relaxed again. "Of course not. I'm sick that you went through that. I'm trying to process it, that's all. I'm not sure what to say or do."

"Look. I understand if this is too much for you. I get it. It changes things. In fact, for me, it has changed everything." She leaned back, putting her hands around her neck and breathed deeply.

"Hawken, no. You're wrong." He shook his head, slowly, tugging at his hair. "I can't think. Will you give me a minute?" He stood up, and before she could say anything, he walked out of the room into the hallway.

Hawken felt ripped apart. Like her insides were hanging out of her body, and at the same time frozen in place. Or glued in place. This was her own personal Event Horizon. There was no after, just the Before that would torment her eternally. She sat alone in the room, unblinking.

It could have been five minutes or five days. Hawken had no sense of time. Henry returned to the room with two bottles of cold water. He sat down on the floor again, across from Hawken and opened a bottle and handed it to her. She reached her arm out to take it but didn't make contact. Her arm felt like it weighed a ton. Like it had been replaced with an anvil.

"Hawken. Look at me." Henry. His voice sounded far away, across an echoing canyon. He reached over and put his hand on her face. "Jesus. You're on fire." He put the water up to her mouth and said, "Here. Drink this." The least she could do was obey his request, so she swallowed a sip. And then another. And then she was gulping down the bottle. He set it down and put his hand on her face again. She felt as though she had just been pulled to the surface from the bottom of the ocean.

"You feel better. Are you okay?" She nodded, unable to find words.

"Hawken. I'm sorry I walked away. I just needed to breathe. And think." He moved closer to her, smashing his knees into hers. "You said that everything has changed, and that is true, but also it isn't." She closed her eyes. He put his hands on her face, rubbing his thumbs on her cheeks. The words *I do not deserve him* were echoing through her head, ad infinitum.

"Listen to me, okay?" He waited. She nodded, eyes locked shut. "I like you so much. So much. Even more. That hasn't changed. Okay?" Another pause. "Hawken, I need to know that you are hearing me." She nodded. "I feel like you've just handed me the lost puzzle piece to complete the picture. After years of seeing something unfinished, I can now see the full picture. And it's beautiful. You are beautiful, Hawken." He waited. And waited. "Don't hide from me, Hawken, please?" Nothing. Darkness and waves. "Open your eyes, sweet girl." She moved her head slowly from side to side. "Yes," he said. She gave in and saw his face beaming so brightly, she felt like she'd been living on the dark side of the moon, now finally exposed to the sun. He was looking at her like he was seeing a shooting star for the first time. Like he was captivated. *I do not deserve him.*

～

AFTER A TIME, he said, "Can I ask you a question?" His voice was tentative.

"Yes. Of course." She was looking down at his collar.

"What happened to him?" His head tilted to the side as he spoke, making fierce eye contact.

Hawken opened her mouth, then closed it again, looking away.

"Nothing. I never told anyone. My parents still don't know."

He immediately leaned back, possibly from the shock of her answer, and blinked.

"How is that possible? How can they not know? You didn't tell anyone?" His face looked wrecked.

"I was ashamed and terrified and when I got home that night, the house was empty. My brother had swallowed a marble or something, so I walked into a dark, empty house with a note on the fridge stuck to a banana magnet. 'At hospital. 7pm.'" Hawken's voice had turned mechanical, cold, robotic. "I looked at the clock and it was eight fifteen. I sat down at the table and when I blinked again it was after nine. I got up and went into the bathroom and stood in front of the mirror. I ripped my clothes off and shoved them into the garbage can by the toilet. My eyes were red. My hair was full of sand. My skin was red and blotchy. I had hand-prints all over my arms and stomach. My legs were scratched and bleeding from the zipper on his pants. I went into the kitchen and grabbed the scissors and cut nine inches of hair off my head." Hawken finally looked up from the spot on the carpet she'd been talking to. Henry looked like he'd been stabbed and was letting himself bleed out. Hawken couldn't stop now, so she continued.

"I stepped into the shower and turned the water as hot as I could and forced myself to stand under it for as long as I could. It made me physically sick seeing his red fingerprints all over my body. This seemed the only way to fix it, the water running over my body, burning it so that was all the same color red. After a few minutes, I turned the water as cold as it would go, standing still while it poured out over me. I don't know how long I repeated the sequence. Over and over. By the time I got out I couldn't even see straight. I put a pair of new pajamas on and got into bed with my headphones on. I had to turn the volume to the maximum level to get his voice out of my head. I just kept hearing him whispering in my ear." She stopped and looked at Henry. This was too much now, wasn't it? Did he want to hear this?

"Henry, I'm sorry." She forced a smile to her face, but it fell flat.

"Hawken stop saying that. You have nothing to be sorry for. None of this was your fault. I can't imagine what you were feeling. When did your parents get home? How did they not know?"

"I had fallen asleep, finally, but woke up around four in the morning. Their bedroom door was closed, so I knew they were home. I walked back down the hall to the bathroom and shut the door. When I turned on the light, I saw someone in the mirror that I no longer recognized. I screamed out and fell backwards against the bathtub. My parents came running in and found me on the floor. They assumed that I got bruised from that fall. Then, when I stood up, I ran to the toilet and started throwing up. They just figured I had the flu and I spent the next week in bed with the blinds closed listening to music in the dark. They never questioned anything else. My mom told me that she was upset that I cut my hair, but that it was probably time for something new.

"So, we moved a couple of weeks later. I never saw any of the kids again that were at the beach that night. I started wearing clothes that I thought would make me invisible. I wore wool hats that covered my hair. Baggy pants." She looked at Henry again. "You remember."

"I remember. I wish I had known." He attempted a smile. "You know what I mean."

"Thanks, Henry." The words came out with feeling, and she could tell he knew she meant it.

"So, what happened then? You don't seem like you're trying to be invisible now. How long did that last? When did you stop?" He picked up one of her hands and started tracing circles on her palm.

"Oh, Henry. This is another secret from the vault. I'm afraid to tell you."

"Please don't be afraid. Not with me." She felt guilty because she had lied to him this entire time. A lie of omission is still considered a lie and she was omitting the truth about his mother. It was time to finally come clean.

"Henry. I've only told this to one other person. Ever. It was impossible for me to trust anyone after that. I walked around in a fog. After we moved to Germany my parents were getting sick of me sitting in the house all day, so I spent the summer running and skating." She smiled at him. His eyes were full of mirth. *I don't deserve him.*

"When school started, I joined the cross-country team, mostly to keep my parents from asking me so many questions. 'Why don't you have any friends?' or 'Why do you sit in your room all day?' We lived off base there, and it was too far to walk home. After practice, I would walk down to the hospital where my dad worked and I did my homework, waiting for him to finish work and then he drove us home.

"One day, I was sitting in the hallway by the nurse's offices working on my math homework and your mom walked over to me, leaned against the wall, and slid down on the floor next to me." Henry stopped moving and tensed. Hawken looked at his face. He looked confused.

"This is why I was afraid to tell you. Are you okay?"

"You knew my mom?" She nodded. "Wait. No. Yes. Tell me." He was smiling now, urging her to continue.

"So, she sat next to me and handed me a 3 Musketeers bar." She smiled at the memory and Henry squeezed her hand. "And she said, 'Tell me your secrets. You can trust me. You can't hide forever. You might as well stop now.'"

Henry's face was on fire. He was smiling and red and looked happy. He said, "That is exactly something she'd say. Go on. Please."

"Well, I was stunned. My parents couldn't see through the façade, but your mom totally called me out. The first time I saw her. She said, 'Whatever it is, sweet girl, I'll help you through it.' Just like that. Just like you did, Henry."

His face could hardly contain his smile. His eyes were nearly slits, his cheeks pressed so far up against them.

"I told her everything. She's the only other person in the world that knew, Henry. I trusted her. I trusted her with everything. I loved her." Hawken could feel the tears form in the corners of her eyes.

Henry moved back and stood up, pulling her with him by the hand. She had a confused look on her face. He said, "I just want to hold you for a minute. Is that okay?" He waited for her response. She nodded, wiping a tear away with her hand. Henry slipped his left hand under her arm and crushed her against his body. He wrapped his right arm around her and rested his hand on her left shoulder. He was so warm, and she felt so safe. In that moment, she felt like the world could fall away around them and she wouldn't care. This was everything. Henry was everything.

She rested her forehead inside the crook of his neck and inhaled. Henry smelled like heaven. Like freshly mowed grass, blueberry pie, hot chocolate, and magic.

After a minute Hawken started laughing. She was feeling like something inside of her had just been set free. This had been such an emotional night and she had a moment of insanity, standing there, floating above the ground.

"What's funny?" Henry made to pull back, but Hawken pulled him tighter.

"Henry, I'm starving." She laughed again and so did he.

"Me, too. Should we go somewhere?"

"No. Yes. No. I'm so hungry, but I feel awful for ruining this." She tilted her head up to look up at his eyes but settled on his chin. She was desperate to kiss him right then but scared about what would happen after.

"You didn't ruin anything, sweet girl." He must have read her mind because he kissed her hair. And then again. "I'm starving, too. We could go eat something. I'll hold onto the key. If we want to come right back, we can, okay?" Another kiss in her hair.

"Okay, Henry."

"Do you realize that we are Those People, Henry?" They were sitting at IHOP, both with a plate of hot pancakes and a scoop of melting butter pouring down the sides. When they had gotten back into the car, they looked at the time and it was only eight o'clock. It had seemed like days had passed, not just a few hours. There was an IHOP right around the corner, so they headed straight there.

"What people?" Henry asked.

"The ones that sit on the same side of the booth, incessantly touching each other." Hawken smiled at him and nudged her shoulder against his.

"You're right. But I don't care. Not tonight." He nudged her back.

Since they left the planetarium, they hadn't let go of each other except to get in and out of the car. With the overflow of emotions that had passed between them, neither of them could fathom letting go of the other.

Henry took a bite of his pancake soup and smiled at her. Every time he did, her body felt an electric charge.

"I don't know how you can eat that much syrup. Here," she said, handing him his water glass. "I don't want you to become diabetic tonight."

"Most of the syrup will stay on the plate, but it tastes really good. Thanks for your concern, Tony Hawk." He grinned and nudged her shoulder again.

"Do you want to know anything else about your mom, Henry?" She put a forkful of pancake into her mouth, glancing sideways at him.

"Of course. I didn't want to push you if you didn't want to tell me any more tonight." He put his fork down and sipped his water.

"She really wanted me to tell my parents. Every time I went to see her, she asked me if I'd told them. She offered to be there with me, too."

Henry stopped drinking at looked at her, stunned. "Every time you saw her? How many times did you see her?"

"I used to go there for lunch or after school to see her at least two times a week, sometimes more." She stopped, waiting for his reaction to the news.

His eyes widened. "You're kidding? Did you talk about other things? Did she talk about me?" He looked like a little kid on Christmas morning.

"We mostly spoke about life in general. Where you'd lived, places she'd traveled to. She told me that she sometimes had visions about her life, and others. She used to try to guess things about my family and she was always on target. I thought she was amazing. She asked me a lot of questions, just like you." Without thinking, she picked up his hand that was wrapped in hers and kissed it. She felt her face turn red but ignored it. This night had turned into something more than she could have ever hoped for and wanted to stay in that place as long as she could. "She's the one who told me about the basically abandoned half pipe behind the elementary school. You remember? That day that you introduced yourself. That was the day that she showed me where it was."

"I remember. I was walking over to Steve Rose's house and cut through the park behind the elementary school. It was getting dark and I kept hearing wheels on cement and scraping. You don't know this, but I stood behind a huge oak tree and watched you for a while. You were amazing. I couldn't believe that you skated, but it was more than that. You were so alive. I was mesmerized by watching you skate. I don't think I've ever seen anyone look so happy.

"I was glad that I saw you there that day. I had obviously seen you around school and knew you were on the cross-country team, but I don't think we'd spoken a word to each other before that night. Do you remember? You picked up your board and walked over to me with your hand out and you said, 'Can you keep a secret?' and held out your hand to me said, 'I'm Hawken Larson'."

"Yep. Then you said, 'Nice to meet you, Tony Hawk.'"

He laughed. It was the best sound in the world.

At nine fifteen, they were back at the planetarium and this time when Henry laid back on the floor, her anxiety having ebbed, Hawken lay against him, her head resting on his chest. He had his right arm wrapped around her, his hand resting on her arm.

"I turned off the narration because it's actually pretty lame. The guy's voice sounds like the narrator in those B action movie previews."

"Okay, but will you do the B action movie preview voice for me, Henry?" He laughed and the movement of his body shook hers.

From nowhere, he pulled out a laser pointer and a red light appeared against the false sky. Hawken couldn't help herself and started cracking up. Really laughing. She sat up so that she could breathe. Henry rested back on his elbows watching her.

His expression looked like he was watching an escapee from the local mental hospital dance around.

"What's so funny?" He was smiling like someone who wasn't in on the joke.

"Oh, Henry." She was still trying to catch her breath. She put her hand on his chest and could feel his heart beating under his shirt. It was an amazing feeling. Like his heart was speaking to her in Morse code. She fought the urge to lay her head over it. That had sobered her.

Henry was still looking at her quizzically. "For the second time today, your inner geek came out, that's all." She laughed again. "Oh, Henry. Will you please show me your laser pointer again?" She was teasing him with everything she had.

He pulled her down to the floor and rolled over onto her, the left half of his body covering hers. Her face went instantly pale. Henry froze, then he pulled her back up to sitting. "Jesus. I'm sorry, Hawken. I wasn't thinking. I was in the moment. Are you okay?"

"Yeah. I'm fine, Henry. Sorry. You just took me by surprise. Don't be mad, okay?" She was worried that his patience was wearing thin with her.

He looked in her eyes. "I'm not mad. How could I be mad, sweet girl? I like you so much." There was a moment when their faces were inches apart and Hawken took a deep breath in. Then she blinked and it was gone.

Inside, she was a mess. They sat in silence, both breathing loudly. She wanted to kiss him. More than anything. But. It wasn't the kissing that made her want to drive off a cliff. It was what came after. She wasn't ready for that. Not even close.

Henry reached up and tucked a strand of hair behind her ear. "You ready to try this again?" he asked, leaning back against the pillow.

"Go for it." Hawken laid back against his side, but it wasn't the same. She rested her right hand on his chest, trying in vain to feel his heartbeat. He turned on his laser pointer and was circling spots in the sky and talking about star formations and supernovas, but Hawken couldn't bring herself back to the present. Her thoughts were on the future. Would she ever be ready? It wasn't like it was now or never. She knew that. She was driving herself insane. In the end, Henry was still there, his arm wrapped around her. He liked her. This was just an overly emotional day. She talked herself out of a breakdown and concentrated on Henry's voice.

"See this grouping of stars here?" She nodded. "This is Gemini. This is my favorite constellation. The story goes that the Queen of Sparta had two sets of twins, each with different fathers. One was with her mortal husband, the other fathered by Zeus, an immortal. Each set of twins had a boy and a girl." Hawken had started toying with one of the buttons on his shirt. She realized that he had stopped talking and she put her hand flat against his chest, then moved her head to look at him.

"Sorry," she whispered.

"You are killing me here, Hawken." He turned his head back to the ceiling as she stiffened her body, trying to keep as immobile as possible. He set the laser down and made a sound in the back of his throat. She could feel the warmth of her body run up to her head. He twisted around so that they were facing each other and pulled her tightly against the length of his body. She put her arm around his back and rested her hand on his shoulder. They stayed like that, frozen, for an unmeasurable length of time. Hawken felt as though she would burst into flames.

Ultimately, he was the one to pull away. He kissed her once on her forehead, then rolled back around. Laser pointer in hand, he began again.

"Each set of twins had a boy and a girl, and one set was immortal. The two boys, Castor and Pollux, were inseparable. During a fight, Castor, the mortal one, was killed. Pollux was grief-stricken. So, he asked Zeus to let him die so that they could be together for eternity. Zeus agreed and they spend half of their time in the underworld and the other half in heaven."

"That sounds incredible, Henry."

"The best part is this star cluster here at their feet," he circled a point of light with his laser, "right here is called M35. It's made up of thousands of stars that are over one hundred and fifty million years old. Most of the stars in clusters that old are pulled away by gravitational fields from the galaxy, but these have stayed together. Like the twins, they are bound for eternity."

"Wow. It's unbelievable that all of this is just up there. For us."

Henry turned off his laser and moved to sit up. Hawken sat up and said, "That was amazing. Even without the lame narrator." He smiled. "Thank you, Henry."

He stood up and pulled her up by her hand. "Anytime," he said, still smiling. Always smiling. It threw her off balance.

"Hey, Henry. You totally dazzled me tonight with your extensive scientific knowledge. I can hardly stand up straight." She laughed and Henry laughed. Then, in a moment of weakness, she pulled him down and kissed his neck.

Henry lit up like a Roman candle. Then, Hawken did burst into flames.

After Henry dropped her at her room, Hawken felt as though an enormous weight had been lifted. She felt like she was finally where she belonged.

What Hawken didn't know was:

A few miles away, there was a boy who had just returned home from an evening with a girl who cracked something open in him. He had a moment, a few hours prior, in which all of the detritus that he called Who I Am Now had parted, shifted, and separated from Who I Am With Her. It wasn't subtle. It was unmistakable, glaring. He realized that every nerve, tendon, muscle, blood vessel, organ, fiber in his body now had a greater purpose. They would expend their energies and focus on her. Making her safe. Making her happy. She was everything.

9

To Hawken: *Are you awake? @9:53am*
   To Henry: *Yes, sir @9:54am*
   To Hawken: *What are you doing? @9:55am*
To Henry: *Cleaning my guns @9:55am*
To Hawken: *Lol. What are you really doing? @9:56am*
To Henry: *Fishing @9:57am*
To Hawken: *Ok @9:58am*
To Henry: *Sorry. I'm lying in bed listening to music @9:59*
To Henry: *Thinking about last night @9:59*
To Hawken: *Me 2 @10:00am*
To Henry: *Happy thoughts? @10:01am*

HAWKEN'S PHONE started maniacally vibrating in her hand. Henry.

"Hi."

"Are you seriously asking me if I am happy about last night?"

"Yes. A lot happened. You've had time to think."

"I don't need to think, Hawken." He sighed, long and hard.

Then said, "I'm so in this it isn't funny. I've never been this happy. I can't stop smiling."

No one said anything else. Balloons were let loose all over the world. Children ran through fields of tulips. Birds cooed. Hyenas laughed hysterically.

"Are you there?"

"I'm here. Henry. All I want to do is be happy with you."

"Let's have breakfast. Or coffee. Anything. I want to see you."

"Okay. Give me forty-five minutes?"

"I'll be there. Hurry."

"WHAT ARE YOU DOING TODAY?" Henry asked as they sat across from each other at the table.

"Building a house." That got his attention. He almost spat his coffee. Hawken laughed and handed him a napkin. "I have to finish my model for my architecture class. Oh, and Kat is taking me shopping." They were sitting in a window booth at the Starbucks just off campus.

"Really? What kind of shopping?" He had picked a corner from his muffin and smashed it into a square, then popped it into his mouth.

"Clothes shopping." She gave him a look and blew the steam from her coffee.

"Seriously? With Kat?"

"What?" She asked, setting her cup on the table.

"Well, I'm assuming this was her idea?" he asked, picking another chunk of muffin and warping it into shape.

"Yes, it was. Why?" She gave him a skeptical look, face askew. He'd never voiced an issue or even an opinion on the subject of Kat before this.

"Hawken. It's just that Kat's style is very different from

yours. Don't let her pressure you into anything. That's all I'm saying." He said it in a way that was obvious that it wasn't all he was saying.

"She says I don't have a style. That's the whole point. All I have are jeans and t-shirts." She looked down at her shirt, making a point.

"You have a very distinct style. You don't *just* wear jeans and t-shirts. As a matter of fact, you don't *just* do anything." He pointed his chin at the window. Hawken turned. "That girl out there. She is *just* wearing jeans and a t-shirt." Hawken looked. Yes, she was. She turned back to Henry.

"What's the difference, Henry?" She reached over and grabbed a chunk of his muffin and threw it in her mouth, perfectly unshapen.

"Look at yourself right now. How many people do you know could wear a t-shirt with a picture of grenades hanging from a tree, paired with a cardigan and pearls?" She put her hand to her necklace, then back to the table. "Oh, and the Vans. Seriously. I'm flagrantly and unabashedly in love with your Vans. Every single pair of them." He smiled and kicked her foot under the table, then leaned forward. "I'm just saying that if Kat tries to dress you like her, I might cry myself to sleep tonight." Now, she kicked him.

"Fair enough. I shall take your tear ducts into account today, Henry." She smiled and took a sip of coffee. "Hey. What are you doing today?"

"Actually, I'm supposed to spend the day with my dad. We are golfing and then I'll take him to dinner somewhere." He batted at a stray hair that had fallen in his face then ran his hand through his hair.

Hawken smiled a devilish smile across the table.

"What?" He reached his hand across the table and took hers. "What?"

"Nothing. I'm just picturing you in plaid plus fours, leaning against a ball washer," she giggled.

He rolled his eyes. "Nice. I'll make you a deal. I won't change my style if you don't."

"Who says I like your style, Henry?" Again, with the kicking under the table. The woman in the adjacent booth sneering at them, which made the pair laugh even harder. She muttered something under her breath, but they couldn't make out what it was. Nor did they care.

As Henry dropped her off at her building, he turned to her in the car and said, "You're different today. Funnier. More smiley. I like it." He rested his hand on the gear shift.

She opened the car door, stepped out and closed it. When she knocked on the window, Henry found the switch and rolled it down. She leaned her face into the car and said, "It's you, Henry. You did this. You are everything."

She turned and walked into the prison, directly to her cell.

"You ready to meet the new you, beeotch?" Kat threw herself down on Hawken's bed after practically breaking down the door.

"Nice," she said, rolling her eyes. "What's wrong with *this* me anyway?" Hawken had thought about what Henry had said that morning over coffee. Kat definitely had her own style that was a lot edgier and sexier than Hawken. She wore plaid with stripes. She wore combat boots with skirts. She wore skirts.

"You just need a little more sex appeal, that's all. Don't get all sentimental. I'm not going to turn you into a mini me." Kat was bent over, retying her shoelaces. The laces that were wrapped and crossed all up and down her calves.

Sex appeal? More like dominatrix, Hawken thought.

"I'm not sure I can pull off sex appeal, Kat. I don't think I want to." Hawken was at her desk, applying her chap stick for the eighteenth time that day. After smacking her lips, she said, "How was Alex last night? What did you guys do?"

Kat turned and looked at her. Really looked at her. "Something's different." Hawken didn't know if she meant with her or with Alex.

"What?" Hawken asked, offended.

"You. You seem different." Kat was looking her up and down, like she was decked out in full leathers.

"No, I don't."

"What did you and Henry do last night?" She was squinting her beady little eyes at Hawken, awaiting the answer, arms crossed over her chest.

"We went to a planetarium and dinner. Why? What did you guys do?" Her tone was defensive.

"A planetarium? Isn't that like star gazing?" Kat asked, smirking.

"Not really. Kind of." Kat was staring. "What?"

"OMG. You totally had sex with him last night." She jumped off the bed and ran to Hawken's side, bouncing up and down.

"No, I did not. Are you kidding me?" She smacked Kat on the arm. "Look at you. What's wrong with you?" This was enough to send her over the edge.

"I don't believe you. You're practically glowing right now," Kat mused. Her face was eclipsed by her enormous smile.

"Nothing physical happened, loser. We just talked. A lot. It was amazing." Hawken rolled her eyes when she said 'amazing' and raised up her shoulders, batted her eyes, like she was in an old movie talking about a boy.

"That's all you guys do. Talk. What on earth can you still have to talk about?" Deflated, Kat fell back onto the bed, crossing her legs at the ankles.

"Seriously? Everything. Let me ask you something,"

Hawken stood up in front of Kat, resting her hands on her hips. "How long was your longest relationship?"

Kat uncrossed and recrossed her legs, looking up, thinking. "Six weeks. Why?"

"Just curious." She thought about that for a moment, but saw Kat looking at her for more. "Tell me about Alex. What did you guys do last night?" Hawken kicked Kat's feet.

"Sex, Hawken. Then we watched a movie with some of his friends upstairs. I watched them all get blasted, then went home. That is a typical date night in the Real World." She bent over and adjusted her tights. "You ready to do this?" She pointed her thumb to the door.

"Absolutely. Let's go." Hawken was thrilled to get out of there. The tiny cell was shrinking with every word that Kat said to her. She understood that most people were like Kat. You see a hot guy, flirt a little, get him up to your room, but she never really thought past that point. At eighteen years old, how many guys *had* Kat slept with? How many girls had Henry slept with?

"DID I say something to piss you off back there?" Kat was blowing pink gum bubbles at Hawken to get her attention. They were in Hawken's car on the way to the mall and she was lost in thought. So much so that she couldn't remember driving as far as she had. They were one light away from the mall's parking lot.

"No. Of course not. I'm just realizing how naïve I really am about life, I guess."

Kat laughed. "You really are. But it's okay. You're just behind the curve, is all. Honestly, there isn't that much that you are missing out on. It sounds like Henry is more like you than like Alex, so that's working in your favor."

"What do you mean?" As Hawken pulled into a parking spot, she put the gear shift into park and looked over at Kat.

"I just mean that someone like Alex probably wouldn't wait around very long for you to get your act together. Most guys will only wait so long, then they move on." Kat pushed the door open and swung her legs out. She turned back to Hawken. "Henry is filthy hot, Hawken. He's probably had a lot of girl-friends. I don't know. But if he's really this patient, then maybe he might be one of," she mock finger quoted, "'the good ones.'"

And he was. He was good. And patient. And kind. As Hawken exited the car and shoved her phone in her back pocket, it vibrated a text alert. Henry.

To Hawken: This sucks. @3:37pm

 To Henry: What sucks? Not wearing plus 4s? @3:38pm

 To Hawken: Ha. No. Wanting to be with u and not being with u @3:39pm

 To Henry: I know @3:40pm

"Are you seriously texting right now?" Kat stopped short at the door to the entrance and Hawken walked right into her. "Oww. What the eff, Hawken?" She shoved her shoulder, causing Hawken to step back.

"Sorry. I'm done." She shoved her phone back in her pocket and looked around at the two floors of overwhelmingness that was about to kill her. "Let's do this."

After two hours of making comments in the realm of "Seriously?" and "I don't think so!" or "I'm not a whore, Kat!" Hawken had found some new pants and sweaters and more t-shirts. Kat even approved of some of it. She did end up with one short leather skirt and black tights that Kat forced her into buying by miming slicing her throat with a box cutter that was left on one of the displays. She folded up the receipt and put it in her wallet to be found later when she returned them.

Kat had walked straight into one of those girly underwear stores and started pulling pink and black lacy things off hangers, leaving Hawken on the verge of passing out, until she realized that they were for Kat. *Bullet dodged.*

On the ride home, Kat must have felt like she put her platform combat boots in her mouth because she said, "I'm sorry if I was abrupt and mean earlier. Maybe I'm just jealous. I don't know. I'm not sure anyone has really cared about me enough to want to ask me personal things. Plus, I'm the queen of beeotches and you were just standing there, so I had to take full advantage of my powers." She grinned at Hawken and all was forgiven.

HAWKEN NOW WAS NEVER MORE than a foot away from her cell phone just in case she happened to miss a call from Henry, like this one that same night that she didn' miss.

"Henry, will you be honest with me?"

"Of course."

"Have you ever been in love?" It took an extraordinary amount of time to get the words out, but there they were. Hanging in the air, floating away.

She heard him swallow. "A couple of weeks ago, I would have said yes."

"And now, no?" She had become somewhat used to her heartbeat increasing on a seismic level lately, but she could barely hear Henry over it now.

"Now I don't think so." He paused, and she let him. She waited patiently for him to continue. "I don't want to say too much here, Hawken. It's too early to know, but I do know that before you, I thought I'd been in love. Like, real love. But everything with you is so different that now I don't think that it could have been."

Silence. Henry couldn't see Hawken covering her eyes with her hands and pushing the tears back in. In this moment she felt like she'd jumped off a cliff and was flying through the air.

"Hey. What are you thinking?" Henry's voice was barely over a whisper.

"I don't know. I'm just really happy, Henry. Like, I don't think I'm even touching the ground anymore."

"I can't believe I won't see you tomorrow." Now he was whispering, his mouth close to the phone.

"I can't even think about that right now. Henry, what did you do before you met me? On the weekends. After school. Whenever?" She was tracing circles in her jeans with her pinky finger.

"I don't know. My roommates have parties usually once a week. I am at school a lot and because of work, I basically stay there all day and do homework or study in-between. Why?"

She took a deep breath. "What about girls? Weren't you dating girls? Going out?"

Now he was breathing laboriously. "Yeah. Some."

"What does that mean?" Her voice caught on the last word.

"What are you asking me?" His voice sounded serious, low.

"I don't know what I'm asking you. I'm not even sure I want you to answer what I'm asking you."

Now Hawken was shaking and turning white. She felt sick. She didn't want to know, but she felt like she needed to know. Would it change anything between them? Doubtful.

"I've dated. I've had a couple of serious relationships. This —us is new for me."

"What about this is new for you?" Hawken's voice was wavering as she asked the question. What was she so nervous about? She was grateful that he wasn't sitting in front of her to see her right now.

"The talking. The knowing you. The not kissing, touching. Being real with you. The feelings. All of this is new."

Instantly Hawken thought of Kat. Kat went into a relationship with someone like a jackhammer through sand. There was never any talking or bonding. It went straight to the physical, then, after a couple of weeks, it ended.

"A good new or a bad new? Do you feel like you're missing out on everything else?" She should just stop now. What was she hoping to get from this conversation?

"Definitely good. I wouldn't mind being able to touch you. Or kiss you. That is hard for me. But I understand where you are coming from and I respect that. "He stopped, but Hawken was in no position to say anything, so she was grateful when he continued. "I like talking to you like this. I've never done this before. I love that you answer my questions. It's funny. I can ask you anything and you always tell me the truth, but you barely let me touch you. So, on the one hand, you trust me with your secrets, but not the rest." He inhaled quickly, then said, "I'm sorry. I shouldn't have said that."

She winced. "No, say what you are feeling, Henry. I need to hear it. I didn't think about it, but you're right. I totally trust you. I've never trusted anyone. Well, aside from your mom. But not even my family. Yet—the other stuff freaks me out. I don't know—I am working on it, though."

"Don't be sorry. I'm not sorry. I told you, this is good. I've never gotten to know anyone else so well, like this. And, you are getting better at the other stuff. You kissed my neck last night. You let me kiss your hair. That was unexpected and amazing."

"Geez. I sound like a feral animal that needs gentle coaxing out from behind the barn."

"No, you're not. Don't say that. I don't mean that at all and I've never thought that."

Hawken bit the fist she shoved into her mouth.

"Sweet girl. Listen to me. If I had the power to change any of this, knowing where we are right now, I wouldn't. I wouldn't change any of it. Okay?"

"I would," she whispered.

"What? What part would you change?" She could hear the anxiety in his voice. No longer a whisper, an octave higher.

"I would have told you to come over tonight. Why didn't we plan on you coming over when you dropped off your dad?"

He laughed. "You scared me. I wasn't sure what you meant. Hey, I told my dad about you today. He remembered you from running."

"Oh great. He probably remembers and ugly, frumpy, loner and I'm sure he's thrilled about your choice." Hawken was laughing.

"Yep. Exactly. Those were his exact words." He laughed, then turned serious. "You could never be any of those things, Hawken." There was commotion in the background and then he said, "Hey. Open your door, sweet girl."

Hawken stood up, unable to contain her smile. When she pulled the door open, Henry was leaning in his Henry way, against the door frame. He stowed his phone in his pocket, then he whispered, "Hey, you. I was sitting downstairs in my car, missing you when I called," into her hair, then kissed her there.

10

Zoom forward an eternity. That was what it felt like to Hawken. By the second Monday night in October, two weeks later, that weekend had seemed like months ago.

She and Henry had been busy with school and work. He worked Monday, Wednesday, and most Friday nights, depending on the schedule of quizzes and tests that the professor administered that week. At first, they tried to see each other every day, but with all the homework and studying, it had become as arduous as finding a lost sock in the communal laundry room. One of them was always missing out on something important school wise. They had figured out that they could do homework together during the day whenever possible, and on the days that Henry had to work, he would call her when he arrived home to his house and they'd talk until they couldn't keep their eyes open. Even after all of that, they couldn't get enough of each other. The anticipation of their next meeting was enough to get them through the day, whatever it held.

Hawken was buried in quizzes and assignments due this

week. After Physics class Monday morning, they had twenty problems to finish by Friday. Another paper was assigned in her English class and Calculus was going to be a nightmare. Homework and a quiz that week, plus she had another model due the next Monday for her Architecture class.

She was home at five, feeling overwhelmed with school, but thrilled that Allison wasn't going to be there. She had left a text message that she would be missing her Tuesday morning class, so she'd just as well stay home.

Hawken sat down at her desk and pulled out her foam core and an X-ACTO blade. Another assignment to finish, yes, but this one was actually fun. Every one of her architecture assignments had been so far. They made her feel like an adult. Instead of pretending at home, building models of buildings that she loved, she was able to create something of meaning, for someone who had an idea about the profession. She was doing this in real life now.

As soon as her phone vibrated a text, she picked it up and went to sit on her bed. A text from Henry.

TO HAWKEN: *I'm at work, thinking of you @5:43pm*

To Henry: *Me too. What are you thinking? @5:44pm*

To Hawken: *about your Vans. They keep me awake at night @5:45pm*

To Henry: *that sexy, huh? @5:56pm*

To Hawken: *On you, yes @5:57pm*

To Hawken: *Tell me your guilty pleasures @5:58pm*

To Henry: *How much time do you have? @5:59pm*

To Hawken: *Forever @6:01pm*

To Henry: *the smell of pipe tobacco, loud music, burnt food @6:03pm*

To Hawken: *Burnt food. Nice @6:03pm*

To Henry: *your turn @6:04pm*

To Hawken: sk8r girls, Vans, strawberry shampoo @6:06pm
To Henry: quite original. How long u working? @6:08pm
To Hawken: 9? @6:09pm
To Henry: K. will I see you? @6:10pm
To Hawken: I hope so. I'll call u. @6:10pm

HAWKEN TURNED her music up and resumed her project. She was busy thinking about school and how amazing these last few weeks had been. Life had turned a page and was finally giving her a break. More than a break, really. An epic shift in genres.

She remembered Henry saying that he was happier than he'd ever been. She felt happier than she ever thought possible. Like in a video game when you spend hours and days trying to beat a level, then when you finally do, there is another level, and another. She had reached a higher level of happy.

She thought about Kat and Alex. They were still together, but unlike Hawken and Henry, they were fine with spending time apart. They even argued like a married couple.

"What do I need to spend all of my time with him for? I mean, I like him. I like spending time with him, but it gets boring. We don't just sit around and touch each other's faces and stare into one another's eyes, Hawk. You and Henry are seven kinds of bizarre. But that works for you. If Alex wanted to sit around and play with my hair all day, I'd stick a gun in my mouth." She had laid this out to Hawken the week before, after they'd all gone to dinner together.

The four of them had been studying at the science building and made plans afterwards to have some fun. Henry had only met Alex once, but had seen him studying with Kat and Hawken plenty of times.

The evening was awkward, to put it nicely. They had gone mini-golfing at one of those blatantly overdone castle themed places where every hole had something mechanical denying a low putting average.

Kat and Alex were smacking each other with their putters like two kids let loose at a circus. They made out like maniacs whenever either of them actually hit their ball.

Henry and Hawken held hands and smiled at each other, exchanging glances anytime Kat smacked Alex on the back of the head, or Alex pulled her hair. It was obvious that they were the boring couple, but it didn't matter. Hawken knew she could never survive in a relationship so volatile, especially with her past. She was growing more and more grateful for Henry whenever she compared their relationship with others.

Henry never pressured Hawken into anything. For her it wasn't only about the fear of getting close, but more about taking the time to really know each other and want to be together. Not just physically, but emotionally. She couldn't do just physical again. Ever. Of course, her perception of lust was an extreme one since she wasn't able to completely discount her past experience. She hoped fervently that Henry would think that the waiting was worth it. *Before she'd killed him*, she thought, grimacing.

After working on her model for almost two hours, she felt like she had made enough progress that she didn't need to feel stressed out about finishing on time.

At that point, her X-ACTO knife blade dulled to the point that it would only cut through the top layer of paper. So, she pulled out her desk drawer and found the extra blades.

Setting down the knife, she unscrewed the small metal screw on the end, then pulled the blade out. Carefully, she inserted the new, sharpened blade in place, but it kept jamming and wouldn't line up with the hole to reinsert the screw. Not thinking, she grabbed hold with her left hand and pushed roughly on the tip with her palm, not realizing what she was doing until blood started pouring out everywhere. Dropping the knife, she held up her hand. Her model looked like something from a horror film, dripping and covered in blood. She pulled tissues from the box, but they completely fell apart, soaked in blood before she could affix them to her hand. At this point, she grabbed a towel from her closet and picked up the phone.

"Hawken? What's wrong?" Henry sounded panicked. She never actually called him before, just texted. And, she knew he was working.

"Are you still working?" she asked, trying to stay calm.

"Yes, what's wrong?" His voice sounded sharp.

"Are you almost done?" She had made it to her door with the intent of shoving something in the doorway so that it wouldn't lock Henry out. Spot began to appear as the darkness took over her vision. She stuck her hand between the door and the jamb, then slowly made her way down to the floor.

"Hawken. Tell me what's going on."

"Well, I cut my hand open with my X-ACTO and I'm pretty sure I need to go to the emergency room." She was laying on the floor with her hand in the air, trying to stop the bleeding.

"Christ. Leaving now. Are you okay? How bad is it?"

"Well, I've wrapped it in a towel, which is almost completely soaked in blood and I'm pretty sure I'm going to have to pass out now, Henry."

"Hawken. Hawken? I'm on my way. Can you hear me?"

SHE OPENED her eyes in the darkness and could just make out Henry leaning over her, tugging at her side. "Where are we?"

He immediately pulled back to look at her face. "Hawken, thank God. You're in my car. I'm trying to get your seatbelt buckled. How do you feel?"

She heard a click and Henry extricated himself from her

side of the car. She grabbed his hand. "Don't leave." She sounded panicked.

"I'm not leaving. Just let me shut your door and I'll get in, okay?" Her Jedi death grip never loosened on his hand. She felt him pry off each finger individually to finally free his hand and shut her door. Half a second later he gave his hand back to her from the other side of the car. She could feel the road pass underneath them, giving her the sensation of flying.

"How are you feeling? Are you alright?" He was looking at her in fast, short glances, paying more attention to the road.

"Stop the car, Henry." She leaned forward in her seat and put her good hand on the dashboard.

"What?" He reached over and said, "What's wrong?" She could feel the car slowing down.

"Stop the car!" she yelled, already grabbing the door handle.

As soon as she felt the movement stop, she pushed her door open, leaned out, and threw up. She felt Henry's hand on her back as she coughed and spit into the grass a couple of times. Sitting up then closing the door, she croaked, "I'm okay, now. Sorry." She looked over at Henry and immediately started laughing without sound. He looked like he had just witnessed her unzip her head and rotate it around on her neck. "Sorry you had to see that."

THE EMERGENCY ROOM WAS PACKED, of course. Fortunately, there weren't any other knife wounds or stabbings, so she was considered Priority One at the time.

Henry tried to sit Hawken down in a chair while he went up to the glass window, but she wouldn't let go of his hand. Not touching Henry right now seemed equivalent to losing her balance on life.

A short, squat man with a comb over and pink scrubs pulled the opaque square glass aside and said, "How can I help you?" looking at Henry, then Hawken, then back at Henry. Hawken had a sick feeling in her stomach. *Is he judging us?* She rolled her eyes. *Yes, I'm aware he's out of my league,* she thought to herself.

Henry told The Judge that she stabbed herself with an X-ACTO knife while working on a school project. Both their heads turned in her direction, and then Henry added, "She passed out and she's vomited on the way in." Hawken rolled her eyes again.

"Did she hit her head when she passed out?" he inquired, showing little care or concern, given his monotonous tone.

"I don't know." Henry looked at her head, as if a sign would pop up with the answer in neon.

Hawken jumped in. "No. As soon as I couldn't see, I laid down on the floor by the door." She looked at Henry. "That's where I was, right?"

"Yes," he answered weakly, then he put his arm around her and kissed the top of her head.

"Okay, so you just need to fill out these forms and we'll call her back next." He handed Henry a catalog of forms which he'd never be able to fill out.

"Okay, thank you," Henry said, then started to turn away from the window.

Hawken stuck her head inside and said, "I'm in desperate need of a toothbrush and toothpaste. Anybody?"

Henry laughed. Out of nowhere she was handed two cellophane covered mini toothbrush kits containing a small tube of toothpaste, a toothbrush, and dental floss. She looked up and one of the women pointed to her right. Hawken turned and saw the restroom sign. "Bless you," she said.

Ten minutes later the double doors opened to a large,

heavily tattooed man, who looked at Hawken and said, "We're ready for you." She stood up and pulled Henry with her.

"Sorry. He's going to have to wait here." The staff at the hospital had to have been the motleyest crew ever. This man looked like he could have been a professional wrestler.

Hawken looked at Henry and kissed her head again. "It's okay. I'll be right here."

She looked at the shaved, tattooed, possibly ex-Navy Seal in salmon colored scrubs and said, "I'm not going back there without him." Her face was serious, sober. Severe enough for him to change his mind.

"Sure," he said, looking at Hawken. Then, to Henry, "We'll pull a chair into the room for you, sir."

AFTER AN HOUR, five stitches, plenty of codeine, an injection of antibiotics, and a bottle of pain pills for the road, Henry and Hawken were in the car, driving back to her building.

"Do you want me to call Kat?" Henry asked. He was holding her good hand, his thumb brushing back and forth over it.

"No. She's busy. I don't want to interrupt." Hawken was feeling euphoric. Her head was spinning. The doctors had told them that the painkillers would leave her groggy, maybe even loopy, but she felt more than that. She felt blurred around the edges. She felt like a mohair sweater.

"Why? What is she doing?" Henry pulled her back out of a trance.

"Alex." Her tone was casual, matter of fact.

"What?" He quickly turned to look at her.

"She's having sex with Alex. That's all they do, Henry. Have sex, watch Star Trek, and have sex again."

"Jesus." A second later Henry laughed. "Poor Alex."

Hawken was watching Henry laugh. She tried to memorize

the small lines that formed from his nose to his mouth and under his eyes. Then, she remembered his comment and asked, "Why poor Alex? What's funny?"

"You know that I like Kat." He turned to look at Hawken, who nodded, then he added, "I can't imagine that Alex would be in one piece after that. I could see him in need of stitches and painkillers, too." He laughed again. Then Hawken slugged him in the arm with her good hand and laughed, too.

She was all laughs in the car. Telling jokes, smiling at Henry, feeling elated. As soon as Henry's car pulled up to her building, she turned somber. She was worried that Henry was going to leave her. Alone in her room. Did the doctor mention something to them about that? She should have asked for a prescription of Henry. With unlimited refills.

He sensed the change and pulled her good hand to his face. "What's the matter? Are you in pain?"

"No. It's fine." She looked at him and swallowed hard, then said, "Henry. Will you stay with me?"

"Of course. I was going to, sweet girl." She couldn't see his mouth with her hand in the way, but she could tell by his eyes that he was smiling.

"Yeah, But all night with me?"

"Yes. I'm not going anywhere. I'm going to get you out of the car and then I'll go park and be right back, okay?" He pulled his door open.

"No. I can walk. Let's just go park and walk together. I'm fine now, really."

"Geez. It looks as though I really was bludgeoned by my room-mate." Hawken had opened the door, seeing the room for the first time. Her model was sitting on her desk, dried blood covering the roof line. There was a pool of blood on her desk and bloody tissues on the floor by her chair. Fortunately, she had taken her towel and wrapped it around her hand, which she left at the hospital. Most of the gore was sitting in that. As she turned to look at Henry, she noticed his shirt had blood covering the lower right side, probably from carrying her down to the car.

"You should take your shirt off," she said as casually as she would say "I'm hungry."

His expression was priceless. One of shock and confusion, leaving his mouth somewhat hanging open. Hawken doubled over, laughing so hard. Henry stood there, watching the spectacle that she became in the last couple of minutes, loopy on painkillers.

"The blood, Henry. All over your shirt. You should take it off." He looked down and started laughing.

A small spot of red had bled through onto his white t-shirt, but it was hardly noticeable. Hawken finally looked down at her clothes and was mortified. She had blood all over her black jeans. She could see it shining in the harsh lighting. She looked up at Henry, who was also tracing the lines of dried blood on her clothes with his eyes.

"Where are your pajamas?" His eyes went back and forth from the dresser to Hawken, who didn't answer. "Hawken. Are you okay?" He was bent over, moving closer to her face.

"Sorry. The drugs. I'm underwater. In a non-drowning kind of nice way, though, I think." Everything seemed pixelated. In her head, her vision, and her ears.

"Do you mind if I look in here?" He was pointing to her dresser. She shook her head.

He opened the top drawer and immediately closed it. Right. Moving on. In the next drawer, she watched him pull out a navy-blue t-shirt and shake it out in the air. It had the letters FDNY on the front in white. He threw it over his shoulder, then closed the drawer. He was bent over now, lifting things and moving things around. Hawken felt like she was watching an episode of CSI in slow motion. He was looking for clues in her dresser. He stood up, with a hand full of pink striped boxer shorts. He held them out to her. "Really? You sleep in these?" She shrugged and sat back against the cinderblock.

He walked over to her and handed her the clothes. "Okay, you put these on, and I'm going to go and fill your ice bag. Okay?" She nodded.

Two minutes later, Henry knocked on the door. Hawken opened it and smiled at him. He looked down at her and frowned. "You didn't change your clothes."

"No, I didn't." She raised her bandaged left hand into the air and nodded at it. "The Bloody Stump doesn't want to cooperate." He laughed at that, which was a good, comfortable sound. "I couldn't get my sleeve over the bandages."

"Okay, I'll help you. Let's take your shirt off first." They stood next to the bed. Henry turned her around so that her back was facing him. She pulled up her shirt with her right hand and he slid it over her right arm and her head, then carefully over her left hand, pulling the sleeve open wide with his fingers. He threw her shirt on the floor and didn't say anything. She could feel his hand close to her back.

Then he did say something. "You have a tattoo," he said, slowly.

"Oh, yeah. I got it right...after." She wrapped her right arm around her stomach reflexively.

"What is it? I can only see the top part." Henry was almost whispering, and she could hear him swallow.

"Here," she said, and with her right hand, she unclasped her bra and took it off, throwing it on the bed. She was aware of the silence and the thickness of the air in the room, but she was feeling so high on the drugs, she didn't care. She said, "It's a hawk, wings spread out, flying into the sun." She'd gotten the tattoo two weeks after it had happened. *Another secret that no one knew about.* It was about four inches high across the full width of her back. Because of the placement, it was easy to forget it was there.

"It's beautiful." Hawken felt his fingertip trace the wings of the bird on her back. Now she was feeling exposed, and shivering, so she bent over and picked up her shirt from the bed and handed it to him. "Right," he said.

After getting her shirt on, she unbuttoned her jeans and pulled them down, then sat on the bed. Henry was sitting on the floor removing her shoes. Then he tugged on her pant legs, sliding them off. She threw him her pink shorts and he slipped them over her feet, then stood up and walked over to the desk, trying to give her privacy, she assumed. She pulled them up to her knees and stood up, raising them to her waist.

"Do you need any water or anything?" he asked, not sure what else to do.

"No. I'm tired. Are you tired?" Looking at the bed, she leaned over and pulled the comforter and sheet down to the foot of the bed, then looked at Henry, expectantly.

"Let me take my shoes off." His voice now seemed thick, almost hoarse.

She sat on the bed as he bent over and pulled his shoes off, not looking at her. Was it possible that he was nervous? Hawken smiled to herself at that thought. She was trying to make mental notes of things to remember from this night. This was one of them.

"Henry. Come here. You are kind of freaking me out." She was patting the bed with her hand.

"Sorry." He put both his hands through his hair and walked over.

"Hey, if you don't want to stay, you don't have to. Really." Hawken looked him in the eye and said, "Thank you for coming tonight, Henry. I am so grateful. I can't imagine having called anyone else." She smiled a wide smile as his expression grew more confused.

Walking over to sit next to her on the bed, his hands cupped her face and he kissed her forehead. Moving his lips to her hair he whispered, "I'm not leaving. I don't want to leave, okay?"

She nodded and then stood up. He looked at her quizzically and she said, "I need to keep my hand elevated. If you get in first, I can lay it on you, thus elevating it per doctor's instructions." He laughed and climbed in, fully dressed, his back turned against the wall. She set the comforter over his side, then placed her ice bag over his hip. She lay down, smashing herself against the full length of his body, intending on being as close to him as humanly possible, a tangle of limbs.

Once she was comfortable, she moved her head up to look at his face. He turned his head down to meet hers, and said, "Hi."

"Hi," she said, "Is this okay?"

He took his right hand and brushed away the hair from her forehead. Then he kissed her there. "It's perfect."

"Henry. I really like you so much. You are too good to me. I don't deserve you."

He kissed her forehead again. "No, you are too good for me, Tony Hawk."

There was silence for a long period of time. Henry whispered, "Are you asleep?"

She shook her head. "I'm just drowning. It's a strange feeling. I'm not sure what's real and what isn't. Does that even make sense?"

"Yes. Just sleep, sweet girl." He placed another kiss to her forehead.

"I love it when you call me that." She paused. "It makes my heart swell to ten times its size, just like the Grinch."

He laughed and pulled her closer. She wrapped her left leg around his, sneaking her foot around his legs. She felt like she was weaving in and out of consciousness, unable to hold on to one place long enough to know for sure what was real and what was a dream.

"Do you think I'm pretty, Henry?" She asked, her voice muted into his chest.

"You are more than pretty. You are beautiful." She felt him sigh into her hair, then whisper, "You are everything." With every word, his chin would scrape against her face. She tried to hold on to that feeling, realizing that this was real, not the drugs.

THE THROBBING in her hand felt like it had been detached and the blood was pulsing from her arm. It took her a minute to realize that she needed to wake up. Then, she realized that she was clenching her hand into a fist, which was pulling on the stitches. She opened her eyes and was disoriented, pulling back away from Henry's chest. The movement woke him. He lifted his head and, with a worried look asked, "Hey. Are you in pain? Do you want to take your pills?"

She looked around the room and asked, "What time is it?"

He pulled his phone out of his pocket and pushed on the screen. "It's three-fifty-two. It's been almost six hours. You should take a painkiller." He sat up and pulled the covers back, climbing over her. Pulling a bottle of water from the refrigerator, he opened it, handing it to her. "Let me grab you a pill."

Hawken stood up and started searching the bed with her hands for the ice bag. She found in wedged between the bed and the wall. She held it out to Henry as he handed her the pill.

When he crawled back into bed, Hawken was still feeling loopy and tired. He set the bag of ice on his side again and put her hand on top. "This okay?" he asked.

She nodded. And nodded. And nodded. He laughed at her

and put his hand on her face. "Hey, fruit loop. How are you feeling now?"

"Fruit loopy. That sounds good, actually."

"What, cereal? Are you hungry?" His face was mere inches from hers.

"I have no idea what you are asking me. Did I just take another painkiller?"

"Wow. You really are out of it. Yes, you just took a painkiller. Go back to sleep. Are you comfortable?"

"Yes." Then. "Kiss me, Henry." For a moment he hesitated, then smoothed her hair and kissed her head. She shook her head. "No. Really kiss me." He didn't move or dare speak. He just sighed. "You don't want to?" She asked into his neck.

"Of course, I want to. Just, not tonight. Not like this." He replied, combing her hair with his fingers.

"Why not?" she asked, reaching her face up as far as she could without pulling herself farther away from his body.

"Hawken. You will not remember this tomorrow. Just try to sleep now."

"So, shouldn't you be taking full advantage of my memory lapse? You know, cracking a sinister laugh and the whole bit. I'm the one asking you." She was smiling. He felt her cheeks rising on his neck.

"No. Sweet girl, I won't do that. I care about you more than anything. More than everything. I wouldn't ever hurt you. I want you to know that and trust that. When you are ready, then it will happen. Besides, being with you like this, like we are-- talking and taking it one step at a time... It's like slow motion, but also high-def at the same time. Like time has slowed for us to enjoy every second. Every touch. Every feeling. It's incredible. I don't want to ruin that."

She tried to really think about what he was saying. She wanted to hold on to this. It was important. Even with all the drugs pushing down on her, she knew that this was something incredible. She was worried that he wouldn't understand. A kiss didn't mean anything to anyone. It **should**. It should be the very start of everything. The starting point of infinity.

A few minutes later, she said, "Tell me something I don't know about you." She wanted to keep him talking as much as she could. It was a new level of amazing to watch his chin move up and down when he spoke.

After thinking for a moment, he said, "My middle name is Burton."

She pulled her face up to look at his mouth. "Like the snowboards?"

"Yep. My mom used to snowboard," he said, combing his fingers through her hair again.

"Henry Burton Lewis. I like that." She burrowed her head back into his warm neck and tried to sleep. A long time had passed, and she said, "Henry?"

"Mmhmmm."

"Are you falling asleep or don't want to talk?"

"I'm awake. I always want to talk to you. How's your hand?" He turned his head and pulled his arm away to check the ice pack. The sloshing of the water was muted by the clinking of ice cubes, so it was still working its magic.

Hawken whispered, "When my brother can't sleep, I sing to him." Henry had resumed his position, wrapping his arm around her. "Do you know the song 'If I Fell' by the Beatles?"

"Yes. Is that what you sing for him?" He asked and she nodded. A minute later she nodded again. "Are you asking me to sing for you?" he said with a smirk. Another series of nods was his answer.

"Only if you want to, Henry Burton Lewis." He laughed.

"Okay, but then you sleep."

On cue, she yawned. "Okay."

He took a deep breath, then against her hair he whispered the lyrics.

11

"I look like Frankenstein's hand double." Hawken had just removed the bandage and gauze from her hand and saw what a bloody mess she made of herself. "Seriously, Henry. Look!" She thrust her hand right into his face, causing him to jump back like she threw acid on him. She started to laugh and chased him around the room with her hand mere inches from his face. When she had enough of tormenting him, she held her left wrist with her right hand and pulled it close to her face. "This is going to leave a nasty scar." She looked up at Henry, who was trying to unroll the wrap that the hospital had given them.

"It's just your palm. There are plenty of lines there already. No one will ever notice. Besides," he said, holding it up to his face with pride, "you have a stab wound. I fervently believe that this may just be the only stab wound you will ever receive, and I bet Kat will be incredibly jealous."

After he set her hand down on her desk and cleaned around the site, he carefully applied ointment with a Q-tip, and folded two pieces of gauze to cover the stitches. Then he wrapped the bandage around her hand and wrist, securing it with medical tape. He kissed her Bloody Stump and started to clean up the desk. Looking at his phone, he said, "It's time for another painkiller. Do you want to take one?"

She brushed the hair out of her face and sighed, contemplatively. "Well, if I take one now, there's no way I'm going to make it through a full day of school. And, I can't miss school, so...no. I'm not going to." She sat back down on the bed, pulling the comforter over her legs.

"Are you sure? I worry about you being in pain all day. There could be an avalanche effect. You feel fine, but then it starts getting painful and the meds take too long to kick in and it can get unbearable. Please take them." He pleaded, unscrewing the cap on the prescription bottle.

"Henry. Do you remember last night? And earlier this morning for that matter? I keep trying to remember talking to you, but I don't think I remember everything. How is that going to help me at school today? And, this is Tuesday, right?"

Henry nodded.

"I don't have any classes with Kat, so I'm on my own. I can take some aspirin. If it gets too bad, I can come home and take a painkiller. I promise." In her head, Hawken was thinking of how unaccustomed she was to someone taking care of her like this. Her parents never did, not after being so overwhelmed with her brother, Rex. She was the one who had to pick herself up after a fall. She didn't have anyone in her life for so long that actually treated her like someone special. Like she had a partner. A supporter.

"I'm just worried. Whatever you want to do is fine. Ultimately, it is up to you." Henry kissed the top of her head and picked up the ice bag from the foot of the bed. "I'm going to fill this, then we'll get you dressed." He didn't look at her, but Hawken thought she saw a smirk on his face when he walked out the door.

While Henry was down the hall, she stood in front of her

mirror, looking at herself. Really looking. She was rather plain. Short, straight, light blond hair. Her body was thin and fit, but nothing to brag to Jennifer Lopez about. What was it that Henry saw in her? Her features were simple. Long oval face, symmetrical eyes, simple, boring nose. Her top lip was the same width as the bottom and her teeth were straight, due to two years of braces. She knew that she could never be considered sexy, no matter what she was wearing. She could pass for cute. Even the girl next door, but not sexy. Kat could be sexy. She had that curvy body and pouty mouth that guys loved. As she studied herself in the mirror between her dresser and closet, she saw Henry step in and stand behind her. She didn't turn, but she watched his face in the mirror.

It is amazing how little things are more pronounced while looking at someone else from the angle of a mirror. Hawken had a dog when she was young that had a small black ring around her right eye. It was hardly noticeable straight on, blending in with her overall coloring. But when she sat in front of the mirrored closet doors while Hawken was getting ready, that ring of black was as blatant as if it were a neon sign.

As Hawken observed Henry, she was awestruck. His eyes were more pronounced and luminous. The angle of his nose was in perfect symmetry with his face. Even the scar above his eye had seemed to all but disappear. He was breathtaking. He was a Mobius strip. No matter what angle you took, he was perfect and balanced. Standing there, his shoulders and head peeking out over hers in the background, she felt in awe. He was here with her. Taking care of her. Caring about her.

She watched him step forward and saw his eyes fill with mirth as his mouth turned upward, slowly lighting up his face. He reached his arms around her, crossing them over her stomach, setting his face in her neck. He kissed her there and pulled her tight against his chest. Hawken watched him in the mirror as he never took his eyes off hers in the mirror. She leaned her head back against him and closed her eyes. She could smell his musky, morning smell and turned her face to kiss his cheek. As she turned her body around in his arms, he said, "You are so beautiful. Don't ever question that, sweet girl."

HAWKEN CHECKED the time on her phone, then panicked. "Henry! It is ten-thirty-seven!" She pushed the phone into his hand and pointed to the screen.

He nodded. "I know. Everything is fine. Sam is in my first two classes, so he can catch me up later when we meet for homework. My next class is at twelve, when you have yours. Don't panic, okay?"

"But—"

"Shhh. I would never have left you here without help. There isn't anywhere else that I need to be, or want to be, for that matter." He looked at her and said, "We should probably get you dressed for school." He stepped over to her closet and slid the door open. He turned and smiled at her. "Hey, I get to pick something for you to wear today, okay?" He was smiling his best crooked smile at her.

"Okay, Henry. You pick. This should be interesting." She sat back on her bed, crossing her legs in front of her. She really was curious to see what he would choose.

When all was said and done, he opted for a black band shirt with knives, "Because what could be more appropriate on a day like this, after being stabbed," he said. He also picked out a pair of dark skinny jeans that she had bought on her shopping trip with Kat. And Vans, of course. That was a given as they made up ninety percent of her shoe options. He chose the shiny silver pair with black laces. He said, "They have a sharp edge."

After Henry was finished playing dress up, Hawken looked at him. "Hey, you have no shirt. Do you have time to go home first?" She was worried about him. It felt good. There was a nice level of equality.

"I texted Sam last night and asked him to bring me clothes. I told you not to worry. I have it all taken care of."

She gazed at him, remembering the last twelve hours and the fact that he dropped everything to race over to help her. And he stayed. Standing up, she walked over to him, put her arms tightly around him, and said, "Henry. You are amazing. Thank you for this. For last night. For forgetting about your life and taking care of me. I am so grateful."

"Hawken. You *are* my life."

HAWKEN MADE it through the day attending all her classes and finding quiet corners to study in-between. She had finally made it home for the day at five o'clock. Henry was going to be at class until seven, then stop by to check in.

As she opened the door, she heard Allison's voice wafting in the air, like a toxic airborne spread disease. She looked down at her now throbbing hand and knew that she had no choice. She had to go in and deal with her roommate so that she could shower, take her painkillers, and ice her hand after a full day without.

"Hawken! You're home, finally." She came running over to ambush her, but Hawken raised the Bloody Stump into the air and Allison comically ground to a halt six inches away. "What happened to you? Are you okay?" She reached out to touch Hawken, but Hawken was anticipating her move and shuffled to the side quickly.

"I got so hungry last night I started chewing my own hand and ended up making a real mess of things. The doctors were able to keep the musculature intact, but some of the nerves are shot." As soon as it came out of her mouth, she felt bad. Allison was always just trying to be nice, but she needed to scale it back about six thousand decibels.

"Are you serious? Why would you do that?" Allison was looking at Hawken like she was the lunatic in the room, her mouth drawn open in shock.

"Just bored and hungry, I guess. What are you doing here? It's Tuesday."

"I have to be at the testing center tomorrow early, so I figured I'd stay here."

Hawken set her bag down on the floor in front of her closet, took off her jacket, then hung it inside. She was dying to take a shower but couldn't negotiate tying a plastic bag around her arm by herself. There was also the fact that she would rather actually eat her own hand than to stay in the room with Allison any longer. Grabbing her phone, she dialed Kat.

"Hey, Kat. I need a favor. Can I come over and shower at your place?" She was talking into her shoulder, ensuring Allison wouldn't hear. When she hung up the phone, she turned around to see Allison sitting at her desk with her earphones on. Grabbing some clothes and her basket of bathroom necessities, she walked out.

"I can't believe you told Allison that and she believed you. That girl has to be the first lobotomized person to go to college." Kat had been hanging out with Alex when Hawken appeared in the doorway, so she kicked him out to give Hawken privacy. Helping Hawken out of her clothes, she tied a plastic bag around her bandaged hand. When she finished showering, Hawken returned to Kat's room to find Kat on the floor, crying.

"What's wrong? Are you okay?" Hawken rushed over in her towel and tried to sit down on the floor without flashing Kat. After deeming the task impossible, Hawken whispered, "I'm the worst friend ever, but can you help me get dressed so that I can sit and talk to you? Please."

Kat, of course, took pity on her. When she was decent, Hawken sat down and put her hand on Kat's back.

"I don't know what I'm doing with Alex. All we do is sit and drink and watch TV and have sex." She turned and looked at Hawken. Hawken didn't know what to say.

"Well, you know that I have less experience with guys than pretty much all of mankind, but I don't know what you expect to get out of this, Kat. I mean, do you guys have anything in common? What does he like to do outside of school?"

"Nothing. Literally. He and Jason just sit around all day playing video games and ordering takeout. It's like when they get together they turn into total morons."

Hawken laughed. She had seen this first-hand. "Well, what about when you aren't with Jason? When it's just the two of you. What do you talk about? Where do you go?"

Kat turned and laid down on the floor, and Hawken followed. They both put their feet up on Kat's bed and their hands on the floor over their head. Hawken's hand was still throbbing, reminding her she needed to find a cold bag of ice, but she wasn't going to leave Kat now.

"Ninety percent of the time we are with Jason. That's the problem. The other part...well, you can guess what we are doing when we aren't around him." Kat turned her head and looked at Hawken. She grimaced, then laughed.

"Well, I don't think you should be crying just yet. I mean, look at the bright side." Hawken leaned over and punched Kat with her good hand. "You basically have two boyfriends and they know about each other and don't care."

Kat smiled, but it didn't reach her eyes. "I don't know." She let out a long breath.

Hawken said, "I suggest taking Alex somewhere alone.

Jason is not allowed. Like a proper date. If Alex gives you crap about it, you know he isn't really into this either, right?"

Kat nodded.

Hawken continued, "I mean, if he can't be alone with you and talk to you about anything relevant to your relationship, do you really want to be with him?"

"You're right. I know you're right." She turned her head and pulled on Hawken's hair. "How did you get so good at this? Why is it that I'm coming to you for relationship advice and not the other way around?"

Hawken shrugged. "I haven't needed any, I guess. Henry is so open, honest, and loving. I know that I could talk to him about anything. I'm lucky. I haven't had a relationship with anyone, including my family, that I could be perfectly nutty-Hawken and not worry that I've let the feral animal out of its cage."

She turned to Kat and smiled. They lay there on the floor for a long time until Hawken shot up and said, "OMG. What time is it?" She searched the bag she brought for her phone, unable to find it.

"It's seven-twenty. Why? You have a curfew?"

"Henry was coming over at seven and I don't have my phone. I have to go." She darted around picking up her clothes and shoved her feet in her shoes. "Thanks for the help," she said and left.

She had too much in her good hand to run, so she walked as fast as she could to her building, her toiletry basket smacking into her hip with every step. She must have looked like a freak show because most of the people that she passed along the way stopped and stared.

As soon as she turned the knob, she had a sick feeling in her stomach. *Please let me not have missed Henry*, she said to herself. Kicking the door open she found Allison sitting at her desk. Grabbing her phone from her bed, Hawken saw two messages and two texts.

I got out early. On my way. @6:34pm
Where are you? Worried. @7:10pm

"Crap!" She pushed play on her voicemails and heard Henry's deep voice, pitched slightly higher in worry. He was calling from his car, concerned when she didn't text back. The next message was Henry calling from his car on his way home at seven fifteen. She looked over at Allison, who didn't appear to notice she was home.

"Allison. Allison." She finally took her headphones off and looked at Hawken. "Did a guy come up here looking for me?" She asked, pleading.

"Yeah. Henry. He seemed a little upset. I told him that you ran off as soon as you got home. Probably upstairs to see your friends." Her eyes pointed up to the ceiling while she was talking.

"What? Why did you tell him that?" She asked, biting her lower lip. "Never mind. Did he say anything? Was he coming back?" Hawken paced the room between both beds.

"How should I know? He just sat here for a long time, watching his phone. He looked worried, then he left."

Great. Henry was exhausted after everything that had happened last night and had an early day tomorrow, so probably wasn't going to want to come back. And, since Allison was here, he couldn't stay with Hawken again. The only other option was to go to Henry's room, but that wasn't really an option. Hawken was terrified of Henry's room. Not just because it was totally private and had a large bed, but because she spent so much time imagining other girls there. So much so, that in her head, it had become a reality. She thought of the pictures that Kat had in her room. What if Henry had pictures of other girls hanging on the walls. Or a box containing the remnants of past one-nighters spilling over underneath his bed. It was too much for her to think about. So, she didn't.

She picked up her phone and walked down the stairway back outside into the cold, harsh air. Her hair was still damp, causing her to shiver as she dialed Henry's number. He picked up on the first ring. Of course he did.

"Hawken? Where are you? Are you okay?" His tone was serious, but his voice muted.

"Henry. I'm sorry. I went to Kat's house to take a shower and she was upset and so I stayed and talked to her, but I didn't realize I forgot my phone until it was way past seven. I'm sorry. I'm back at my building now. Will you come back?"

"I can't. I just got home, and I told my roommates I'd go out with them. We are on our way out now. I'm sorry that you weren't there. I was in agony all day thinking about you and how you were feeling. How is your hand, sweet girl?"

"Fine... Not really. It's hurting now. I need to ice it, but I haven't had a chance."

"You need to. Go do it, okay? Please? It's just going to hurt more and take longer to heal. What's wrong with Kat?"

Hawken could hear voices in the background and Henry's voice now sounded like he was talking into his hand. "Nothing. Just Alex issues. She'll be fine." Hawken paused. "Henry, I don't want to have missed seeing you tonight."

He sighed. "Your roommate is there. She's completely insane, you know." He said it as a statement, not an interrogative.

"I know. I keep thinking that there is someone walking around out there with a butterfly net and a picture of Allison."

Henry laughed. "Funny girl. I probably won't be home for another hour and a half at least. I have to be up early tomorrow. I don't think I can come back tonight."

Hawken said nothing.

"You should take a painkiller and go to bed, Hawken.

Okay?" He sounded serious, but also like he was ready to hang up.

"I want to see you, Henry. Please?" It came out more pathetic and desperate than it should have. Maybe the pain in her hand was worse than she thought. It seemed like her nerves were exposed now.

"Well, you can come to my house, Hawken." There was an edge to his voice, to the tone he used.

"I can't." The words flew out, without hesitation.

"Why? Don't you trust me? After last night how can you say no?" He sounded tired and irritated.

"I just can't. I don't want to go to your house."

"You need to explain to me why, Hawken." She was getting impatient at his tone and his apathetic attitude towards seeing her tonight. If he was unwilling to come over, then she would survive. She had noticed that he was saying her name now, instead of nicknames. That had to mean something, too.

"I can't go there, Henry. It will be too much. It's overwhelming and scary and I'm not ready."

"Not ready for what? Nothing is going to happen. We just talked about that. I've promised you that." He paused. "You don't trust me? Is that it? You think I'm lying to you now? That you'll come to my house and what? What Hawken?"

"You know what, Henry? Go have fun tonight. Maybe I'll talk to you tomorrow." Hawken hung up the phone.

12

Hawken woke to the sound of typing. In the aftermath of the previous night's events, she wondered if she was dreaming. Or dead.

When she hung up on Henry the previous night, she turned off her phone immediately and went up to her room. By some miracle Allison wasn't there. Her desk light was still on, illuminating the trio of picture frames on her desk. Picture frames holding images of people that Hawken had assumed were family members. The bad news was that she would no doubt be returning.

After swallowing a painkiller, Hawken picked up her empty ice pack from her bed and threw it at the window. Hoping to what? Break the window? Break the ice pack? Probably. Henry had said that it was important for her hand and he wasn't there to care, so it was her way of rebelling against him, she supposed. Instead of alleviating her anger, it made her feel worse. It made her feel like a spoiled child having just been sent to her room.

Quickly, she realized that she was an idiot. The entire time that they had been dating, he was a prince. He came over constantly, called her, texted her, waited for her. He was tired and needed a night off from Crazyville, and a night on his own again. Of course, she could understand that now, given that she had time to think, but she didn't have much experience with this. She was always on her own, and this was a new experience. To have someone know you. See you. The real you.

She was afraid of letting go. Of giving him space to realize that he would never be able to be with someone like her. Someone as messed up as her.

Hawken convinced herself to give Henry space, but then started thinking about the cluster of stars that he described at the planetarium. M35. She remembered that he had explained about the stars and how they are pulled apart by gravitational forces from other galaxies, but that cluster had somehow bound together for eternity. The concept was so foreign to her. Eternal. Infinite. Being bound to someone. She had never understood the notion of spending forever with someone, but lately the image had been more comprehensible to her. Like she suddenly believed in the idea of happy. No longer an abstract idea, but something concrete that she could possess. Hawken could *have* happiness. With Henry.

She lay down on her bed and pushed the hair away from her face. She was starting to feel overcome by the drugs and was trying desperately to think about Henry. She would apologize tomorrow, first thing. It would be her mission. She turned her body towards the wall and pulled her blanket over her, taking a deep breath. Her lungs filled with the scent of Henry.

WHO IS TYPING? *Is Allison still here? She should be at school. Why does my hand feel cold?* She curled her fingers and felt the ice bag underneath her bandages. Her heart started beating out of her chest. Making a conscious effort not to attract attention by sudden movement, she slowly turned her head in the direction of the clicking. She could just make out the back of Henry's head from her obscured view beneath the corner of the desk. He was leaning back in her desk chair, looking towards the window. She slid her body a fraction to the right and could see that he had his feet propped up on the windowsill, his laptop on his lap, ear buds in his ears, typing on the keyboard. On the screen he had a Zoom session running of what looked like one of his classes. In the bottom corner of the screen was a notepad collecting the notes that he was busy typing.

Hawken turned back and focused on the ceiling. This was unbelievable. He must have come over earlier when Allison was still here to let him in. She had a mega-scandalous smile on her face that she couldn't shake off. She turned to look at him again. His hair was perfect. He was wearing a navy long sleeved thermal shirt with a red t-shirt over it. His tan pants were fraying on the left pocket from overuse. Hawken fought the urge to rub the worn edge between her finger and thumb. He was wearing shoes that she didn't remember seeing before. They looked new. A pair of grey Vans with black laces. She smiled again, then slowly started making her way out of bed. Using all of her acquired stealth capabilities she crept up behind him. He was still busy typing away and she hesitated, like an animal stalking its prey, deciding her next move. She leaned over and kissed the back of his neck, just between his hairline and his shirt collar.

He jumped, which she expected, which is why she immediately stepped back, unable to contain her smiling face. He pulled his ear buds out by the wire lying across his chest and turned his head. Once the initial surprise left his face, it was replaced with a smile that hitched on her heart. He quickly placed the computer on her desk, righted his feet and swiveled the chair in her direction. Without a word between them, she walked over, and he pulled her into his lap. They sat there, time flying by or stopping, neither could tell. Her head was resting against his shoulder, his head leaning against hers. She was wrapped around him so tightly, anyone watching would have thought that he was saving her from falling. His arm was curled around her back, his hand tracing lines up and down her side.

Hawken broke the silence with, "Thank you for the ice pack." She could feel his cheeks raise in her hair. She made him smile.

He remained wordless, so Hawken continued. "I'm so sorry Henry. I wasn't trying to—"

"Shhhhh." He interrupted and squeezed her tightly. "You have nothing to apologize for." Craning his head around so that he could see her face, he continued. "I'm so sorry. I shouldn't have said what I did. I didn't mean any of it. I—"

"Henry." Hawken had to stop him. How could he be apologizing to her for being patient and caring and present? She couldn't let him. This was all her. "Stop. I'm sorry that I didn't give you space last night. I was acting like an idiot. I should have understood, but I was being selfish."

"Hawken, you don't have to be sorry for wanting to spend time with me. I want to spend all my time with you, too. I'm sorry for pressuring you to come over. I shouldn't have said any of it. I feel like such an ass. And a criminal."

Hawken laughed. Henry hitched up an eyebrow in a mixture of confusion and surprise. "It wasn't you, Henry. Not even a little. I trust you. How could I not?" She looked up to the ceiling, then back at Henry and said, "It's the room. Your room."

She could tell that he was processing that, so she waited. Finally, he said, "Okay, explain that then."

She took a deep breath, trying to organize her thoughts. Honesty was best in most situations, right? She would be Abe Lincoln. Here goes. "I hadn't really thought about any of this until I was in Kat's room. She has a wall full of pictures of herself with various guys groping her, kissing her, hanging on her." She looked at Henry, who was attentively listening. "She also tends to save various things, just random things that she collected from some past boyfriends, but has kept, and uses or talks about during conversations that I've had with her. It's that kind of thing, Henry, that sends me over the edge of a cliff without a parachute." She sat up, looking him in the face.

He looked back, then to the ceiling, gathering his thoughts. Finally, he said, "I hear what you are saying." Casually, he placed his hand on her cheek, then removed it. "The thing is, you can't know everything about me, or anyone for that matter, before you feel comfortable enough to relax and leave your little bubble. It doesn't work that way. I've been here in your room many times now and I haven't been looking for signs of past secrets or clues." He looked around the room, to make his point, then continued. "And, I can't sterilize my life either. My past is my past. I may be a different person now, but you just need to trust that. Trust me." He looked at her again, emotions running through his eyes. "Look, I promise that I don't have anything in my room to worry you." His face held a grin and his voice a timbre of teasing. "I should probably tell you, sweet girl, that you are on a wholly separate plane from anyone else that I've ever been with. You are the only one that matters. The only one that I would want to hold on to anything from."

Hawken rested her head against his neck, her nose against his Adam's apple. "I'm sorry for being so juvenile about all of this. And irrational. I will work on it, I promise."

"Don't be sorry. Just promise me we'll always talk like this. About anything. About everything."

"I promise." She sat up again and asked, "How are you here? It's late and you have classes at eight on Wednesdays." She looked panicked and then said, "Crap. I have class at ten. What time is it?" She moved to stand up, but Henry pulled her back down.

"Relax. It's after eleven, but I called Kat from your phone

this morning and asked if she would *actually* take notes in class today so that you could skip. She agreed and said to tell you 'Thanks.'"

"Wow. You really did that? Thank you, Henry." She ran a hand through his hair, finding it too irresistible not to, being so close. "What about you? How are you getting your notes?"

He looked at the computer and said, "Sam was recording the lecture and I was taking notes. I'm meeting up with him in a little while to do homework. It's all under control."

"When do you have to go?"

"I am meeting him at twelve thirty. Why? What do you want to do?" His face had an air of mischief embedded into it.

"I don't know. Maybe I should get dressed and we could eat. Have you eaten?"

Henry shook his head. "I can get something later, if you want to do something else." His eyes were burning into her face.

"Henry, what are you suggesting?"

"I'm suggesting we get back into bed and talk more. What do you think?" He threw her a sly smile.

"Ummm. I guess that would be okay." Her voice thick with sarcasm. He picked her up and set her on the bed, but she immediately stood up. "I'm going to take a two- minute bathroom break and be right with you. Hold that thought." She grabbed her toothbrush and ran down the hall like she was in the race of her life.

BACK IN HER ROOM, she and Henry were lying chest to chest, legs entangled on the bed. Hawken wanted nothing more than to stay wrapped up in him forever. Just Henry. Touching Henry and smelling Henry.

She decided it was time to ask him some questions for a change. "Henry? Can I ask you something?"

"Anything." He answered immediately.

"Really? Anything?" Hawken didn't hide the surprise in her voice.

He angled his face down to hers, finger under her chin to face him. "I can't imagine that there would be anything that you couldn't ask me. Or that I wouldn't answer, sweet girl."

She smiled and rubbed her nose on his chin. She was thinking of kissing him right then. She didn't want to wait anymore. It was time. Then, she remembered that he was leaving soon, so she decided against it.

He spoke first. "Now I'm curious. Why were you surprised that you could ask me anything?" He tucked his head down to look at her in the eye again. "Could I ask you anything?"

She laughed. "Yes. Go on then. Ask and I shall answer." A test.

"Do you remember things from Monday night when we were lying like this here and you were asking me questions?"

Hawken winced. Obviously, she would answer, but she didn't want to. "Yes. Some things."

"What things?" He had lowered his voice, his hand in her hair.

"You sang to me. I distinctly remember that. Well, until I fell asleep." She waited for his response, hoping that he would leave all the other stones unturned.

He didn't.

"Do you remember asking me to kiss you?" He asked her this softly, his lips bumping on her forehead with each syllable, like eleven tiny kisses.

"Yes." She quickly added, "But I also remember thinking that I didn't know where any of that was coming from. I heard my voice asking you things, but it was like someone else was talking for me. So, to answer your question, yes. And I very much appreciate your answer, Henry. Truly I do." He was silent for a pause.

"What did you want to ask me?"

"Oh. Nothing major. I was just wondering what you used to do, really, to take up your day before I took over your life."

"Well," he said, rubbing his leg on hers, "before you, I went to school all day, worked, and hung out with my roommates. I have three in total. We used to hang out a lot. I played baseball on Saturdays when we weren't studying, too."

"Henry. Your roommates and friends must hate me. You should spend more time with them. Seriously."

"They don't hate you. At all. They're happy for me, and they know I want to spend time with you. I was with them last night. That should be enough for a while. Don't worry."

Hawken let out a breath. "I want you to have friends, Henry. When you grow bored of me, who will you turn to, to keep you up at night and bother you at work?"

"Well, how about if I promise to never grow bored of you, then it won't matter. The perfect solution."

"Nope. At least one day a week you will hang out with your friends. Besides, I could come watch you play baseball, Henry. It would be fun." She reached up and put her hand in his hair.

"Okay, we'll see."

They were both quiet after that, enjoying the closeness of each other. After a few minutes, Henry put his mouth against her forehead and said, "Tell me what you are thinking about. Please?"

Every time Henry's mouth moved against her face, she felt like she would stop breathing. The feeling of his mouth, his breath so close to her, was enough to stop her lungs from contracting, possibly even her heart from beating. "Honestly? About what you just said. I was thinking that there is going to come a time when you realize how boring and nutty I am and you'll run away screaming. That will be the worst day of my life." She buried her head in his neck.

He pulled back instantly, pushing her away so that he could see her face. She held on as tightly as she could, but gave in, keeping her eyes locked on his chin. "What?" he asked, his voice gravelly, like he had spent his voice at a concert. She just shrugged, closing her eyes, reaching to bury herself in his neck once more. "Hawken, please. Don't say that again." He chinned her face up as far as he could and said, "Every time we talk you surprise me. I am constantly left wanting. I want to know you more and more. You are never boring. Please look at me." He reached his hand up to her face, his fingers in her hair. "I've never met anyone like you before, Hawken Larson. I can't imagine being any happier than I am right now, with anyone, anywhere else." He kissed her hair and said, "Do you believe me?"

"Of course, I believe you. Henry. You know that feeling you get after it has just rained and everything is glowing bright and the world smells fresh and new?" He nodded, his chin bumping her forehead again. "That's what you are."

They stayed curled up in each other for another few minutes, until Henry pulled out his phone, glanced at the display, then set it back on the desk. "It's that time. School calls." He said it in a way that made Hawken think he was trying to talk himself into sounding happy about it.

She pulled him tight and rubbed her nose on his neck. "Thank you for being here this morning. That was extremely sweet, and I'll never forget it."

"You are welcome." He said, extricating himself from her grip and pulling himself out of bed. He stood up and turned to say, "Promise me something."

He looked at her seriously, solemnly now, like he was about to tell her that her best friend had died. "Promise me that you won't ever turn your phone off again. Not ever. Okay?"

WHEN HAWKEN MET up with Kat at school, Kat was uncharacteristically nice to her. As in, "Thank you for coming over," and "You really helped me out," and she actually didn't call her "Beeotch." Rather, she called her Hawk.

"You are totally freaking me out, Kat. What happened after I left?"

They were sitting in the lounge working on their English homework together, but both were wearing masks, hiding behind a thin layer of skin. Kat opened her mouth to say something, then dropped her head to the table with a loud bang and stayed that way, leaving Hawken dealing with the twenty pair of eyes staring at her.

She could only think of one thing to do, so that's what she did. "Oww. What the eff, loser?" Kat shot up and grabbed her arm. "Did you just pinch me?" Her eyes were bloodshot, and her hair was in a messy bun, uncharacteristic of her normal, curly ponytail.

"Seriously. Talk. Now." Hawken gave her the evil eye and stared her down.

"Okay, fine. Good Lord. Alex and Jason showed up after you left and I asked Jason to please leave and give us some space, you know, nicely." Kat smiled a hideously sarcastic smile that would have scared kids away from candy.

"Well, that doesn't sound so bad." Hawken relaxed back in her chair, then immediately sat forward again, the wooden spindled chair back cutting into her skin.

"Well, I didn't think so either, until twenty minutes later he was banging on the door saying, 'You done? Let me in.'" Kat did her best impersonation of Jason which was on the nose. Typical pot-head loser voice.

"Why did I ever think that he was a nice guy, Kat?" Hawken

asked, shaking her head. "So, what happened for the twenty minutes? Did you talk at all?"

Kat pulled her elastic out of her hair and shook it out, much to the pleasure of the predominately male room. "I asked him questions about Sacramento, and he said things like, 'I guess' and 'sure' and 'what do you think?' I'm not sure that this is going to work, girl. Maybe I've outgrown the guys who just want to sit around and drink and make out. Maybe I want more." She narrowed her eyes at Hawken, then pointed her finger in her general direction. "This is your fault, ass hat."

"Lovely. Thank you." Hawken mimed tipping her hat. "So, did you guys break up, then?"

"No. I'm waiting for the right time. Maybe right before Thanksgiving. Then we'll have a nice four-day break from each other, and we can come back fresh."

Hawken laughed. The idea of spending time like that with someone that you don't want to be with was so foreign. Like studying the day after a test. Waste of time.

"Well, I am glad that you figured yourself out. I was worried."

"Liar. Your halo just slipped an inch to the right." Kat mimed shooting a gun directly over Hawken's head, then blew on the smoking tip.

13

"Hey, T- Rex. How was school today?" Hawken was Zoom-meeting with her parents and her little brother after she had returned from her last class of the day. This used to be what she looked forward to most each week, to be able to see Rex and talk to him. It was something that held her together at the beginning. Until she met Henry. Again. Now, she tried to call home when Henry wasn't around or in-between classes, so it didn't take any time away from them being together.

Hawken's parents had always been amazing until Rex was born. They were always there for her. Her dad shuttled her to and from soccer practice and sometimes, if it was light enough outside, they'd kick the ball together and she'd amaze him at her newly acquired skills of dribbling through cones or heading the ball. He was the one who taught her how to kick a corner kick so that it arced around back into the goal. He was proud of her and she loved him for that.

Her mom had woken up early every single morning to make "an athlete's breakfast" before school. It was always eggs and bacon, or pancakes and sausage, or oatmeal, or freshly baked muffins. She also packed Hawken's lunch for school every day, without fail. "Mom, I'm getting too old for you to pack my lunch. People are laughing at me. Every day I open my lunch bag and there's a handwritten note on my sandwich and the kids pass it around the table laughing."

"Well, they are just jealous. You are lucky to have a mom that takes the time to show you how much you are loved."

"Wow. That ought to be a winner comeback line. *You're just jealous that my mommy loooooooves me.* Sure. I'll just go practice not crying in the mirror."

Her seven-year-old brother, Rex, was a surprise. Apparently, he wasn't a surprise to her mom and dad, but he sure was to her. "I can't believe you are having another baby now. Seriously? I'm eleven years old. I wanted a brother or sister years ago. I'm over it. Don't expect me to change diapers or babysit. Well, I'll babysit, but you are going to pay me the going rate. No exceptions!" Of course, as soon as Rex was born, Hawken would have done anything for him. He was so cute and snuggly, and smelled that wonderful new baby smell that someone should really bottle and sell. She instantly fell into the role of big sister. The little onesies with the feet were so adorable. Rex was the perfect baby. He was always happy. He loved riding around in the car and would laugh and laugh just looking out the window. Hawken used to tiptoe into his room in the night and slide the rocking chair over next to the crib to hold his little hand and sing to him. There is nothing sweeter that a sleeping baby. It would always relax her. Her parents would find her asleep on the floor next to his crib the next morning. "Sweetheart, the baby whisperer was here again," her dad used to say to her mom.

But then things had changed. Or not changed as much as they should have. At a year and a half, Rex still wasn't walking or talking. He was happy consistently, but he didn't seem to be achieving milestones at the rate that the stacks of baby books had warned.

By Rex's second birthday, his pediatrician recommended taking him to a Developmental Specialist. His name was added to the six-month waiting list and they prepared for bad news. Once he was finally seen, there were hours and hours of questions and tests, needles, and packets to be filled out. It seemed like an agonizing amount of forms and questionnaires. After they had run a battery of tests, Rex had put together puzzles, and matched toys to a color wheel, they came up with a diagnosis.

"What exactly is Autism Spectrum Disorder? How long will he have it? What caused it? What will happen to him? What do we do now?" These were the questions that were asked by Hawken's parents to the doctors, then by grandparents, then by friends and neighbors. There were no simple answers to any of their questions. So much remained unknown. Hawken's mom spent months online and at the library reading every book she could find on the subject. In the end, Rex was still the happy kid that he always was. He was just a little more difficult at times. He struggled with talking, so he was enrolled in Speech Therapy. Every Thursday morning Angie would show up at the door with a bag of books, toys, and candies. She would sit on the floor with Rex and pull out a toy for him to play with. She would tell him what it was called, and he would have to repeat the beginning sound before he could play with it. "Boat. Buh. Buh. Buh. Boat." Angie would say, pushing her finger on Rex's bottom lip and moving it down. "Buh," he replied. Angie would hand him the boat and the family would clap, laugh, and make a production about what a great job he was doing.

Rex also had Occupational Therapy and Hippotherapy (where he had treatment while riding a horse) and Habilitation

Therapy once a week. Their parents seemed to be busier and busier with Rex and his needs, so that Hawken was forced to become more independent. She started packing her own lunch most days and would buy a slice of pizza on Fridays at the school cafeteria. She stayed after school to work on homework with friends and helped with tutoring one day a week.

Over the years, Rex progressed, and life got a little bit easier, but the crack in the foundation between Hawken and her parents never resealed. Two years later the Incident happened, and the crack became a chasm that seemed unlikely to be repaired.

But the weekly phone calls to her family were still important. She and Rex had really bonded when they moved from Germany to Phoenix, Arizona. He was starting school and she was finishing her final two years of High School.

"Rex. Look at me. How was school today?" Hawken asked, sitting at her desk in her jail cell, a lit candle next to the window was filling the room with the smell of clean linen. One of the better smells that she had tested.

"Good day," he said, looking away from the screen.

"Do you have therapy today, buddy?"

"Yeah. Speech today." Then he looked up, like he was going to talk to the screen, but dropped his head back down so that his chin rested on his chest. "Bye. Love you," he said then got up from his chair and walked away.

"He's been saying 'I love you' a lot lately without prompts. I'm thrilled that you were able to hear it." Hawken's mom appeared in front of the computer screen and her dad hunched over like Quasimodo in the right corner of the screen.

"Rex looks like he's happy. Tell him I love him, okay?" Lately, Hawken and Rex had become buddies. She spent countless hours over the summer watching Sponge Bob Square Pants episodes with him on his flat screen in the game room upstairs.

It would take an hour sometimes to watch one full episode because he would hold the remote in his right hand, his index finger poised over the rewind button like a trigger, and each time one of the characters said something he thought was funny, he would press the button and watch the scene over, and over, and over again.

"Well, honey, we have some good news!" Her mom was grinning so wide she could see all the way back to her molars. Then her mom turned to her dad as if expecting him to finish the thought.

Suddenly the door opened. "Hey! Look who I found out in the parking lot," Allison said as she walked in and threw her backpack down on the foot of her bed. Hawken turned around to find a smiling Henry. Allison removed her boots and threw them one by one into her closet as he loped in the room.

The smile on Henry's face could make the sun jealous. He always lit up the room. "Hey, Tony Hawk. I was in the neighborhood, so...hey, are you okay? You look weird." He had narrowed his eyes, trying to piece together her deer in the headlights expression.

Hawken had panicked. She hadn't talked to her parents yet about Henry. What was she waiting for? There was no reason that this relationship should be a secret, was there? She and Henry had never had The Conversation, but they had spent so much time together, laughing and talking that 'boyfriend' was sort of implied at this point, wasn't it?

What was she supposed to say to her parents right now with him in the room? This is exactly the scenario she was trying to avoid. Obviously to no avail. If she had a superpower right now, she would make herself invisible.

"Hello, Allison. Is this your boyfriend?" Hawken's mom was obviously attempting to ease the tension in the air from 400 miles away.

"Oh, hey, Mrs. Larson. Sorry, I hadn't realized that Hawken was on the phone. Wait, you haven't met Henry? He's not *my* boyfriend. He's Hawk's boyfriend." Allison responded matter-of-factly, and then sat down at her desk and turned her earphones on.

Call 911, Hawken thought to herself. *Yes, it is an emergency. Someone is having a heart attack. Mayday. Mayday. The plane is going down.* She could see the shift in her parent's faces.

"Hawken?" An echo. One voice from the computer and one voice from the doorway.

After a second, she finally spoke. "Mom and Dad, this is Henry," Hawken said, her voice shaky. Standing, she reached for Henry's hand, not looking at his face. She was sure her own was fifteen shades of crimson. She pulled him over to the chair and sat him down, whispering *sorry* in his ear. His smile was brighter than the yellow highlighter on her desk.

"Hello, Mr. and Mrs. Larson. I'm Henry Lewis. We've never formally met, but I actually knew Hawken from High School in Germany. I'm sorry to have interrupted your conversation, but it is really nice to see you again." He beamed that perfect, crooked smile at them and Hawken could see her mother touching her face and smoothing her hair. His smile could safely land planes in a snowstorm.

"Good to meet you, Henry. I remember you, son. I worked at the hospital with your mother. I'm so sorry about her accident. She was a lovely person. How is your father?" Hawken's dad was genuinely nice, which didn't surprise Hawken in the least.

"He's quite well, thank you. He lives close by, which is nice. I see him about once a month for dinner. He's still teaching math at the local high school here, which keeps him busy and happy. I don't want to take too much of your time from chatting with Hawken, so I'll step away, but it was really nice talking to you again. Bye." He turned and smiled at Hawken and stood up.

"Do you mind that I'm here? I'll just sit on the bed and wait, okay?" He kissed her on her head and quietly sat on her bed, pulling his cell phone out of his pocket and swiping the screen to unlock it.

Hawken slunk back into her chair pushing her hair back behind her ears and said, "So, that's Henry. We saw each other in the lounge of the science building at the start of school and we've been hanging out a lot. So, what is the good news that you wanted to tell me?" Jesus. She was talking so fast she was almost stuttering. She never introduced anyone to her parents before, let alone a guy. In her room, for an added bonus.

"Oh. I forgot about that. Yes. Well, we are going to be coming out to Los Angeles for Thanksgiving next week. Rex is dying to go to Disneyland and Sea World for a couple of days over the Thanksgiving break, so we wanted to know if you would join us at Disneyland. We'd love for you to bring Henry, wouldn't we, sweetheart?" Hawken could see her mom twitch from kicking her dad under the table.

"Of course. We'd love it!" Replied Hawken's dad, side eyeing her mom.

"Um—I'll talk to him about it and let you know, okay? I'd love to go. I can't wait to see Rex. I'm sure he is dying to see Sleeping Beauty's Castle." Rex was probably on Google all day memorizing the park maps in preparation.

"Okay, wonderful. Well, we'd better get going. Rex has Speech in ten minutes, and I've got to get dinner made. We are so excited for you. It sounds like you are doing really well!" Hawken's mom just winked. As in—winked. Seriously? "We love you. Bye, Hawk."

"Bye guys." Hawken closed the screen on her laptop and bit her lower lip. Maybe Allison did her a favor. Henry didn't seem to mind meeting her parents. She walked over and sat down next to him on the bed. He put down his phone and ran a hand through his bangs, making them stand up out in all directions.

"So, your parents didn't seem as nervous as you." He laughed. "Do I need to get you a paper bag to breathe into or are you okay?" he smirked.

"Ha ha. I'm sorry I didn't tell them about you earlier. I just didn't know what to say. We haven't had the best relationship for years. It has mainly been cursory unless we are talking about Rex. Thank you for being such a nice guy. It means a lot to me. I'm pretty sure my mom was swooning when you smiled at her." She picked up his hand and kissed his palm.

"If only I had that effect on you." He pulled her close to him and kissed the top of her head.

"Hey, guys. I can hear everything you are saying. Why don't you get a room?" Allison's shrill voice echoed in the increasingly miniscule space of their joint cell.

They both looked at each other and rolled their eyes. "Why don't I take you to dinner? I've got my car here," Henry proposed.

"Yeah. Okay. Sounds good. Allison, I'll see you later." Hawken pulled her black sweater out of her closet and Henry held it for her while she put it on. He opened the door for her, letting it click shut as they walked down the hall to the elevator.

"I'm sorry. I'm an idiot. Please come." Dinner didn't go so well. Henry had taken Hawken to a sushi bar a couple of miles from campus. It was one of those places that you fall in love with the first time you visit. There was a wooden sign hanging from scrolled wrought iron above the door that read "One Fish Two Fish." When they walked inside, Hawken beamed.

"I love this place. It is everything you would never expect a sushi bar to be. Isn't it incredible?" Henry was holding her hand and guiding her through the entrance to a table.

"Are you sure we just seat ourselves?" Hawken was amazed.

The restaurant was just a large square room, but the walls we covered in dark cherry wood providing the look and feel of a library. There were built-in shelves on each of the walls that were filled with thousands of books. Hanging directly from the center of the wooden inlayed ceiling was an enormous chandelier. It must have had a hundred or more light bulbs hanging from its massive, wrought iron core. It was the kind of place that exudes comfort, like a warm scarf. Hawken hadn't stopped looking around since they walked in. She looked like a little girl seeing snow falling for the first time, eyes to the sky, mouth slightly open.

"You are going to make yourself dizzy," Henry said. "I know the owners. They are this amazing couple that bought this space about ten years ago. The husband wanted to keep it a bookstore, but his wife was worried that they wouldn't be able to make enough money selling books and wanted to open a sushi bar. So, they compromised and ended up with both." Henry had pulled out a chair for Hawken before sitting into his own on the opposite side of the table.

They both ordered an assortment of vibrantly colored fish laid atop rectangles of rice as well as a platter of avocado rolls. During the meal, Henry asked if Hawken was going to invite him to go to Disneyland with her family over Thanksgiving. He had a bottomless smile that quickly faded. She responded with, "Ummm. I don't know. Would you even want to spend a day with my parents and brother? It will probably be really crowded because of the holiday."

"Oh. Right. Sure. I just thought it would be a great time to meet your parents again in person. And I've never spoken to Rex. But it sounds like you don't want me there. Is that what you are saying?" He set his chopsticks down on his plate, the bite of avocado roll still between them, and looked up at her. Hawken had never seen him look so incredibly sad. And she had done this to him. Was that what she was saying? That she didn't want him there? This was all so new for her. She'd never brought a boy home. She'd never even discussed boys around her parents.

In Phoenix, Hawken found a group of friends that would include her if she wanted to go out, but they never missed her if she wasn't around. Her parents had never met any of them.

"It isn't that I don't want you there. I would have to be insane to not want you around. Really. Truly. I'm sorry. It is just that things are going so well and then you surprised me when you came in while I was Zoom chatting with them and I just needed a minute to readjust, that's all. I promise. Okay?" She reached over to grab his hand, but he pulled it off the table into his lap before she could reach it. "Henry. I'm sorry. They've never seen me with a guy before and I panicked." Hawken understood that this was a pivotal conversation. The kind that teetered on the edge of starting something real or ending something that she never even gave a chance. It was time to decide. She owed it to Henry. Either she was going to be all in, or it would be all over. Go hard or go home.

"I'm done. Are you ready to go?" Henry turned in his seat and motioned with his finger for the check. Now she felt awful. She had to make this right. What was she thinking? There was no question that Henry should go with them. At this point they were practically inseparable anyway. Her parents had always created that air of panic in her. She absolutely wanted him there.

Of course, she did. This was just scary because it was uncharted territory for her. This was stepping off a ship onto soil in America in 1492. Or landing on Mars. She cared about him enough for this. She could take that leap. She *would* take that leap. Henry could be trusted. He wasn't like anyone else, and she knew it, deep down in her core. She trusted him and owed it to him to prove it.

They got back in the car and Henry was silent. He wasn't ever silent, so Hawken knew that he was undeniably upset. She sat nervously in the passenger seat of his BMW and anxiously rubbed her right hand back and forth along the door handle. It was time to act. Reaching over, she rested her hand on top of his on the gearshift, curling her fingers over his. He didn't pull his hand away. That was a good sign. Or did he *have* to leave it there to shift gears? Hawken sneaked a glance at his face. The corners of his lips were turned up, like he might be smiling. Maybe this night could still be salvaged.

"Hey, Henry, let's go back to your house, okay?" Hawken asked. She was a new kind of superhero now. Brave Girl.

His head whipped around, and his face looked stricken. "You never want to go to my house. You've never even *been* to my house. No. Not tonight," Henry said, sounding frustrated and completely done. She was just compounding his irritation, but she didn't want to let this go. She knew that if she didn't make this right, to show him she was in this, she'd regret it. Henry meant everything to her. He needed to understand that.

"I figured it is time to see how the other half lives. Come on. I'm asking." Smiling and batting her eyes at him, she pleaded, "Please?" The muscle in his jaw flexed, tensing, clenching.

"It's getting late and I have an early class tomorrow. I don't want to have to drive back to campus." They had just pulled up to the curb in front of her dorm. He slid his hand out from under hers then ran it through his hair, front to back, keeping his hands on the nape of his neck.

"Okay. Here's the deal. I'm not ready to say goodbye to you tonight. I want to come over. I'm going to get in my car and follow you home. I can drive myself back in a while." Jumping out of his car, she ran down the sidewalk towards her dirty red

Honda Accord in the parking lot. She wasn't about to give him a chance to say no. Not tonight.

He waited for her car to pull out onto the street. Following him for about four miles off campus he slowed and turned into the driveway of a small yellow house with S-shaped roof tiles the color of mud. It was an older, Spanish style home with a small patch of green grass out front. There were two other cars in the driveway. Hawken parked her car on the street, grabbed her purse and walked up the front to meet Henry.

"Wow. This is nice. How long have you lived here?" Henry had been waiting for her behind his car and when she stepped close enough, she grabbed his hand. He threaded his fingers through hers and kissed the top of her head. Progress.

"I moved here after my freshman year. My roommate, Sam, and some friends from the dorm all moved in here together." They made their way up the driveway and into the entrance of the house. There was loud music playing in the family room that sounded like U2.

The downstairs was a huge open space with a family room at the front, massive kitchen in the back, and what was originally a dining room separating the two, now home to a giant, dark brown scrolled-wood pool table. The felt was the color of sand and there was a wooden cue hanger attached to the wall on the far side between two windows. Hawken was surprised by the feel of the house. Cozy. The ever present dirty sock aroma was missing, and there weren't mounds of dirty laundry piled in the corners like she'd expected.

Henry shut the door behind them and one of the guys on the couch yelled out, "Henrietta, is that you?" without turning his head. She looked at Henry with a gleam in her eye.

"Hey, guys, this is Hawken. Hawken, this is Matt and Joe." Henry had pulled her in the door and stepped behind her, resting his hands on her shoulders as he made his introductions. She couldn't see his face, but she could tell by his breath on her hair that he was smiling.

The blond guy sitting on the well-worn leather reclining chair stood up and reached out his hand. He gripped hers warmly and said, "Wow. So, you're the girl who stole our little Henry's heart." He smiled a broad smile at Henry then glanced at Hawken and said, "Nice to finally meet you. I'm Matt. We hope to see a lot more of you around here. Seriously. Welcome. "

Hawken smiled and nodded and said, "Thank you."

Matt pointed at the curly haired guy sitting on the leather couch in cargo shorts, flip flops and a gingham shirt, completely unbuttoned. "This asshole here is Joe. He never blinks or stops playing Wii U unless a scantily clad girl wanders in-between him and the screen. Even then it's unpredictable. Could go either way." He turned back to Hawken and Henry. "Hey, did you see Cecelia outside? She said she was coming over tonight."

Hawken could resist. "Cecelia? Don't let her break your heart or shake your confidence, Matt. And definitely no begging on your knees."

Both Matt and Henry stared at Hawken. *Oh crap.* This felt like a scene from a teenage comedy movie where she showed up naked to a dance. Their faces slowly became animated again, both turning to look at each other with such cheesy grins they could have filled their own can of Cheez Whiz. They raised their hands and high fived each other.

"Hell, yeah!" Matt.

Even Joe got in on the action. "Are you kidding me? Henry, hang on to this one. If you don't, she's mine. I effing paused the game for you, Hawken. Simon and Garfunkel? That was effing sweet."

"Great. Thanks. We'll see you guys later," Henry said, taking Hawken's hand again to lead her across the hallway and up the flight of stairs. He leaned into her, saying, "Sorry about them. They really are the best, though." He continued leading her up to the second floor and turned left at the top. Turning his head to the right, he waved his hand at a door. "This is Sam." Continuing down the hallway, he pointed to a closed door and said, "Matt." At the next door he said, "Joe" and pointed to the half-opened door. They turned another corner and walked to the end of the hallway. Henry squared himself and looked at Hawken. "This is me," he said, grinning. "Welcome." He opened the door and stepped back so that she could enter first.

The room was massive. It was the master bedroom, complete with a private bathroom containing a walk-in shower and garden tub on the left. A few feet past the bathroom door was another door leading to the walk-in closet. The wall across from the entrance housed a queen-sized mattress on a frame, no headboard. An oak nightstand stood on one side of the bed with a black shade over a lamp and an alarm clock. The comforter was a plaid pattern covered in pillows with matching pillowcases. Along the wall to the right stood an oak entertainment center sandwiched by two towering speakers housing a TV and stereo inside. As Hawken spun around back to the door, she saw a black Fender Stratocaster electric guitar connected to a large, black Peavey amplifier.

She turned to Henry. "So, is this your secret weapon?" she asked, pointing to his electric guitar. "Is this how you lure women into your bed?" She was smiling, but it was obviously forced. The words had just fallen out of her mouth and she wanted more than anything to take them back.

"Don't. Please," he said, his face a visible grimace.

Walking in her socks to the foot of his bed, she systematically studied the room. A panoramic view of Henry. *This is where he spends his time*, she thought.

"Wow. This is incredible. I love this wall." She said, walking over to the wall in-between the closet and the bathroom. It was full of pictures and hand drawn artwork. "This is beautiful. Did you draw all of these?" There were sketches of birds attached haphazardly by thumbtacks, some layered over others, so she had to delicately lift the bottom corners to find what was underneath. When Henry didn't answer, she turned to look at him. He was beaming.

He shook his head and answered, "My mom." Then said, "You look strikingly beautiful in my room, Tony Hawk. Jesus, it was worth the wait." He started to walk towards her, warmth in his smile.

She could feel herself losing her courage, changing direction towards the guitar. He turned and followed her across the room. "I never knew you played," she said. "Will you play something for me?" She picked up the guitar from the stand and handed it to him, as he bent over and switched the amp on. She pulled herself into the middle of his bed and sat waiting, legs akimbo, smiling with her eyes.

"Okay. Any requests?" He asked, setting up. He looked like a rock star standing there, guitar slung over his shoulder, his guitar pick in-between his lips as he adjusted the knobs on the amp. His soft brown hair was hanging in his eyes and he brushed it aside with his right hand, then grabbed his pic between his thumb and index finger.

"Anything. Everything. You decide." As she watched him, she couldn't get over how strong and corded his forearms were. How natural he looked in his room with a guitar in his hands. Hawken knew she'd never forget this moment. And then, he started playing. Hawken recognized the song immediately by the first few chords. A soft smile played on her lips. Then Henry started to sing.

His voice was amazing. Yet another aspect of Henry that she was unprepared for. The words were like a warm caress against her skin, his voice holding her still.

By the end of the song, Hawken had a smile hanging on her

face that rivaled Henry's best. Henry set his guitar down gently, then slowly sat down next to her on the bed. "Wow. I should have played for you weeks ago. Look at you." He took his finger and traced the smile on her face with it.

"Henry. I'm in awe. You have so much talent, it's mind-blowing. It's like you are superhuman. Like you're Superman. But you make Clark Kent look like a dolt-wad." She made a fist with her hand and gently tapped his chin with it. Then she hopped off the bed and turned to Henry, walking backwards saying, "My turn?" in the flirtiest voice she could conjure.

"You can play?" Henry's jaw dropped a little. He quickly recovered, but Hawken made a mental note. She had impressed Henry. Score one for the mere humans.

"I can't sing, but I can play a bit. Now that my hand is a mess we'll have to see. I'll play you one of my favorites."

Henry watched intently as Hawken played the full song, quietly humming the lyrics, even though she was no match vocally. No one was. As soon as the song ended, she set down the guitar, placed the green pic on the amp, then flicked the switch to OFF. Henry was sitting on the bed, somehow in awe of her this time. Hawken couldn't even begin think about that.

You can do this. You want this. The voice in Hawken's head was overpowering.

She made her way across the room and crawled onto the bed. Kneeling next to Henry, she studied his face. His eyes were a shade of blue that could only be described as aquatic. Mesmerizing. The skin underneath had a pale purple coloring now, reflective of the long, tiring couple of days they had. Her eyes made their way down to his lips.

Jesus. His lips.

Hawken never let herself focus too long on his lips. They were perfect. The same size, both top and bottom, and more of a red than pink. They were salvation.

She let herself really look at them now. *Good Lord.*

Her gaze trailed back up to his eyes. He was looking at her face now. She could tell he was hesitant. This was uncharted territory. Back to Columbus. Back to Mars.

He spoke. "Why did you come here tonight, Hawken?" It was almost a throaty whisper.

She placed her hands on his shoulders and pushed him gently down so that he was lying on the bed. He straightened his legs as she lifted one of hers over his waist and straddled his body. He put his hands on her waist and squeezed her tightly. Then he ran his hands up and down her sides, slowly driving her mad. With every touch her nerve endings were ablaze. This was the happiest she had ever been. This. Right now. With Henry.

Quickly, panic hit. Her eyes flashed up to the windows above his bed. Her heart had somehow made its way into her brain and was beating in her ears like a dozen galloping horses. *Not now. Get it together,* Hawken thought. This is Henry. Beautiful, honest, warm, Henry. She looked back down at his perfect face and saw his perfect crooked smile. She could feel her heart hitch back in her chest.

This wasn't uncharted territory. This was Henry. This was home. This was everything.

She smiled back.

"Henry."

"Tony Hawk."

"Don't flinch, Henry."

She leaned down and rubbed her lips gently back and forth on his widow's peak. His hair smelled of sunshine. Then she moved down to his eyes. They were closed and she gently kissed one, then the other. Henry made a sound from the back of his throat.

"Hawken. Come here." Henry ran his fingers through her hair, put them on the back of her neck and pulled her face an inch from his. "I'm going to kiss you now, sweet girl. Don't be scared. I like you so much. I would never hurt you. Okay?"

She nodded and he pulled her so that her lips were against his.

And then.

And then two worlds collided. Stars exploded. Black holes were created. It was perfection.

14

Hawken spent the night with Henry. In his bed.

Nothing happened.

Well, *something* happened.

There was kissing. There were buckets of shooting stars falling over them all night, mostly thrown by Henry.

Hawken's clothes remained buttoned and attached. Henry's shirt did not.

His shirt was on the floor, but all other articles of clothing remained undisturbed, of course. He was the perfect gentleman, as promised.

This did happen:

Hawken rubbed his entire face and neck with her lips until they were raw.

She ran her hands through his hair until she became truly worried that it would all fall out.

She pulled his shirt up to his neck and Henry sat up, pulled it off, and threw it on the floor. She ran her hands over his stomach, fingering each ridge in his abs. (Seriously. He just got better and better.) She rubbed his broad chest with her lips until they were so swollen, she was sure they would break open.

Then, she ran her tongue over the small sparrow tattoo she found over his heart. "Why a sparrow?" she whispered.

"That's what my mom always called me." He pulled her face back up to his and kissed her hard on her mouth. Even after rubbing her mouth over every inch of his head and chest, she still kissed him for hours. And hours. It seemed like there would never be enough air, but as soon as their mouths broke apart, she realized she couldn't fill her lungs without kissing him either.

Hawken set the alarm on her phone for seven am. She couldn't imagine actually leaving his bed. She couldn't imagine being separated from him for more than two minutes. It would be physically painful.

And yet. She had class. He had class. They agreed to meet later for lunch before her lab and before he was scheduled to be at work.

Hawken needed to stop at her dorm room to shower and get her backpack for school, so she kissed Henry goodbye ninety-six times, then walked out to her car. As she started pulling away from the curb, she saw Henry out of the corner of her eye running through the lawn. He was still in his jeans and he'd put his t-shirt back on, but his feet were bare, and the sprinklers were on, leaving the bottom of his pants soaking wet. She rolled down the window just as he approached her door. "I have to tell you something."

"Okay. What is it?" Hawken couldn't stop smiling.

"God. I can't breathe. Hang on a sec." He must have run all the way down the stairs from his room because he was standing with his hands on his knees trying to catch his breath. Hawken laughed. He stood up and rested his hands on the door of her car. Leaning in just a bit he tilted his head, silently taking in her face. Then he said, "I've fallen in love with you, Tony Hawk. Jesus. I need to start running again." He took another deep breath and shook his head before he continued. "I love you. I'm seriously, madly, head over heels in love with you." He let out another breath, accompanied by a smile this time. "If this were a cartoon, you'd have bonked me on the head with an oversized mallet and I'd have stars and hearts circling my head." He reached through the window and pulled her face closer. Then he leaned in and kissed her. This wasn't a goodbye kiss. This wasn't a *hello, it's been a while* kiss. This was a drumroll, crescendo, freeze frame, credits roll, life changing kiss that left them both breathless, yet so full of air they were floating. Soaring. And neither of them ever wanted to come back down.

HAWKEN WAS SITTING in the lounge of the Science Lecture Hall at a table with Jason. "Hey, Hawk. What's up with you? Have you seen yourself today?" Jason had flicked one of his dirty playing cards at her with his thumb and middle finger.

"What are you talking about, perv?" Hawken plucked it off her shoulder and threw it back.

"You look like you got your hair done or have more makeup on or something. You look different. Like, happy?" His head tilted to the right a bit like a dog's might when it hears a high-pitched sound.

"Uh, thanks?" Hawken asked, absolutely a question as even her eyebrows pulled together above her nose.

"I mean, it isn't like I always thought you were unhappy, but now that there's something to compare it to... yeah, happy." Jason's eyes peered over Hawken's shoulder, and a strange look ran over his face. Leaning forward onto the table, he whispered, "You know that we *have* to get this project done before break next week, Hawk."

"I know. That's why we are here, working on—" Hawken felt a warm hand on the back of her neck. She turned to see Henry leaning down to kiss the top of her head. His face looked like he'd just conquered Everest. "Hey, you," she whispered. Then she asked, "What are you doing here?" pulling him down by the arm into the next chair.

"Hey, Jason. Sorry to interrupt." Henry's eyes never left Hawken's face.

"I assume I am going to have to carry on without you for a while?" Jason asked, sounding irritated, as usual.

Hawken shot him her meanest scowl. "Go take a nap with your cards, perv." Jason laughed.

"Fine, but this just means we have to work later tonight." Jason stood up and pulled his backpack strap from the arm of his chair. "I'll see you at the lab?"

"Yes." Hawken swatted the air like she was batting away a fly then turned to Henry. "I can't even tell you how happy I am to see you, Henry." She said, studying his face, her mind replaying the previous night.

Henry was sitting sideways, his hands on her leg. He was wearing a long-sleeved black Henley shirt with khaki pants and red Vans. His hair was perfectly tousled on top of his head. All Hawken could think about was how to make out with his hairline in the middle of the lounge without being taken to the nearest asylum. She couldn't stop staring at his mouth and thinking of his lips on her neck, on her face, on her own lips.

"I couldn't wait until lunch to see you. Now that you have some time, let's run away. What do you say?" He smiled a smile that could raise the dead.

Hawken leaned into him and whispered into his ear, "I am going to burst if I don't touch you in the next five minutes."

Henry's eyes lit up. "You are going to kill me, Tony Hawk. I'm not joking..." He pulled her up by her hand and they quickly walked out of the building. "Can we go to your dorm? Is Allison home?"

"She's home working on her English Lit paper. That's why I

was in the science building. Where is your car? We could go to your house." They increased their stride towards Henry's car.

"C'MERE." Hawken stood in the middle of Henry's room. It smelled like his cologne, something else distinctly Henry, and Hawken almost lost her breath when she saw the sun tracing diagonal lines across Henry's chest from his blinds. He was looking at her like he couldn't figure out what color her hair was.

"Are you okay? What's wrong?" she asked, her eyebrows knit together above her eyes.

"God, Hawken. Nothing. I'm just—" He rolled off the bed and made his way over to her, pulling her tight into his body, arms wrapped around her waist. "I'm speechless." He put one hand on the back of her head and the other on the side of her neck and kissed her. It was soft at first, but then grew harder and more urgent.

Henry pulled away first, catching his breath. "I meant what I said this morning. I've been pushing the repeat button from last night all day. I've been smiling like an idiot. I can't stop. I'm so worried that I'm going to scare you away, but I've never felt this before. It's excruciating to breathe when I'm not touching you."

"Henry, when you say things like that, I feel like you're pouring buckets of stars on me."

An hour later:

"I'm worried that I'll never be able to leave this bed if you are in it." Groaned Hawken.

"You never have to." Henry responded, puller her closer still.

"So, we'll just live here? On your mattress? Forever?"

"Forever sounds good to me."

"What if we get hungry?"

"We'll call delivery."

"What about class?"

"What do we need a college education for if we are living on a mattress?"

"I don't think I can be responsible for you giving up your future and happiness to live on a mattress like a hermit."

"I wouldn't be giving up my future. You are my future, and my happiness for that matter, which is why I'd be living on my mattress."

"Henry. I think we should get up." Hawken was starting to sit up, but he pulled her back down.

"Bad idea." Henry slowly rolled over on top of Hawken and kissed her on the throat. "Terrible idea." He kissed her on the corner of the mouth. "Worst idea." He kissed her mouth. "This right here." Another kiss. "Best idea."

Fifteen minutes later:

"Okay, you need to study. You have a test this afternoon, right?" Hawken sat up and Henry pulled her back down to him on the bed.

"I hate studying and I love you. You win." He brushed her hair out of her face with his fingers, then kissed her ear.

"God, Henry. If this is what it's like kissing you, I can't imagine actually having sex with you. I already feel like I can't get enough." Hawken finally got out of bed and stood against the wall by the door. "I need you to get out of bed. I know you have flash cards for your test. I'll help you study until I have to go, okay?" She was hoping that the wall behind her would somehow bind her to itself. She was wavering in the self-control department.

"Okay, but first, tell me something nice." He was sitting up, watching her.

She looked to the floor, biting her lip, then back at him. "Henry. I'm not good at wearing my heart on my sleeve. It is hard for me to express my feelings and I don't want you thinking—" She paused. "I'm the happiest I've ever been. Ever. You've completely altered my chemistry. It's like I've been living in black and white and now everything is in Technicolor."

He leaned backed against the wall behind the bed, his face a flurry of emotion she couldn't discern. "You can't say things like that and expect me not to want to touch you. Come back. Just two more minutes, okay?" He was sitting in a shadow against the wall and he looked so vulnerable, so meek, so amazing.

As Hawken walked back over, crossing the room, Henry crawled back down onto the bed. She climbed up over Henry and laid her body directly on his, matching up their legs, feet, and arms. He rolled her over onto her back, pinning her arms over her head with his hand. Hawken visibly stiffened. Henry let go and jumped off the bed.

"Oh, God. I wasn't thinking. I'm so sorry, Hawken. Are you okay?" Henry's voice shook as he watched her with wide eyes.

"You don't have to be sorry. You didn't do anything wrong. I thought I was getting over this. I'm the one who's sorry." Hawken sat up and walked over to him. "Don't be mad. I'm sorry, Henry."

He grabbed her hand. "How could I be mad at you? You are everything."

She smiled. "Well," she said, "at least I got you out of bed."

15

"Dad, this is Hawken. I don't know that you've ever officially met." Henry turned to Hawken. "This is my dad." Henry was, of course, beaming at him.

"James. Please, call me James. It's really, really nice to meet you, Hawken." He held out his hand and when Hawken reached hers out to shake it, he pulled her in for a hug.

It was Sunday night and Henry had planned to spend the evening at his father's house, so he called and asked if he could bring Hawken. "Of course. I would love to see her. Please do." So, there they were, sitting around his round, wooden kitchen table, eating takeout Chinese food and laughing at stories of Henry as a child.

"Henry used to hide his notes home from his teachers underneath the living room couch." James looked at Hawken and leaned forward, accentuating the next sentence. "He got a lot of notes at one point. Anyway, the movers came to pack up the furniture into the truck and there they were. A full stack of papers fanned out on the floor. Years of them."

Stories upon stories of Henry were told by James who was

absolutely effervescent and glowing as he relived the memories. Hawken sat there, Henry on the left of her, James across
the round table, contemplating how different their lives must
have been. She grew up in a household where her parents
nodded to her in passing, left notes on the refrigerator, and,
most nights, food in plastic dishes were left for heating up
meals.

She thought of Henry's description of his relationship with
his father. Superficial, he said. She glanced at Henry now,
sitting across from his father, a low, wide smile played across
his face. James was similarly uniformed, a glint of pride
splaying across his own wide smile. They just needed a third
party to recharge the batteries. While she regarded them, she
felt Henry grab her hand under the table. Barely turning in his
direction, it was enough to see his smile radiating enough
energy to power a thousand-watt light bulb. She squeezed his
hand under the table. She could feel the transfer of energy
within a nanosecond and then she herself was matching his
smile, watt for watt.

Once they had finished eating, Hawken excused herself to
the hall bathroom. As she stepped from the kitchen into the
hallway, she lingered at the pictures that were lining the walls.
There must have been twenty pictures and collages hanging on
display. Pictures of Henry as a baby, held by Anna and James.
Henry's school photos, yellowing in their frames. It was a life
she never knew existed. That there were families who enjoyed
spending time together. In her house, the pictures that lined
the walls were reprints of famous works of art. Pictures of
strangers. Sterile.

She washed her hands and checked her teeth in the mirror.
There was a smile on her face that wouldn't retreat. It was so
overwhelming she pulled the shower curtain to the side and sat
on the edge of the bathtub, catching her breath. In the small

space, she raked her memory for a time when she was this intoxicated with joy when it wasn't centered around Henry or his family. After a couple of minutes, she still couldn't find anything in the recesses of her mind. She ended up drowning in those recesses. Then, there was a knock at the door, and a whisper.

"Are you okay?" Henry asked. She could hear him running his hand along the square molding on the opposite side of the door.

Hawken turned the lock then sat back down. Henry rotated the handle and slowly pushed the door open to find Hawken, red faced, sitting on the edge of the bathtub, wiping her eyes with a square of toilet paper.

He walked in and closed the door. "Come here." He pulled her up and wrapped his arms around her. "I have no idea what this is about, so you are going to have to tell me." He kissed her eyes, then pulled back so that he could see her face.

"I'm sorry. This is so embarrassing, Henry. I didn't mean to come in here and do this. I just...I've never been part of a family like this." She waved her arms around. "This house. It's an actual home. You walk face first into happiness here. It's like an alternate universe." She looked at his face. "Even you. That smile at the table. Henry." She shook her head. "I've never been this happy. You radiate so much life. You could make a flower grow just by looking at a seed, Henry. How do you do that?"

"I love you. I've only been like this with you." He kissed her then. Soft at first, stopping to look at her in-between kisses.

Hawken left the bathroom first and headed down the hallway to the family room at the back of the house. It connected to the kitchen via an archway, lined with white columns on either side. When she took a seat on the couch, Henry walked through the room, under the archway into the kitchen. Then James appeared asking if she minded if he sat with her while Henry cleaned up the dishes.

James was all smiles but asked if he could talk seriously with Hawken while they were alone. "Of course. Please," she answered.

"He's had a very hard time these last couple of years since his mom died. They were more than close. They were like the same person, like the same mold was used on Anna, then again on Henry. Really, it was more than that. You know when you are so similar to someone that you end up fighting over the same things and resenting the other person for being just like you? It wasn't like that with them. Sure, they fought, but it was mostly normal teenager/parent arguments. It was always over just as quickly as it began. When Henry and I would argue, it was like lighting a candle. It would begin strong, then flicker around until someone finally snuffed it out, usually Anna, but there was still smoke billowing about in the air for a while. And later, always later, you would realize that it would never be gone. It had embedded itself in the fibers of the room, in the paint, in the air itself. With the two of them, it was more like someone flipped the light switch on, then, with the flick of the switch, it was over. Forgotten.

"They had this... this symbiotic energy between them. Words weren't even necessary half of the time. They always did this thing that used to drive me crazy. We would be sitting on the couch watching television, or at the table at a meal and I would say something, or gesture, and they would exchange the tiniest glance and it was like they'd just had a full conversation. I always did feel like the outsider with them."

"Oh, James. I'm sure that they didn't mean to make you feel that way. Really."

"Don't worry, Hawken. After more than seventeen years, I was used to it, but..." He pulled his glasses up and rested them on his forehead, the rubbed his eyes in circular movements with his fingertips.

"What is it?" She inclined forward in his direction.

He lowered his glasses back to his nose and smiled at Hawken.

"Seeing you and Henry together—" He paused in hesitation. Hawken watched his eyes turn heavenward, as if deciding whether to continue or not. Slowly he looked back at her, sighed, then said, "I feel it again." He smiled and Hawken sat immobile, confused. "You and Henry have a similar language. Flow. You get each other. Your rhythm is the same."

Hawken leaned back against the pillows and sat quietly, processing.

"I'm sorry if I've said too much. I certainly don't want to overstep, but I can see how taken with you he is. He's never been like this with anyone before, Hawken, and I think that it is better for you to know. I also feel that I need to come clean about something else, before this gets too awkward and muddled." He glanced around Hawken, to the direction of the kitchen, verifying that Henry was still out of earshot. Then he continued.

"I hope this in no way diminishes your respect or love or feelings for Anna, but Henry told me what you told him, about knowing her." He stopped, as if waiting for a reaction, then continued, "Hawken, she told me. Back then, in Germany, she told me about you."

Hawken sucked a deep mouthful of air in and raised her hand to her mouth. James dropped his hand onto her other hand, left abandoned on the couch. He patted it twice, then pulled away. He was silently apologizing, comforting her.

"She was worried for you and she had to talk to someone about it. Henry never knew. He still doesn't know that I knew. I just really thought it best if there wasn't this...this thing between us because I knew. Do you understand?"

She winced at 'this thing', but she could understand where it would be difficult. She nodded, smiling at him, and then said, "Apart from that, what did she say about me? Anything?"

He could see it then. He could see her eyes change to a warmer, softer hue of blue. He could see the mirth settle there and it made his smile crack open. "I could always guess the days that you went to see her because she would come home with an air about her. She looked like the cat that ate the canary." He smiled to himself, in remembrance of a particular memory, Hawken assumed. His face turned more serious and he looked her in the eye and said, "She loved you, you know. She wanted the world for you." He looked at his lap, then looked around the room. He blinked, swallowed hard, then said, "I had never thought about it until just right now. Is the anniversary coming up hard for you, too?"

Hawken's face dropped, but she caught it before it hit the floor. She leaned forward, impulsively, and whispered, "That was the worst day of my life. She was my only friend. She was the only one who knew me." As she drew up her hand to stop the tears from falling, she said, "Yes. It's hard for me, but mostly because no one else knew that we were close. There's been no one else to share it with." She smiled at him. "Until now," she said.

James sat up quickly and Hawken followed suit. Henry padded down the hallway and walked in to find them both smiling at him. "What?" He asked, returning the smiles.

"We're just catching up. Come here and sit with Hawken. I'll leave you guys for a little bit while I make a few phone calls." As James stood up, he patted Hawken on the shoulder and gave her a conspiratorial wink as she smiled at him. She had never felt so much a part of a family in her life.

As soon as he was out of the room and Henry sat down in his place on the couch, he said, "Did my dad just wink at you?" Hawken smiled and shrugged. "Well, you certainly won him over. Seriously. Did you see him?" He turned to look at the invisible wake his father left when he walked out of the room.

"He's awesome, Henry. I'm sorry that you guys aren't closer.

He seems really easy to talk to." She put her head on his shoulder and he ran his fingers through her hair.

"I'm glad that you see that side of him, sweet girl. I love you." He kissed her hair.

16

"I can't believe we are going to Disneyland. And you are meeting my family. And you aren't even nervous. How are you not nervous?" There was an audible hum billowing from Hawken's nervous-excited body.

"I am nervous. But I'm happy, more than anything else." Henry was smiling at her visible anxiety.

They were in Henry's BMW merging onto I-5 towards Anaheim. The last week had been hectic at school for both of them. Papers and projects were all due in before Thanksgiving break and Henry had been spending more time at work grading papers and assignments. They had both felt pangs of guilt about putting school priorities ahead of each other but what choice did they have?

Hawken was sitting on her hands in the passenger seat. "I'm just so excited for this break to spend time with you again without worrying about anything else. I feel like I've been aimlessly wandering in the desert this past week and I've finally found water. And I plan on diving in, so be warned." She had told this to Henry when he came to pick her up the night before they were leaving for Disneyland.

"Warning heeded and I fully intend to ignore it. I can't wait to be with you, either. This has been the longest week of my life. It has made me see how much I need you, though. If we hadn't been able to talk on the phone, I would have had to quit work. Seriously." He reached his hand over to find hers in the car. She took it and rubbed the back of it on her cheek.

"My parents sent me our tickets for Disneyland. Actually, my mom overnighted them so that we could just meet them in the park tomorrow whenever we get there."

"They didn't have to buy mine. I was planning on paying for myself."

"You wouldn't be going if it weren't for them visiting. They expected to pay. Don't worry about it. I am so excited for you to meet Rex. He's going to love you. They all are." She said and traced his knuckles with her lips.

They spent the night at Henry's house, then got up early to drive to Anaheim to meet Hawken's family.

Hawken loved riding in Henry's car. She had an unobstructed view of him. She also loved that she could look at him without getting caught. So that's what she did.

She looked at his hair. Then put her hands through it.

She looked at his ear. Then leaned over and kissed it.

She looked at his nose. The way that it had a little bump about halfway down that gave him character. He told her he got into a fist fight in high school and his nose had been broken. *But you should have seen the other guy,* he'd said.

She looked at his lips. They were perfectly shaped, symmetrical, and the lower lip curved down towards his chin in the center. She touched her fingers to them, and he kissed them.

"Penny for your thoughts?" He tilted his head and looked over at her with just his eyes.

"A penny? No way. I'd need a lot more than that to tell you what I'm thinking. How about some music? I made a playlist for the trip, actually." She shifted her body in the seat and pointed her finger at him. "Don't laugh. It's all of the songs that make me feel like the world is sublime and I'm the luckiest person in it."

"Wow. That must be quite the playlist. I can't wait to hear what makes you *sublime*. Put it on, love." While Hawken plugged in her phone, Henry asked, "Will you tell me the songs in advance, or do I have to let the suspense effectively torture me?"

"I'm not sure. How much do I want to torture you is the Question of the Day. Hmmmm. I'll give you the first one. 'Almost Gold' by The Jesus and Mary Chain. It has to be one of the most romantic heartbreaking songs. It makes me feel happy every time I hear it." She looked over at Henry. He ran his fingers through his bangs and made a fist. "Henry, are you okay?"

"It's just amazing, isn't it? This? Us?" He stole a glance at her and she blushed in return.

Henry was quiet for a while after that, listening to the music. Hawken was thinking about her parents and how close she had once been with them. Like the Three Musketeers. And then Rex was born and things changed, as they naturally do when there is a baby in the house, but she realized now that she was always waiting for the day when it shifted back to them being a team. A family. Where she felt important, not superfluous. Maybe it was too late. Maybe she was an adult now and that ship had sailed. Now she had Henry. Beautiful, perfect Henry. He made her feel important. No, more than that. He made her feel essential.

A few songs later, Henry squeezed her hand and said, "Tell me something ridiculous," and grinned at her.

"Ridiculous? Okay." She paused in thought. "So, there's this disorder called Exploding Head Syndrome where when you sleep you hear gunshots and explosions and fireworks. In essence, it would be like the worst kind of torture, wouldn't it?

You can't sleep, and if you do you end up in the middle of a war zone?"

"You never cease to amaze me, Tony Hawk. Exploding Head Syndrome? Why do you know these things? You're a walking encyclopedia of maladies."

"I've got more in the vault." She threw him a sideways glance.

"Tell me something that is both happy and sad at the same time. A dichotomized question of sorts."

"Give me a minute to think on that one." She took his hand and held it up to her face, touching his fingertips to her lips. "Okay, I've got it. Here goes—I think your mother, in some ways, loved me more than my own mother ever has." She turned to Henry to assess his reaction. He looked sad. "Oh, Henry. Don't be sad. I'm not sad. I consider myself to be the luckiest girl in the world to have had the relationship that I did with your mom. She gave me the unconditional love that I needed at that time in my life. She made me feel safe. She was everything. You are so much like her, you know. You change people. I don't know how to say it right. The atmosphere can be cold and dry and hard, and you walk into it and it's like the air swirls around and becomes pleasant and light. Does that make sense?" She touched his shoulder and he turned to look at her briefly.

And then he said, "You know that feeling when you walk out of a dark movie theater and everything is so bright and warm and unexpected? That is what my life is like with you in it."

"I CAN'T BELIEVE we are here. Together. And you are meeting my family. Henry, you are the most amazing person in the world for walking into the lion's den like this."

"I hardly consider meeting your family a suicide mission, Hawken. Now, stop freaking me out and relax, okay?" They had parked the car and were collecting the necessary items from her purse to transfer into the backpack that she'd brought to carry. He reached over to her, grabbed her by the waist and dropped his lips onto hers. She put her hand on his neck and Henry pulled away, shaking his head, smiling. "Let's go. Don't forget the shoes."

Hawken had gone shopping for the trip and found the most amazing pair of Vans. They were Star Wars inspired and had both Luke and Leia as well as Darth Vader on them. So, she bought a pair for herself, then noticed the same pair in the men's section and the little boy's section. "Can you believe this?" she said triumphantly when she showed them to Henry. "We can wear matching shoes at the park with Rex." She looked at Henry. "Oh, crap. Is this the worst idea ever?" She stilled, gauging his reaction. "Are you mortified right now, Henry?"

He laughed. Then he pulled his out of the box and put them on. "The force is strong with these. I can feel it." She rolled her eyes so hard it hurt.

"Shut up. Seriously, what do you think. Is it too much?" She pulled hers out and held them up.

He was contemplating them. "I think that in a vacuum, these are awesome shoes." He looked up at her now. "If you want us to match, I want us to match. It will be fun. Like we're Rock Star Nerd Ken and Barbie." He had the cheesiest grin on his face so she leaned forward to kiss it off.

"I hope Rex likes them. He was totally into Star Wars this summer." Hawken wanted everything to be perfect for Rex. When she spoke with him on the phone, he told her how excited he was to see the Castle and go on the rides.

～

"Okay, they said to meet them in front of 'It's a Small World' at nine o'clock. What time is it?" Hawken was anxiously looking around through the bustling crowd. There was no way she would have made this trip by herself. Just standing among a sea of people was giving her anxiety. Holding Henry's hand had been soothing. His voice was always so calming. That's why she would always fall asleep on the phone with him at night. She couldn't help it. His voiced lulled her to sleep. Then, she'd wake up the next morning with a red rectangle on her cheek where she'd been sleeping on her phone all night.

"It's nine-oh-five. Have patience, my love. They are probably on a ride. C'mere." He pulled her into his body and wrapped his arms around her. "I can't imagine coming here with anyone else for my first time," he said then kissed her on the head. He was the perfect height for that. He was six foot three and she was five foot nine.

"Hey, there they are!" Hawken pulled away from Henry and grabbed his hand, leading him through the mass of humanity.

"Hi, Dad." Awkward hug. "Hi, Mom." Awkward hug. "Hey, T-Rex." Mega hug. "This is Henry." She made a sweeping gesture towards her parents and said, "This is Paul and Nancy."

Hands were clasped and backs were patted. *Nice to finally meet you*'s were said.

Drumroll, please. "This is Rex. Rex, this is Henry. Can you say, 'Hi, Henry?'"

Rex looked over towards Henry's legs and said, "Say Hi, Henry."

"Hi, Rex. It's nice to meet you, dude." Henry held out his hand to Rex and Rex high fived it.

"Star whores. I like it," Rex was pointing to Henry's shoes.

Laughter erupted from their group. Hawken pulled her backpack off and pulled out the shoes for Rex. He said, "Thank you," and put them on right away. "Darf Bader. I like it!"

After all the introductions and small talk was complete, the decision was made to go ride Space Mountain. Rex had been watching videos on his computer and was excited for the 'ups and downs'. Hawken's parents had gotten a pass for Rex because standing in line was so difficult for him, so they were all able to stand in the disabled line instead. "This way, we'll be able to go on as many rides as we want today even though it is so crowded." They all started walking towards Tomorrowland, with Paul on the left of Henry, asking questions about his father, school, and his plans for the future. Henry was holding Hawken's left hand and Hawken was holding Rex's hand with her right. After a few steps, Rex let go of Hawken's hand and pulled Henry's hand from hers. Henry and Hawken looked at each other. Then, Rex took Henry's right hand in his left and Hawken's left hand in his right and continued to Space Mountain linked in the middle of the human chain. Henry was still talking to Paul when they got there.

Paul asked, "Who wants to ride this one?" and everyone but Nancy raised their hand. "Okay, looks like I've got Rex with me, you guys."

"No. I want Henry." Rex grabbed Henry's hand and started pulling him forward.

"Wow, Henry. It looks like you make quite an impression on the Larsons. Honey, do you see this?" Paul's jaw was hanging loose in observance. Nancy was speechless. Hawken worried that her mother would be upset, but she looked ecstatic more than anything. Like her baby had just solved a Rubik's Cube. That was the general consensus of the adults, anyway. Hawken felt like she had won a Pulitzer.

Rex was glued to Henry all morning and most of the afternoon. They held hands and Henry asked him lots of questions like, "Do you like school? What is your favorite color? Which is your favorite SpongeBob character?" Rex was thrilled. He would walk ahead and then look backwards holding out his arm and request, "Henry's hand."

After lunch, Paul and Nancy asked Rex if he wanted to ride some rides with them so that Henry and Hawken could spend some time together. He said, "No. I want Henry ride." He looked at Henry, right in the eye and said, "I love you," then kissed him on the cheek, just exactly like he would to Hawken. Hawken and Paul both craned their necks at Nancy, who had a tear in her eye.

"I love you, too, Buddy," Henry said and put his arm around Rex's shoulder. Henry looked at Nancy apologetically and shrugged. "What do you say we let Mommy and Daddy have some time alone and you come with me and Hawk?"

"Yessss," said Rex and pumped his arm over his head. Again, everyone laughed and looked over at Nancy. She was blowing her nose into a napkin and dabbing the corner of her eyes.

"You kids go have fun. Let's meet back here at five o'clock and we'll trade, okay?"

"Sure, Mom. You and Dad go and relax. Don't worry." Hawken squeezed her mom's shoulder and stood up with Rex and Henry.

The trio walked down Main Street through Sleeping Beauty's Castle to Fantasyland and stood behind a couple with two little girls in pink Mickey ears running in circles around their parent's legs. It was obvious that the parents were too tired to care what they were doing, as long as they weren't touching other people. They were all standing in the Handicapped Accessible line for Peter Pan, which the sign said would be a fifteen-minute wait for them. As Rex wouldn't let go of Henry all day, Hawken had to settle for whatever part of his body was left over to touch. There were many Henry Sandwiches as the day went on. Rex would stand with his back to Henry's chest and pull Henry's arms onto his shoulders, so Hawken would hug Henry from behind, wrapping her arms around his waist.

Hawken was worried that Henry would be irritated after a

while and finally asked him while they were sandwiched in line, "You are being extremely nice. Are you okay?" She had the side of her head buried in his neck.

He turned his head as far as he could to answer with, "Of course. This is the best day ever. Seriously. How could I possibly be having a bad time? Come here."

Hawken let go of him and walked over to his side. He pulled one arm off Rex and put it on Hawken's face and kissed her. He kissed her hard and urgent on the mouth, and when she pulled away, he gently bit her lip. "I'm so crazy in love with you. And your brother. Don't worry. There is nowhere else in the world I'd rather be."

They rode every ride in Fantasyland, some twice. Rex always wanted to be with Henry, so Hawken sat out on the rides that only had two seats. She could tell that Henry felt bad, but she was happy.

How could she not be happy? As she waited for the Dynamic Duo to appear from Mr. Toad's Wild Ride she was thinking about Rex. And Henry, of course. Henry had altered her life in such a way that she realized was a permanent trans-formation. She had been so shy and timid and insecure in so many ways. She had been emotionally barren and scarred. She thought she was scarred. Hawken was under the impression that through talking to Anna after the Incident happened, she had started to grow scar tissue to heal over the wound. Since she had been with Henry, she was realizing that there was just a scab covering the lesion. A scab is easily picked off and then you were left with an open, bleeding gash. It was Henry who was healing her. Henry. She had felt differently after she told him her story. She had felt raw. Like the scab had been washed away. Each time he touched her, smiled at her, new skin would grow, covering the injury. Each gentle touch, each kiss, each time he poured buckets of stars on her she was being made whole. She had never felt this with anyone else that she had known. This was all Henry.

She thought about all the moments they shared in the past weeks and found herself smiling like an idiot on a bench amidst a sea of screaming kids and tired parents. Most of the things that Henry said to her had made her embarrassed at the time, but scored on her heart when she thought of them later. Conversations like this:

"I love you so much, Hawken. When you smile at me it is so genuine and sweet it makes me feel like I'm going to explode. I'm not kidding. Look out, Los Angeles. The first human supernova has been spotted on Southern California University's campus."

Or this:

"When I am sitting in my lecture and I know that you are in the same building in the lobby studying, with your cute as hell nerdy black reading glasses and your perfect nose in a book, I sometimes find myself doubting your existence. Like you can't possibly be real. Just a figment of my imagination. Then my class finally, painfully ends and I hold my breath walking down the hall while my lungs hitch and I have to catch my breath from the shock and awe of you."

And this:

"I wish I owned a satellite in orbit around the earth. I would press the Record button so I wouldn't miss any moments of you."

God, he was so patient. He hadn't made her feel bad at all after she made him wait weeks to kiss her. She wouldn't even touch him for weeks.

Hawken was starting to wonder what was taking so long. When she looked up, she saw them, hand in hand. They were walking towards her, both with Mickey ears on the top of their heads and matching smiles covering their faces.

"Don't worry, Tony Hawk. We didn't forget you." Henry

pulled a set of purple ears from behind his back and placed them on her head. "Perfect. A perfectly matching hatted and shoed family."

Hawken couldn't help it. She wrapped her arms around his neck and kissed him so hard their teeth clacked together. "Sorry!" she laughed.

"Wow. I should put you in hats more often. I love you." Their matching smiles reached all the way up to their Mickey Mouse ears.

They met up for dinner with Paul and Nancy at The Blue Bayou restaurant. It was magical, until it wasn't. The restaurant was nestled inside of the Pirates of the Caribbean, seating you next to the water to watch the boats drift by. There are thousands of twinkling lights that look like lightning bugs. It seemed like it would have been relaxing for everyone after such a full day, but it was too dark for Rex. He was covering his ears, walking around the table, and he kept asking to go outside. Henry volunteered and walked him out of the restaurant.

Hawken's mom pulled her purse onto her lap and started to fish through it with purpose. After a second, she pulled out an envelope and handed it to Hawken. Hawken slipped a photo out of the bent envelope and looked at her mother.

"When you told us that you were with Henry, I went looking through our photos that we had from your cross country meets. This is the only one I found that had Henry, but I thought you might like to have it." She smiled at Hawken, and Hawken was touched.

She studied the picture, holding it carefully by the edges. The shot was focused on Hawken. It was an action shot of her crossing the finish line, dressed in her red school uniform (which left little to the imagination), with black yoga pants and a black shirt underneath. She had a black wool cap on her head, pulled down to her eyes. Her standard uniform for invisibility. Less in focus, to the right side of the photograph, was

Henry. He was standing about twenty-five feet behind the finish line, on the yellowing winter grass of the football field. Immediately to his left was his girlfriend, Amanda, who was caught mid speech. Henry's body was in line with hers, but his face was turned towards the finish line, watching Hawken.

She put the photo back in the envelope and tucked it into her backpack. Looking up at her parents, she smiled and said, "Thanks, Mom," then took a sip of her soda. She felt the immediate need to run through the door and find Henry, but stayed seated, testing her willpower. Luckily, her father broke the silence.

"Baby, your mother and I have been talking and we wanted to discuss Henry. Would that be okay?" Paul and Nancy both leaned forward and folded their hands in their laps at the same time. Uh oh.

"What's wrong? Are you guys serious?" Hawken felt immediately defensive. How could they have anything negative to say when he had swooped in and befriended Rex all day. Couldn't they see how much he meant to Hawken?

"Don't be like this, Hawken. Look. You haven't exactly been forthright about this relationship. Your mother and I just found out, what, ten days ago? We have no idea how serious this is and we are worried for Rex as well as you. It is hard to see Rex so attached to someone. Anyone. You know how hard we work with him and how difficult it has been for him to engage with others. He never lets anyone touch him. You know this. We were taken aback this morning." Paul sat back in his chair and wiped his forehead with the back of his hand. Throughout the day Hawken had noticed that it had turned a bright shade of red.

"I don't understand. Shouldn't you guys be dancing on the ceiling? This is a monumental breakthrough for him. Why do you sound like this is the end of the world?" Hawken started leaning forward on the table herself.

"Hawken, listen, we just think," Nancy started, "that it is going to be hard on Rex when Henry leaves tonight. It isn't fair for him. Not only that, we are worried for you. We've never seen you with a boy. This is new for us and for you. We just want to make sure that you are okay. Do you understand?" Nancy tilted her head at an angle and reached her hand across the table to touch Hawken's.

"I think I do. Instead of being happy that Rex is able to feel comfortable with someone he just met, you think it is upsetting? And, basically, you have the same worries for me. I'm almost nineteen and Rex is seven and you think it is better for both of us to stay in a cage and not meet people because we might get hurt? God, you guys. How in the world did we get here?" Hawken pushed her chair back and moved to stand up. Her father grabbed her hand.

"Hawken. Don't. Just listen to me. Okay? Please." Hawken stalled, upset, but then sat back down.

"I don't know what happened to you. You were so outgoing and fun and full of life. And then it was like the spark died out. Overnight you turned into a shadow. You barely left your bedroom and when you did your mom and I didn't even recognize you. When we moved to Phoenix we saw a gradual improvements, but you were never the same. We've been so worried about you. Fast forward to today. You look like yourself again. Actually, you look like a better version of yourself. We've not seen you this animated, this *alive* in years. You seem so happy."

"Isn't that a good thing? Isn't that want you want for me? Somehow, I think I'm missing the point here." She was exasperated. She felt as if she were sitting at the Mad Hatter's Tea Party, everyone talking in nonsensical, circular references. When the mouse flew out of the teapot, she would explode.

"Yes. Of course, that is what we want for you, but it scares the hell out of us. Just like with Rex. You know him. He won't be the same after this. He'll be talking about Henry for months and months. He'll draw Henry in all of his notebooks. He'll ask about Henry. If Henry doesn't stick around in his life, it is going to be that much harder on him. Do you understand? We are so afraid that if something happens and Henry is no longer in the picture—" Paul took a deep breath. "Hawken. We love you so much. We can't see you go back to that place again. We didn't even recognize you. It would be too much." He reached up and wiped his left eye with his napkin. "Let's not turn this into a bad day, okay?"

"I want to know what you think of Henry. Everything you just said is ridiculous. None of this has anything to do with Henry. You are making it sound like you'd prefer if he was an ass so that Rex didn't like him. And, you'd rather see me alone. I'm done with this conversation. I want to know what you think of Henry. Not how he makes me feel, or Rex. Just him. As a person." Hawken sat back in her chair and crossed her arms.

"Oh, honey. How could we not love him? He radiates happiness. He would make a fortune if he could bottle that and sell it," Nancy said. "He is perfect for you and he seems to really care about you. We are thrilled to see you together and this happy. Of course, we are. But. Just be careful. You are young and you have your whole life ahead of you. I know that this sounds cliché, but it is true. Just be careful, okay?"

"Yes. Thank you," said Hawken. After a minute, she said, "Can I just say one thing?"

They nodded in unison.

"Rex is growing up. He's not a baby. He needs friends. He needs space. Let him grow up a little bit, okay? You should have seen him with Henry today. I've never seen him laugh or smile so much. I'm afraid his cheeks are going to be so sore tomorrow."

They both looked at each other with tired eyes. "We hear what you are saying. It's hard to let your babies grow up. Especially Rex. We just want to take care of him." Now Nancy was crying. Hawken stood up and hugged her.

When Henry and Rex returned to the table the bill was paid and they were all standing up pushing in chairs. "Thank you, Henry. He certainly looks better now," Paul said.

"Of course. You have an incredible kid, here." He looked at Hawken, then back to her parents. "We should probably go find somewhere to sit out there. The fireworks are going to start soon," Henry said and motioned to the door.

"I'm not sure that Rex will do fireworks. They might be a bit loud for him. Why don't we let you guys have some time together and we'll meet up after the fireworks at the castle." Paul proposed.

Henry put his hand on Rex's shoulder and said, "Buddy, I'll see you in a little while, okay? Go have fun with your mom and dad."

"Yeah. Okay," Rex said and started walking away. Once again, everyone started laughing and Paul caught Hawken's eye.

She walked over and hugged him while he whispered, "Maybe we were wrong. We just want you to be happy and it seems like he makes you twenty shades happier that we ever thought possible. We just love you so much, Hawk."

"You, too, Dad."

Hawken grabbed Henry's hand and they walked away. "Do you want to watch the fireworks?" she asked him.

"I want to do whatever you want to do. I've missed you today. Even though we've been next to each other, it hasn't been the same, has it? I need my required allotment of Hawken." He pulled her hand up and kissed it.

"I like that sound of that—required." She looked up at him. "Henry Lewis. You need me?"

"I do." He leaned down and kissed her nose.

"Let's go sit somewhere quiet, okay?" She couldn't remember the last time she'd been this happy. Something inside of her was clawing its way out, forcing her stomach to knot up like a Mickey Mouse shaped pretzel.

"Tony Hawk. Are you suggesting performing semi-naughty acts in a darkened corner of Disneyland?" He raised an eyebrow, but his smile was one of a co-conspirator.

"Naughtiness is now officially a daily *requirement* of mine," she said and laughed maniacally. "I feel like I should be twirling the edges of my non-existent handlebar mustache."

They walked over to an outdoor auditorium and sat on a bench in the back under the towering Jacaranda trees whose trunks were lit up with little white sparkling lights. The moon was a Cheshire cat moon and bats were swarming around the turrets of the Castle.

Hawken took Henry's hands in hers and squeezed them. He said, "You seem nervous. What's wrong?"

"It's my turn," she said.

"Your turn for what?" he asked, questioningly. His eyes were lit up and full of mirth under the lights.

"To throw buckets of stars at you," she said. His face opened up revealing another layer of happiness. "You are blinding me with your smile, you know. And I haven't even said anything yet," she laughed.

He laughed. And then he kissed her.

And then he laughed again. Another kiss. Another laugh.

"Henry. Do you want to hear what I have to say or not?" She asked, smiling.

"I can't decide which will be better. Kissing you here, under the stars and twinkling lights, or you pouring stars on me," he paused. Kiss. Then, "I'm ready. Tell me, love."

A minute went by. And another.

"Did you change your mind?" he asked, pulling her chin up with his index finger so that he could see her eyes.

"No, Henry. I'm just trying to remember this. Everything. I want to freeze frame this moment with you," she said.

"Jesus, Hawken. I know. I can't stand it. I just want to hold you until we stop breathing," he whispered and rested his cheek on her shoulder so that his nose was touching her neck.

"You are so much better at this that I am, Henry," she said.

He laughed. "You think so? I have no practice. It's never been like this before. You aren't as bad as you think, sweet girl." He kissed her neck.

"Henry, look at me, okay?"

He did. Now she was nervous. His face reflected pure love.

"Okay, maybe don't look at me," she said, laughing. "I have so many things that I want to say to you right now and I don't know where to start."

"I'm not going anywhere. Take your time." He looked upward, then back at her, adding, "Actually, should I be worried here?" with one raised eyebrow.

"No. Okay. I'll start with Rex," she said and took a big breath in. "I know you realize how paramount today was. There aren't words. The earth tipped on its axis today, because of you. He's never touched anyone like that. Or spoken to anyone so much. My parents are crying. And worried that he won't be able to survive without you," she said, taking another pause and another deep breath. "They're worried that I won't be able to survive without you, either." She stopped and looked at him. His eyebrows knit together, and he exhaled.

"What? What does that mean?" He was searching her face for an answer, but not finding one. "They are worried that I'm going to leave you?" He was incredulous. Hawken could feel his muscles tense in her hands, the muscle in his jaw tighten.

"No. Yes. No." She put a hand on his jawline. "They are worried because they see how much I like you and how much you like me—"

"How much I love you," he corrected her.

She put her other hand on his face and pulled him close so that they were eye to eye.

"And how much I love you," she said.

She watched him inhale. Then she watched his face crack open. His smile. In the same instant, the whole world lit up.

Or maybe it was just the sky above Disneyland. The fireworks had started, but Henry and Hawken were missing them.

"Do you think there is such a thing as the perfect day?" Henry looked over at Hawken, who had a permanent grin on her face. They were driving back towards LA after saying their goodbyes to Paul, Nancy and Rex. They were all unsure how Rex would react, but he hugged Hawken and kissed her cheek, and then hugged Henry and kissed him as well. He tried to give Henry his Mickey ears, but Henry didn't accept them. "Dude, those are for you to remember me, okay?" Henry told him.

Paul and Nancy each gave Henry a solid hug and surprised Hawken by whispering in his ear. He later told her that they both said, *We love you.*

"A perfect day or 'The Perfect Day?' I think there's a distinguishable difference. I think that you can have lots of Perfect Days, but I'd hate to think that there can be only one of The Perfect Day. Am I talking in circles?" she asked Henry.

He shook his head. "I can't stop smiling. My cheeks are getting sore, but I can't help it. I can't imagine being any happier than I am right now. I feel like I don't deserve all of this. Like I've stolen an entire country's ration of happy and used it all on myself in one day."

"I know. Me, too." They sat in silence for a few minutes until Henry said, "Tell me something I don't know about you. Not something trivial."

"Something meaningful?" She thought about it sincerely then answered, "I knew that you watched me skate." She paused to look at his expression. He looked surprised. "I used to see you come down the hill by the park most days after school when I was there skating on the half pipe. You would carefully, purposefully walk between the trees and then you would stop next to one. Sometimes you would stand there by the tree and sometimes you would sit behind it so that I could only see your knees poking out. Then, you would stand up and walk back into the thick trees and make an exaggerated arc around the park. I would stop skating and watch you. I figured you wouldn't mind since you were watching me, too." She was watching Henry's expression change from surprise to something she couldn't read. "Are you upset?" she asked.

"No. Not at all, actually." He grinned. "I guess I wasn't as stealthy as I had thought. I thought that it was my secret. I had no idea you knew. You were my outlet, you know that? Watching you skate was hypnotic. That sounds so lame, but it was true. I wasn't happy at that time and that first day that I saw you and you introduced yourself, you were alluring. Really. I walked through the park the next day and you were there again, so I decided to sit and watch you. Maybe it was the repetition of movement, but you were so fluid, like a wave on the ocean. It made me happy. So, I just kept doing it. You were my therapy, of sorts, I guess."

THAT NIGHT, in Henry's bedroom, Hawken sat on the floor, legs bent in the air with her arms crossed on her knees. Henry was playing his guitar for her. His acoustic guitar. He switched songs and when he did, he sat down in front of her, so that their legs were touching. Hawken smiled and inhaled deeply when she realized what he was playing. One of her favorite songs. It was 'Such Great Heights,' a song that was so intense, and the words so meaningful. She immediately had tears in her eyes.

When the song ended, Henry put the guitar down and

wiped the tears away with his thumb. "Don't cry, sweet girl. I love you so much."

"I love you, Henry." She gave him her best smile.

He looked directly into her eyes and, without hesitation said, "I think you might have unknowingly unlocked the universe for me."

Hawken's breath hitched in her throat. "Henry? Do you ever feel like your feet aren't even actually touching the ground anymore?"

17

"What do you want to do today?" Henry asked as he rolled over onto Hawken. She had decided to spend the night at his house again and was desperately hoping that he had an extra toothbrush.

"Aren't you getting sick of me? I'm afraid that if I spend the day with you again you'll be bored of me," she said, teasing him.

"Impossible. Not in a million years. I can't imagine ever having enough of you. I didn't know I could be this happy. I didn't know I could want things and have them, too. And I do. I want you. So badly. Just to be near you. Just this," he said, waving his hand over their fully clothed bodies, "You've changed something in me permanently. By its very definition, you've mutated me." They both smiled at each other like idiots. "I want to spend every waking minute, and every soporific minute with one person. With you." A smile pulled the edges of his mouth to his eyes. "Love, I can't imagine being apart from you."

"Henry?"

He laughed. "Yes?"

"Why are you laughing?"

"I'm just thinking about how you always start or end a question or statement with my name." He looked at her and realized that he'd made her feel bad. "I'm sorry. I should have prefaced that statement with this...I've never wanted to hear my name as much as I do when I'm with you because you always include it in any thought of yours." And with that, he batted his eyes at her. And she punched him in the arm.

"Just for that, I'm going to be self-conscious about what I say, Hen—crap."

He laughed. "Say it. I really do love it." She rolled her eyes.

"My question to you was this...Why Electrical Engineering? Was that always what you wanted to do?" As soon as the words left her mouth, Hawken watched Henry flinch.

"I don't know. I guess so. My mom and I used to talk about it a lot. I was always really good at math and science and we just decided that it sounded good."

"Do you love it? You never really talk about the future. What do you want to do?"

"I like it. I'm good at it. What about you? Why architecture?" He was deflecting.

"That's what I've wanted to do forever. When I was in third grade, I fell in love with graph paper. I loved the perfection of it. Perfect squares morphing into other perfect squares. I would sit for hours with my mechanical pencil and ruler and draw floor plans of homes, offices, and schools. Anything. Everything. I have books of them at home. Anyway, ever since then I've wanted to be an architect."

"Henry," she said and laughed. "What did you want to be when you grew up? I can't imagine you telling people at age ten that you wanted to be an engineer. There had to be something. What was it?"

"Why is this so important to you?" Now he was sitting up, irritated.

"Wow. It isn't as if it's a state secret, Henry. Is it?" Hawken sat up, too, wondering where the sudden change of temperature came from.

"No. I just—I don't know." She could hear the mild irritation in his voice and decided to press the issue, but he got up and walked into the bathroom before she had the chance.

THEY HAD DECIDED to spend the day together after all, of course. Henry drove Hawken home to shower and change her clothes. The plan was skating. Henry found a skate park nearby and he wanted her to skate for him and to teach him some moves.

"You ride goofy," Hawken said.

"What? Are you making fun of me?" Henry stopped and jumped off his board. Hawken started laughing and glided over to him.

"No, I'm not, Henry. It just means that you ride with your left foot in back. I ride regular, see?" She had her left foot in the front.

Hawken was trying to get an idea of how much Henry knew about skating. "What kinds of tricks can you do? Can you Ollie?"

"Yes?"

"Good. Can you heelflip?"

"Uh, no. I can pretty much just Ollie."

"Okay. A heelflip is a good place to start then. So, you are going to do your Ollie, but you'll kick the board with your back foot and then slide your front foot off the side, toe down so your heel kicks the nose up and it flips completely over. Here, I'll show you," she said and got on her board and skated down the street a bit, then turned around. She came towards Henry quickly, smiling, and when she reached him, she kicked the board up and spun it around while she was in the air. She landed back on the board and coasted to a stop. "You up for it?" She was grinning like a maniac.

"You make it look so simple. I'm thinking that I should have been more prepared; meaning knee pads and elbow pads. I'll do my best." Henry followed her instruction and the first time the board went flying off to the side. The second time, it landed upside down and he had to run to keep from falling. The third time he was pretty close to landing it.

"Very nice, skater boy. You just need some practice." Henry spent the next half hour practicing and Hawken watched him while smiling like an idiot and saying things like, "so close, do it again, you had it that time, try again."

"Okay, my ego has been sufficiently wounded for today. Why don't you impress *me* now. Don't hold out on me, okay?"

"Okay, but I'm a bit rusty. It looks like the halfpipe is open. Let's go over there."

For the next hour, Hawken dropped into the halfpipe and showed Henry how to Rock and Roll, Axle Stall, Rock to Fakie, and the Indy Grab. His favorite trick was the hand plant. "That was amazing. I can't believe you can hand plant. What can't you do?" he asked as he took her hand.

"Ha. You've now seen all of my skills, I'm afraid. I pretty much suck at everything else in life."

"You don't suck at anything. I don't deserve you," he said. Henry's words were raw, his voice breaking. "Seriously. What is a girl like you doing with a guy like me anyway?" They had stopped walking and Hawken could tell that he was half serious. He was looking at her, but also through her. What could he possibly be thinking? She noticed then he had a glossed-over look, like he'd closed the windows and dropped the blinds and was just living inside in the dark.

How could he be asking her this? He had it all wrong. Backwards. She couldn't understand what he saw in her. She was shattered when he met her. She was mending now, but she still wasn't whole, which is what Henry deserved. She could make herself whole again, she thought. With Henry.

"Are you serious?" she asked.

"I don't know. I suppose I'm asking the question, so, yes. You are beautiful and talented beyond measure. You are sweet and good and smart and happy all the time. I guess I've just been thinking a lot today. I'm sorry. The anniversary of my mom's death is coming up and it makes me really take stock of where I am." He had been looking down at their entwined hands. He looked up at her and said, "Tony Hawk. I'm sorry. Forgive me. I'm just a little off today. I'll be fine." Hawken nodded.

They strolled back to the car and Henry didn't open her door. As he said, he had a lot on his mind. They were completely silent in the car on the way back to Henry's house. When they had pulled into the driveway, the clouds had settled just above them, blocking the path of the sun's rays. It seemed eerily dark. Henry didn't make a move to get out of the car, so Hawken stayed immobile, surveying his face.

Henry had laid his head back against the headrest, pushing the palms of his hands into his eyes. He almost whispered, "I'm actually really tired. Do you mind if I just take you home now?" He never turned his head to look at her.

"Uh. Okay. Sure, Henry." She slumped down in her seat while he started up the car. "What about dinner? We were going to take your dad out tonight, remember?" Hawken didn't want to leave like this. She couldn't understand what had happened. What had gone wrong. Did she do something? Say something? "Right. I forgot. I'll pick you up later, okay? How about seven?" he asked.

"Okay, that sounds great." But it didn't. Wasn't it just this morning that Henry had told her that he wanted to spend every minute with her? She felt sick deep in her stomach. Something had happened, but what? She sat the rest of the way gazing out the window, her mind reeling.

She started to backtrack the entire day, but his voice halted her thoughts.

"We're here. I'll see you later, okay?" Henry reached over and touched her cheek. She opened her mouth, but nothing escaped.

"Bye, Henry," she said and closed the door. Before she stepped onto the curb the car was gone.

HAWKEN WAS DISTRAUGHT. After Henry had dropped her off, she took the stairs up to her room, fumbled with her room key, dropped it, picked it up, dropped it again and slid down the door and sat on the floor in the hallway. She let out a deep breath and pulled her knees to her chest. Then the tears came. At first in single tears, but then the torrential downpour started. She couldn't make herself stop crying. What was the point anyway? Henry was probably at home thinking about how to get out of this. How could she not see this coming?

The longer she sat, the more upset she got. Mad at herself for thinking that he was different. For thinking that he loved her. But. He did love her, didn't he? She thought back on all the stars he'd thrown at her.

"Nobody can be worth this many tears. What the hell did he do to you?"

Hawken jumped and turned to see Jason sitting on the floor, his back against the opposite wall. "You scared me. You can't just sneak up on someone like that," she hissed. "What are you doing here?" she asked, wiping her eyes on her sleeve and sniffling like an idiot.

"I was actually looking for you. I knew you didn't go home for break and I didn't either. I was bored and thought I'd see what you were up to," he said. He was on his knees crawling over to sit next to her.

"You look like hell, Hawken. Tell me what happened." His head was slightly tilted, and he put his hand on her shoulder for a moment, then set it down on the carpet between them.

She thought about the question. What had happened? She had no idea. Everything was fine until this morning. But what had she done? She wasn't showing off at the skate park...Henry had asked her to teach him tricks. He had gotten weird when she asked about his major. Maybe he just needed space. "I don't know what happened. I don't really want to talk about it." She stood up awkwardly and picked up her keys. Jason followed suit.

"Wait. What do you think you're doing?" she asked, turning around in the doorway.

"Oh, I thought you might need some company?"

"Uh, no thanks. I'd rather be alone right now, Jason."

"I would prefer to hang out, if that's okay." He was smiling at her in a way that made her take pity on him.

"Don't you have a list of 'hot girls' (yes, she did the finger quotes) that you can booty call?" she asked, sarcasm in her voice. She was pulling tissues out of the pink floral tissue box on her desk and attempting to wipe away the wreckage of the last twenty minutes.

"I do have quite an extensive list, but I'm always keeping my options open. There's plenty of this to go around," he said, pointing to his body. "Where is your roommate?" He was now sitting on Allison's bed looking through her cd collection.

Hawken rolled her eyes. "Don't touch anything. She'll think I was rifling through her stuff. She's probably at work. She works at Thai One On up on Washington. It's a bar that has open mike nights and live bands. And they serve Thai food. She's probably working tonight. You should go." She could only imagine what Allison would think about seeing Jason show up at the bar looking for her.

"Maybe I will. You should come with me. What else do you have to do?"

Hawken scowled. "I'm going out with Henry tonight, actually." She was reapplying her makeup and looked over from her mirror to accentuate her point.

"Then what was with the water works?" He asked, tilting his head slightly.

"Honestly, Jason, I just really need some time alone. I'm sorry. You understand, right?"

"Yeah. Okay. Let me know if you change your mind, Hawken." And with that, she was all alone.

HENRY CALLED Hawken that afternoon and told her that he wasn't going to be picking her up. He needed some space, some time. The fear and worry had left her when he dropped her off earlier. Now she was merely angry with Henry. She spent all day thinking about what had changed in those few hours and his comments throughout the day. She decided to ask him point blank.

"Henry, what's going on with you? Specifically, with you and your future?"

"My future? What are you talking about?"

"Every time I ask you a question about what you want to do or be or where you see yourself, you unzip yourself and hide inside your skin. You never have a straight answer and you are pushing me away. I think I deserve an explanation." Straight away she started biting her nails.

"Wow. That was semi-hostile. Where did that come from?"

"You aren't answering the question."

"I don't know, okay? Do I really have to have all of this figured out right this second, Hawken? Jesus."

"It's that right there, Henry. That defensive attitude. If you asked me about my plans, I could tell you in generalization without getting upset. You aren't telling me what's going on. I want to know why."

"I know that we've spent a lot of time getting to really know each other, but that doesn't mean that you have the right to know everything. You don't."

"Are you serious right now? Henry, listen to yourself. Why do you want to hide something? You can tell me anything. Anything."

"It's my mom, okay? I don't want to talk about it. Let's just drop this."

"No. What about your mom?" Henry was quiet and Hawken was running the conversations in her head on an infinite loop. And suddenly, it clicked into place. "Henry, did you plan all of this with your mom?" No response, just breathing. "And now she's gone, and you don't know what to do next? Is that it?"

There was silence on the other end of the call. Hawken left it for a minute.

"Henry?"

Nothing.

"Henry. I love you. Please talk to me."

More silence, then a loud breath. "I don't know what to say." Hawken could hear the pain in his voice as he continued. "Yes, we planned everything together. She got me here. She's been responsible for everything that I have and now there is no map without her. I have no plan. I have reached the point that I have nowhere to go."

"Henry. She isn't responsible for any of it. You did the work. You got yourself here. She loved you and she helped you decide, but she didn't do the work. You made the choices, Henry. It was you. You don't have to feel like that. I want to help you. Your dad would love to help you, I'm sure of it. You aren't alone here."

"I have to go. I'll call you later, okay?" His voice was sharp and quick.

The line went dead.

∾

HAWKEN SAT on her bed for what seemed like an eternity, staring at a corner of cinderblock painted off-white above Allison's bed. She stared at it until she could no longer see it for what it was. A fuzzy line. A buzzing sound. A buzzing sound under her hand. Her phone.

She quickly picked it up, adjusting her eyes to the now darkened room. Her screen lit up the wrong name. She pulled the covers over her head and lay in the darkness. She had no idea how much time was passing. When she turned her phone off and willed herself to sleep, she felt this sick darkness coil in her belly. Laying in the dark, she silently sang songs over and over in her head, thought about darkness, blackness, oceans, fog. Eventually she found herself carried away into a fitful sleep whereby all her fears had come true.

She dreamed of falling and woke with a start, her covers on the floor next to her.

She dreamed of flying and the thrill of the wind in her face, but when she looked down, she fell. Again, she woke with a start to find herself sweaty in her sheets.

The next time she opened her eyes the light was shining in through her windows. She turned her body towards the wall and threw her pillow over her head.

The room was still and quiet. There were no sounds emanating from either of the side walls, nor from upstairs. It was Saturday. Most everyone wouldn't be returning to school until Sunday after spending the holidays with their families. Hawken was alone. She fought the urge to turn her phone on. If he hadn't called her, she decided she wouldn't be able to handle it. The abyss of not knowing was better than knowing that he chose not to call. She felt as though she had a phantom limb. The ghost of Henry always with her. She could feel him but couldn't see or touch him. He was always just out of reach.

Slowly, the sun grew higher in the sky, and Hawken was still lying in bed. She was devising a plan. A plan that consisted of not caring about Henry, but not staying in bed. So far, it was a twofold plan.

1. Get up
2. Don't think of Henry

That was as far as she got. She failed miserably at both.

"Starting...now," she said, smashing her eyes closed. "Dammit."

Eventually she turned over and went back to sleep. When she woke, the sun was highlighting her closet door, the wall over Allison's bed. She lay there, realizing that it must be after six at night. It was time for a new plan. After fifteen minutes, she'd created one.

1. Don't think of Henry

It was a simpler plan in theory, but she couldn't muster the energy to enact it. She decided that thinking about Henry would be okay as long as she didn't call him. He would have to call her. She'd wait one day. Two days. Five days. Twelve days. Twenty-nine days. Four hundred and seven days.

"Who am I kidding?" She threw her pillow at the closet and got up. One swift motion and there she was, standing. After running to the bathroom to wash her face and brush her teeth, she walked into her room and stared at the phone. There was no movement, no sound, no light. Changing her clothes, she threw her phone into her back pocket and closed the door to her cell.

Hawken quickly found herself sitting in her car, starting the engine. She tried not to think of that day when Henry drove her to the bowling alley. She tried not to think of the things he said to her, sitting right there, in the Taco Bell parking lot. After a few minutes she had decided to drive to the movies. She parked under a light and sat in the cold car for a minute. When she looked down, she realized that she was wearing a black hoodie and black jeans. She smiled to herself, thinking of the past, how it was now catching up to her. As she stepped out of the car, she pulled her hood over her head and walked up to the entrance.

There was a group of five teenagers standing next to the curb. Two were girls, standing on their toes in their short skirts and tight shirts. *They must be freezing*, Hawken thought. She made her way through the groupings of people, couples, dates, finally getting in line. There was a romantic comedy in twenty minutes or an action movie in fifteen. Opting for the action movie, she slipped into the theater and took a seat five rows from the back, two in from the aisle. The theater smelled like popcorn and hot dogs. As she sat there, her hood still over her head, she looked at the rows of people ahead of her. Out of the thirty-seven people, twenty-four were couples, the rest were groupings of males. She was the only person sitting alone.

As the lights started to dim, a couple of guys walked in and turned at the bottom of the stairs, looking up, in Hawken's direction, for seats. She glanced over to her right and noticed that there were three empty seats next to her. She said a silent prayer that they wouldn't sit there. As they made their way up the stairs, she could hear and feel her heart beating like a heli-copter propeller. *What am I doing here?* Mercifully, they stopped, two rows beneath her and climbed over a couple, taking the seats adjacent to them. The previews were starting, and the theater glowed in the reflection. One of the guys took his hat off and Hawken saw his curly hair. He turned to say something to his friend, and she knew it then. It was Sam. *You've got to be kidding me.* Hawken was stunned. She was stuck in her seat, unable to feel her legs. She could only hear the blood pulsing through her ears, see the light flashing across his face as he said something amusing to his friend, who laughed. She caught the moment when he reached his hand in the air, palm facing the screen. She let her eye travel the trajectory of his and saw Henry, making his way up the stairs, three drinks in his hands. Her hands immediately went to her hood, pulling it tightly around her face, the same time shrinking down into her seat. She watched Henry, now only feet away from her, climb across the couple and sit next to Sam, distributing the drinks among them. She was frozen in place, staring. When she finally blinked and looked up, the movie had already started. She twisted in her seat so that she was facing Henry, trying to get a good view of his face. Right then it was paramount to know whether he looked upset, or tired, or, god forbid, happy.

She couldn't read anything from it in the dark. There were only flashes of light, not long enough to get a good look at him. More than once, she noticed that he did look down into his lap. She assumed he was checking his phone but couldn't be sure. She pulled hers out then and turned it on. What if he had left her a message and he was waiting for her response?

It seemed to take centuries to reboot, but finally the screen came alive and she had seven voicemails and two new text messages. Her heart stopped. Then it restarted.

All the voicemails were from Kat. Jason must have said something to Alex. Of course, they had been talking. One message was from her parents. The other text message was from Henry. Henry. She looked at the time. It was seven thirty-nine and the text was from that morning at nine twenty-six. Henry was thinking of her at nine twenty-six. The message was just two words. She didn't read them, just counted. It wasn't three. Just two. Two words. That couldn't be right, could it? She looked at them. *I'm sorry.*

The two words left her gasping for breath. What did it mean? Sorry for what? For acting like he didn't care? For hanging up? For leaving? For not calling? For breaking up with her? Is that what this was? Did he break up with her and text her *I'm sorry*?

She looked over at him. He had his face resting in his hand, leaning on the armrest. She had to get out of there. Did she want to leave? If she left, she wouldn't come back. If she stayed, she was going to torture herself. Hawken stood up. She quickly flew down the stairs, rounded the turn at the bottom and pushed through the doors. Without stopping she made her way through the lobby and out the double doors to the cold, dark night. Then, she ran. She ran through clouds of cigarette smoke, crowds, row after row of cars, until she found hers. She stopped and leaned against it, crying. The minute she heard voices close to her, she opened the door and fell into the seat.

Within twenty minutes she was back in her room, music pumping through her headphones directly into her ears. She was too tired, too heartsick to cry anymore. She fell asleep to the feeling of abandonment.

SUNDAY. Hawken laid in bed as long as she possibly could. She counted swirls on the ceiling and played music. She pulled out her phone and flicked through her pictures. When she scrolled through, she stopped on one that she took of Henry and Rex at Disneyland, both sitting in the model car outside of Mr. Toad's Wild Ride. Rex was holding on to the steering wheel, his eyes turned up towards Henry. He looked genuinely happy. She tried not to focus on Henry in the picture. Then next photo was a close-up of the three of them in their Mickey ears, Henry's arm sticking up, holding the phone to take the picture. Both Hawken and Rex's eyes were pointing in the direction of Henry. She thought of that night under the fireworks. Was it really only three days ago?

It was ten fifteen. Time for a new plan. Today was going to be all about Hawken. She would get out of bed and go running. It had been days since she had run, and she knew that she needed it. Then, she would shower and dress and go skate. Laying there, wrapped in the cocoon of her covers, she felt herself actually smile. Some part of her knew, no matter what happened with Henry, that she'd be okay. She'd live. Actually live. Not as an invisible, but as Hawken Larson. Someone capable of friendship. Of giving herself to other people. Knowing people. Letting them in.

So, she got up.

She ran six point four miles, according to her phone app. She concentrated on leaving all her anger, hurt and emptiness in her Dri-FIT Technology fabrics, pulling them away from her skin, dropping them in tiny splashes on the sidewalk.

After showering, she pulled her skateboard out from under her bed and headed out to her car. She stopped at Qwik Trip on her way and bought a thirty-two-ounce Diet Coke and a bag of Skittles. Dave, the cashier, according to the name tag attached to his shirt, smiled at her and offered a humorous commentary on her lunch. Hawken smiled back. As soon as she pushed the door open, she was thinking of Henry and the smile quickly faded.

The skate park was full of boys of all ages. Feeling slightly deterred, Hawken sat in her car and ate her candy with her music filling up the sound in her head. After a while, she realized that while some people were, in fact leaving, others pulled up in their place. She decided not to waste the day and grabbed her board and walked up to the half pipe. There were fewer people than she thought. Most of the park was full of observers, just watching and taking video of their friends. Hawken dropped in and relaxed.

"HEY, YOU ARE REALLY GOOD." A guy in a black t-shirt and ripped jeans had stopped off to the side and was watching her. He stood in the grassy length along the side of the ramps with his right hand across his forehead, blocking the sun, and his body leaning against his board. "How long have you been skating?"

Hawken stopped and looked over. "A few years. I'm rusty, though. I haven't been out much lately." She turned away from him and asked, "What about you? How long have you been skating?"

He stepped towards her and put out his tattooed arm in front of her. "I'm Jon." Hawken took his hand and shook it, thinking how weird it was that she had shaken so many hands lately. As a kid and teenager most people settle for a nod or a wrist flick. Adults evidently shake hands. She'd have to get used to it.

"Hawken." She responded slowly.

"I've been coming here for years. Probably six or so. I live close by. There's another park in Culver City that is bigger, but more crowded."

"Ah. Nice." She turned to pick up her board and said, "Nice to meet you, Jon."

Hawken walked over to the curb and dropped her board, hopped on, and spent the next twenty minutes practicing grinding on the curb and bench. After a while she grabbed her drink and spread herself out on the grass, letting the sunlight wash over her. A shadow encroached over her, then the sunlight was back to blinding her. Propped up on her elbows, she found Jon sitting next to her, leaning back on his hands, face to the sky.

"Oh, hey. The sun feels good, doesn't it?" Hawken felt like she had been interrupted and was silently hoping that he'd leave.

"Yeah. The thing is..." He turned and looked at her. She could see the sleeve of tattoos running up his arms and the tail of one of them peeking out from his collar. "I was wondering if you want to get something to eat, or a coffee some time?"

Stunned wasn't the right word for how Hawken felt by the question, but the way her heartbeat kicked up to a gallop and she could feel herself start to sweat, she knew she wasn't ready for this. She'd come a long way this year since meeting and giving pieces of herself to Henry. She'd let herself let go of the wheel a bit with Henry, trusting that he'd be there to course correct or guide her to safety. Without him here, though, she felt as though she was on shaky ground again. And she didn't have enough sturdy pieces of herself to continue on the path.

"Jon. Thank you, but I have a boyfriend. I appreciate you asking me, though." She smiled at him, but he was looking ahead, not seeing her gesture.

"Yeah. Sure. Okay." With one swift move, he stood up and grabbed his board and walked off into the parking lot. Hawken looked around and noticed that she was the only one left. Feeling tired and sad, she picked up her board and got into her car. There was only so much she could handle in one day.

Monday morning came and she started the day with a run. She met Kat for coffee on campus before Physics class. They hadn't spoken since Kat left for Thanksgiving. She ended up going to Sacramento with Alex after trying to break up with him the night before. Alex had no idea that she was upset (typical) and told her that they could spend the entire holiday weekend together (with his family).

"Okay, Kat. Spill. Are you guys still together? What happened?" They were sitting on a bench outside of Starbucks, sipping their hot, spiced coffees. Hawken was looking at Kat, but Kat was staring straight ahead, watching a flashback in her head.

Kat smiled, devilishly, then turned to Hawken. "The skinny is this...We are still together. We spent a full day driving up there, just talking. It was unbelievable." She smacked Hawken on the arm. "You were right. We talked about all kinds of things, mostly history. Our life history. I got to know him so much better."

"That's amazing, Kat. How was his family?" She took a sip of her coffee, burning her tongue.

"Insane. As in, lock them up and throw away the key, mad." She shook her head, laughing. "They made me sleep on the couch and flipped when I snuck into Alex's room the last night. He has them thinking that he is this perfect, straight arrow. Then he brought me home." She started laughing so hard Hawken had to hold her coffee so it didn't pour flaming hot lava all over them.

"I don't know that I'd call them insane for not wanting their goody two shoes son sleeping with his freak girlfriend in their house." Hawken laughed and handed Kat her coffee cup back.

"Oh, it wasn't that. They are insane because his dad chased him down the street with a hunting rifle promising to kill him if he got me pregnant." She glanced sideways at Hawken. "That, my friend, was not my idea of a welcome wagon."

At that, they both started cracking up. It felt good for Hawken to laugh like that again, after the weekend that she had.

Kat glanced at her watch. "Hey, we have to go if we are going to Physics on time." They both grabbed their bags and started heading in the direction of the lecture building. "So.... How was your Thanksgiving with Mr. Perfect?"

"It was good. We had a really great time at Disneyland with my family. My parents were really impressed with him. Rex totally fell in love with him." Hawken paused, looking at the sidewalk, then said, "I totally fell in love with him."

"OMG. Did you tell him? You two really are a couple of made-for-each-other-losers. Seriously. This is like the start of some kind of ridiculous Disney movie." She looked at Hawken's face and stopped walking, pulling Hawken by the arm. "So, if you are so in love, what the hell is that face for?"

"Nothing. Let's just get to class. We'll be late." Hawken started walking again, but Kat grabbed her arm and swung her around. Hawken looked around to see if anyone had noticed them. "Kat, leave it alone. Okay?"

"Uh, no. Not okay. What the hell?"

"He broke up with me on Friday. I don't know anything else." She turned and started walking towards their building. Kat grabbed her bag and ran to catch up to Hawken.

"What a bastard. I can't believe this. What do you mean you don't know anything else?"

"I mean, he called and said he needed time and space to think, then he hung up. He texted me Saturday and said, 'he's sorry.'"

"Sorry for what? Leaving? Hanging up? Needing time? What?"

Hawken stopped. She looked into the distance and sighed, then looked Kat in the face. "I don't know. It doesn't matter. It's over. He doesn't want to be with me anymore and I'm trying to accept that. Okay?" Kat nodded, then swallowed. "Can we please not talk about this anymore?" Hawken pulled the door open and walked through it.

For the next few days, Hawken lived in a world that wasn't reality, but was the opposite of fantasy, too. Kat, Alex and Jason all treated her like she was a fragile Faberge egg. If anyone bumped into her in the hall or on campus, they would give their best Mike Tyson impression and leave the innocent bystander running away in fear. No one ever brought up Henry's name or spoke of him at all. They had all decided that it would be best if they still met at the science building like they always did, just so that if Henry happened to walk in, he would see that she wasn't the injured party. "You shouldn't have to change your life just because he's an asshole," they had said. To this, Hawken got angry.

"He isn't an asshole. Okay? I love him. He's just... I don't know. Confused. Just don't say things that you can't take back, okay?"

She saw the three of them give each other looks when she ran to his defense. She watched them silently, blatantly scanning the room for him, just to make sure she didn't accidentally run into him. That was the problem, though. She did want to see him. At least, she thought she did.

At night, they invited her to go out, to stay in and watch movies, to do homework, to study, sleep over, anything that they could think of so that she didn't have any time to herself. Which is just what she wanted. She wanted time to think.

She thought about being underwater and being unable catch her breath. The first instinct would be to panic and feel as though you are dying. That you are drowning with no one to come and save you. And you look left. You look right. No one is there to throw a life preserver. And you think, *this is it. This is the end.* But. You remember something. Wait a minute. You have legs. And arms. And you move them and realize... you can stand up.

That is what this week had given to Hawken. She had the realization that she was okay. Did she love Henry? Yes. Did she miss him more than the tides would miss the moon? Yes. Did she want him back? Of course. But. If none of those things happened, would she be okay? The truth was, in her head she thought she would be. She felt like she would be. On paper, she would be fine. But. She pulled out her phone and flipped through his pictures and started crying, yet again. She wouldn't get over him. He'd given her everything. To never have the chance to talk to him again, to touch him again. It was too much.

So, Thursday night came and took her away again, back to the ocean. Fighting for breath. Fighting to stay afloat.

FRIDAY BROUGHT the worst of it. Morning came early, along with the piercing sunshine through the blinds. Those ridiculous holes in the sides where the cord is woven through were letting the rays shine directly into the mirror, reflecting perfectly into Hawken's swollen eyes. She had already called Kat, begging for the morning off. Today was the day. Today was the Anniversary. Today was the worst day of the year. The end.

Once again, Hawken had a plan. She would miss school to accomplish what she needed to but would be back in time for her Physics lab that afternoon. So. Time to get up.

The plan was this:

1. Run
2. Shower
3. Henry's house
4. James' house
5. Physics lab
6. Who cares?

Once she accomplished the first two tasks, she crossed them off her list. Right. The big one. She had decided that she would take some things over to Henry's house and leave them for him.

She'd written a note for him that she wouldn't allow herself to rewrite and edit and rip her hair out over. One note. No more, no less. It simply said this:

I'm sorry I'm not what you need. I know today is pitch black, but there will be sun again tomorrow.

With love. H.

She took the Mickey Mouse ears along with the picture that her mother brought her of the two of them (well, three of them) and the note, to Henry's house. His car was in the driveway. She immediately looked up at his window. Blinds closed. Henry is closed. She left everything on the doorstep, rang the bell and slowly walked to her car. Without a second glance, she drove away from him.

She pulled over and parked her car in front of a florist, the entrance set back in the corner of a shopping mall. She was sitting in the driver's seat, praying to have the strength to walk inside. She knew that stargazer lilies were Anna's favorite, so she bought a bouquet of them in a glass vase. She wasn't sure if James would be home that day or at school, so she had them ice the water, which would hopefully keep them safe if she were to leave them outside.

When she pulled her car up to the house, she took about seventeen deep breaths before she was able to push through the fog in her mind and open the car door. Halfway up the concrete walk, the front door opened, revealing a small, thin, pale James, with tissues in his hands and his glasses pressed to his forehead. Without a word, he took her into his arms and hugged her.

"I can't believe you came over here. This was really nice of you, Hawken. I so appreciate it." James and Hawken sat at the kitchen table, a box of tissue between them. He hadn't stopped smiling since she got there. "You certainly know how to cheer up an old man."

She picked up her water glass and drank half of it in one

gulp. "I wasn't sure if you would be home today or not, but I have a lab this afternoon that I can't miss, so I thought I'd take a chance and come now. I'm sorry if this is an intrusion." She suddenly felt like maybe she shouldn't have come. After all that had happened, she wasn't sure she'd still be welcomed.

"You are always welcome. Like I said, it is nice to see a friendly face that knows what we are going through." He tilted his head to the side, then asked, "How is Henry today?"

The question hit her like an explosion. "What do you mean? I haven't talked to him in a week." She tightened her face, trying to monitor her expressions. Her skin felt hot and prickly.

"A week? Did something happen?" He was obviously stunned by the sudden impact of the information.

"Henry needed some space, I guess. I haven't heard from him since last Friday. When was the last time you spoke to him?" Now she was worried. What if something had happened to him?

"He came over last night. He didn't mention anything." He was rubbing his chin, as if there was a ghost of a beard there. "I asked him where you were, why he didn't bring you over and he just said you were busy with a test or some such thing." He looked directly at her. "I'm sorry. I'm not sure what to say."

"Don't worry about it. I'm sure he just didn't want to put you in the middle. I'm sorry." Hawken turned instinctively to the door. "Maybe I should go."

"You don't have to leave, but I can understand if you need to. Henry won't come around today. I never see him on the Anniversary. Ever. He always stays inside. Doesn't answer his phone, doesn't talk to anyone. Just give it time, okay?"

"Sure. Thanks for—you know." She stood up and pushed her chair back underneath the table.

"Please, Hawken, come back, okay? Anytime. I feel like you

are part of the family and would love it if you felt that way, too."
He was smiling now.

She felt like she had to get out of there before she burst into
tears. "Thank you so much for that, James. I'm sure I'll see you
soon."

Halfway back to campus, Hawken pulled over, stepped out
of her car, fell to the ground and sobbed. Right there next to a
dumpster behind a Whole Foods store, half a head of wilted
cabbage staring at her.

"HAWK, you look pale. Are you feeling okay?" Kat was about
two inches from her face, her hand on her forehead.

"Fine. Get off." Hawken reached up and batted Kat's arm
away. "Just a First Class Crappy Day all around. I'm fine. I'll be
fine." She gave her a grateful look. "Let's just get this lab done
so that I can get the hell out of here."

They had almost finished their project on rotational inertia,
which had sucked most of Hawken's available brain power
reserves and left her shaky and tired. The only thought that she
could focus on was getting back home and crawling into her
bed, sleeping a sleep of the dead. Quite fitting for the day.

"The radius shouldn't be the center of the mass, but the
radius of gyration, like that of a cylindrical weight." Kat
explained this to the group and Hawken laughed.

"Sorry. It is just funny to hear you say things like that when
you are wearing a Hello Kitty shirt with suspenders."

"It's quite possible that I'd kick your ass right now if you
weren't such a sad sack." Kat squeezed Hawken's shoulder and
proceeded with the equation.

The second that they were finished, Hawken grabbed her
bag and headed for the door. "Hawken, wait." She turned to see
Kat, loping towards her, knee high boots comically shaking

under her. As she approached her, Kat hugged her. "Just promise me that you are okay, please?"

Hawken pulled back and looked her in the eye and replied, "Of course. I'm just tired and a little sad, but I promise I'm fine. I love you for caring. Okay? I'll call you later." Hawken turned and Kat let her go.

As soon as she was out of the building, she heard her name again. She ignored it, wanting to think of nothing but her bed.

"Hawken." This time it was clearer. Closer. Henry. She turned and saw him, walking towards her. He was in jeans and a long-sleeved black shirt, a red baseball cap on his head. His cheeks were pink, flushed. As soon as her brain registered this information, she turned away and started walking, fast.

"Hawken, please. Stop." He reached his arm out to her and when she whipped her head around, he let go. "I'm sorry. Please. Let me talk to you. Please." His face was almost crumpled in agony and Hawken felt her insides turn slick.

"Okay, Henry. Go on, then." She pulled her backpack off her shoulders and rested it against her leg, then folded her arms across her chest, defensively. He watched every move she made as if he was cataloging them for a future date. When she stopped moving, he looked around, finally noticing that they were in of a crowd of people brushing past them, moving towards their classes.

"Not here. Can we go somewhere, just us?" His voice held a pleading tone. His face was creased. He looked like it was all he could do to be standing in front of her.

She sighed, still not sure she wanted to hear what he had to say. Anger was the primary emotion currently floating to the surface. "Fine. We can go to my cell. Allison shouldn't be there."

Without a further look at him, she bent over and swiftly pulled her bag over her shoulders and continued on, as briskly as she could, towards her building. Henry followed, staying just barely behind, out of her immediate peripheral view. He never tried to speak to her, never tried to touch her. She felt strangely like he was her security guard, following her about, waiting to be given instructions.

Once they made it to her building, Henry bolted ahead and pulled the door open for her, then filed in behind her. She took the stairs and Henry stayed three or four down from her the entire way up. Once she'd pushed her room door open, she set her bag on the floor and gestured for him to sit on her bed. As she made her way over to the desk chair, she realized that the walk over had diluted most of her anger and now she actually wanted to hear what he had to say. She wanted to let herself off the hook for being angry at him, but most of all, wanted an answer. Why did he treat her like this? Was this really over?

As she watched him sit on her bed, raking his hands through his hair, she thought about the times before, times when Henry was sitting in her room, the smiles they had mirrored on their faces. She sat, watching him in anguish, and she knew. She knew like she had been struck by lightning. Every cell in her body rang out at the same time. She would love Henry forever. Here he was, visibly in pain. All she wanted to do was put him out of his misery. She asked herself then, *How much am I going to make him suffer?*

As if he could hear her thoughts, he looked up at her. She smiled a forced smile at him, then moved to the bed, sitting down next to him, legs touching.

"I'm so sorry. You were right. About all of it." His voice wavered, but Hawken looked directly into his eyes.

"Henry. Just talk to me, okay?" She took his hand and waited for the rest.

"I spent my entire life planning out everything with my mom. Every trip, every sport, every year of school. It was all on paper. Every summer before school started, we would pull out her computer and she would make me type out goals and plans for the year for school, for sports, for life. This is what I knew.

She was always there, championing me. I had never felt like I was lost. I had direction." He was looking down at their entwined hands but paused to look at her. "Obviously, things changed, but she always supported me. After she died, I kept the plans the same. I would come here to school and major in EE, but that was as far as we had ever gotten. And here I was, now, on my own." He shook his head. "Saying this out loud makes me feel like a child."

"Henry, she was your mom. I get it. She was your world."

"Thanks for that." He looked down and squeezed his fingers around hers. "I've been struggling lately with this. The past couple of years I started thinking that I was living in a tunnel. Life was streaming by me at warp speed, like taillights in the darkness. Zooming past, fading to black. But all I could do was stand still. I kept thinking, what should I do now? It scared me. I would build up this wall around me thinking about it. I always had a next step. After my mom died, I didn't do anything. I sat around. I didn't finish school and graduate. Did you know that? I sat at home and took the GED and somehow this institution took pity on me and accepted me. That's when I decided to turn it around. To make my own way.

"But I went crazy. I went out and partied. I drank and went out with a lot of girls. I was unstable, unreliable. I swear, Hawken, I was a different person. Until the first day I saw you in the lounge—" He stopped talking and looked out the window to the sky. A minute later, he leaned into her and his face was heartbreaking. It made Hawken shudder. His eyes were wild.

"I saw you sitting there, and I kept looking over. My heart was beating out of my chest. I can't explain it. Something changed. I wouldn't have gone over to talk to you, but something was pulling me to. A force. As soon as I touched your hand that day, I couldn't let go. I didn't want to. I went home and couldn't get you out of my head. I drove Sam crazy all week looking for you again. Every time the door to the lounge opened, I would reflexively look towards it in anticipation."

"Henry. You don't need your mom to tell you your choices are the right ones. You have to feel it for yourself. And I happen to know that you have."

"I know. I know that now. I panicked, Hawken. I did. I started thinking about you and how close we were and how it felt meeting each other's families. It all felt so good. So right. But then you started talking about what I wanted to do with my future, and I couldn't help but think of my mom and agonize over these first choices that I'd made without her.

"I'm an idiot. I walked away from the best person in my life. In my world." He looked down at his lap and shook his head, erasing a memory. Then he turned to her. "This is going to sound terrible. So awful. I hope you can forgive me for this, but —" His face was pained, his eyes sad. "I think leaving was the best thing that I could have done. It made me realize what I'd been hiding from. I wasn't living. I was trapped and it took me dealing with this to figure out that I can make my own choices. That I can have things that I choose to want for myself and not feel guilty that she isn't part of it."

Henry had figured this out for himself and he seemed lighter. He held himself straighter. His face was replete with confidence. Hawken hadn't realized that she was zoning out as she thought about Henry and his mother. How easy Anna had made life seem. Hawken could fully understand feeling stuck in a cul-de-sac, unable to push through. To move forward. She had been living in one until she met Anna. Henry had been living in one since Anna. It seemed like somehow, they were now both on a straight, infinite road with nothing standing in the way as far as the eye could see. Now, the question was whether they took the journey together, or went their separate ways. She knew what she wanted. She smiled outwardly.

He laughed, and she looked up. His eyes met hers, searching. She opened her mouth to speak, but he beat her to it.

"I know that I promised you that we would always talk about everything. You were so brave at the planetarium that night." He paused, hands in his hair. "I wanted to be the one person that made you safe. I let you down. I should have come to you with this, but I really do think that I had to do this on my own. I promise that I'll never do that again. I love you more than you can imagine, sweet girl. But I also understand how much I hurt you. I can't bear that I left, but I can't take it back. I'll do anything to earn your trust back. Anything." He pleaded.

"Henry." She smiled at him. He looked up at her through his eyelashes, hesitant, waiting. "Henry. Do you remember what you asked me years ago on a meet bus? You said, 'Tell me something that you know is true.' Do you remember that?"

She watched as the memory flickered in his eyes. "You said something about people being in your life for a reason, right?"

"Yes. I said that there are some people who come into your life that open doors and windows and throw rainbows at you. At the time I was specifically speaking of your mom, but I can honestly say that every person in your family has been that for me. I feel like a metal ring. Like you have all stretched me and shaped me into something so much better and now there's no going back. Especially you. You have given me so many things, Henry, and taught me so much about life and loving someone. I know that I'll be okay now. That I'll be safe." She looked at him and could tell that he wasn't sure where she was headed with this. She loosened her hands from his and stood up.

"Here's the thing, Henry." She looked right into his eyes, willing him to understand. "I can't just let you off the hook. You hurt me. You walked away. You ripped my heart out and took it with you. No contact. No reason. No explanation." She started shaking but pushed through. This was too important. "Now you show up here and I get it. I completely understand why.

Okay? You have to know that, but it's going to take a while for the stitches to heal. I want to trust you, but this impacted us."

Henry nodded, then stood up. "I know. I'm willing to do anything. Is there anything that I can do?" He walked up next to her, six inches away. She could smell his cologne, his shampoo. His eyes were searching hers. *This. Right here. He's suffered enough. I've suffered enough.*

"Tell me something that you are afraid of." She stepped back, six inches away from him.

"Losing you. I'm afraid of losing you." He stayed put, his shoulders sagging.

"What else?" One more step back.

He swallowed. "There is nothing else. I could handle anything else." His voice was now a whisper.

"Promise me that you will never do this again." She retreated one foot closer to the door.

He looked at her. Or directly through to her, like he had opened a porthole into her and stepped through. She felt ethereal, empyrean. "I promise that I'll never hurt you again. Believe me when I say I love you. I've seen what it is like without you and I can't do it. I am willing to start from the beginning if that is what it takes to trust me again. I'll do anything. I love you. I love you."

Hawken closed her eyes and took a deep breath. In that instant, she saw the Henry that bought her Mickey Mouse ears. She saw the Henry who carried her to his car, bleeding. She saw the Henry who walked into the bathroom at his father's house and saved her from herself. She saw the Henry who gave her a family.

When she opened her eyes, she saw the Henry with a broken heart. With a sad, pleading face. With so much love bursting inside of her, she closed the distance by jumping up, arms spread, right onto him, sending both of them onto the floor, a tangle of limbs. She laughed at the shock on his face and kissed him until it was gone. "I missed you," she said, brushing the hair from his forehead. "I missed this face." She kissed his right eye. "I missed these eyes." Then the left eye. "I almost stopped breathing without these lips, Henry." She kissed them. "Don't take them away from me again."

18

"I am not surprised to see you both here, together. I'm thrilled, but not surprised." James had opened the front door and offered Henry and Hawken the same kind of smile that was enough to supply power to a small lamp store. "Come in," he said, his arms pulling them in the door by their shoulders.

"We just stopped by to make sure that you were okay." Henry looked sideways at Hawken and smiled. "I know it has been a rough couple of days, Dad." Henry turned and held Hawken's jacket as she slid her arms out of the corduroy sleeves. He hung hers on the metal hook by the door, then peeled himself out of his, placing it on top.

"I'm fine. I keep thinking that it will start getting easier every year that passes, but it hasn't. Although," he turned and gestured at Hawken, "this one certainly made it more bearable this year. Did you know that she came over here with flowers on Friday, Henry?"

Henry turned to her and said, "Seriously?" With a crooked smile, he kissed her quickly on the mouth, then pulled back and said, "That was awfully thoughtful of you, sweet girl."

James walked down the hallway into the kitchen after offering drinks. He looked a little lighter in his step as well.

Hawken put her hand on Henry's shoulder and pulled him down to her, kissing him on the mouth. "I love you. I love your dad and was worried about him. I just came over here for a few minutes." She let him go and looked down at his feet, clad in Star Wars Vans. She laughed. "You know I went to your house, too, right?"

She watched Henry wince, then he said, "Yes. I have your hat. I'm giving it back to you."

"What about the picture?"

"I'm keeping that. It is already on my wall. I had to do some minor cropping and adjusting, but I'm keeping it." He smiled wide.

They walked into the kitchen and sat down at the table as James was clearing away papers from its center onto the spare captain's chair.

Henry looked at him quizzically and asked, "What is all of that, Dad?"

James brushed the air with his hand and said, "Oh, I was just going through some of your mother's things this weekend." Hawken watched him glance at her, then at Henry. He continued, "I actually have something for you that I think it's time you look at." He pushed back in his seat and started rifling through the papers in the box. Henry looked at Hawken, then stood up and walked over to the box.

He put his hand on his father's shoulder and said, "What is it? I'll help you."

James shook his head. "Henry, just go sit down for a minute. I have it here. It was in this pile. Just give me a second." Henry returned to his seat, wide eyed, and peered over at Hawken who was trying not to intrude. She smiled back at Henry, focused on what James was doing. He finally pulled out an envelope, its flap hanging open, folded at a scalene angle. He smiled at them collectively and set the envelope down in front of him as he resumed his place at the table. He sighed, then said, "Hawken, you remember that my wife had a sort of sixth sense?" He looked at her, waiting for a response.

Hawken looked sideways at Henry, then answered, "Yes, she told me that. She used to ask me questions about my family and tell me things that she was sure would happen." Hawken looked up and smiled, then said, "And I'm pretty sure that they all did." Henry smiled at her, then gave his father an interrogative look.

"What do you have, Dad?"

James let out a short, muffled laugh. "Henry, you never did have any patience. Okay." He said, fingering the envelope, then handing it over the table to Henry. "I am not sure if you will want to read this alone or with me here. It is a letter from your mother to you."

Henry's head flicked up from the envelope to his father's face. "What?"

"She wrote this letter to you about a week before...the accident. We had a conversation about what is in this letter and I told her that I thought she should wait to tell you. It was about one of her visions. You know how she had them all the time? That was why she always thought it so important that you write up your goals every year. She wanted you to keep in mind what you wanted for yourself so that if she ever saw or felt something different for you, she could let you decide what you wanted, always knowing and reminding you of what your first choice was."

"That's why we did that? That was why she had me write out everything? I always thought she was worried that I wouldn't be able to make good choices alone." Henry looked down at the envelope in his hands.

"Henry," James continued, leaning into the table, "she trusted you to make the decisions that you wanted for your life.

She was worried that you would always change them, based on what she saw, and she didn't want that. She trusted you more than she did her visions."

Henry looked at Hawken and took her hand in his. "Dad, you've read this?"

"Yes. She and I talked about what she saw for you at the time and decided that you shouldn't know until the time was right. Read the letter, Henry." James nodded at the envelope in Henry's left hand. "It's fine. I promise you. There isn't anything in there that hasn't already happened, which is why I waited until now to have you read it."

"What do you mean, 'hasn't already happened?'" He looked at James with skepticism.

James returned the look with mirth. "Just read the letter, Henry." James stood up and leaned over the table. "I'm going to give you two some privacy." Hawken looked at him like he was locking her into a cell and throwing away the key. He smiled at her and said, "You should stay. You are in the letter, too." And with that, he left the room.

Henry looked at Hawken. Hawken looked at Henry. They shared the same look of disbelief. Hawken took her hand back and said, "Henry. I can leave you alone to read this. Really."

He sat for a moment regarding the letter, then turned to her and said, "If this is about us, you should be here." He moved his chair closer to hers and looked her in the eye, then pulled a single sheet of paper from the envelope. He slowly unfolded the page like he was opening the Declaration of Independence, then laid it flat on the table, running a finger down on the seams. He looked at Hawken, then asked, "Should I read it out loud?"

"Henry, this is your letter."

He grabbed her hand and held it on his lap, then picked up the paper in his left hand and began reading to the room.

. . .

SWEETHEART,

I know that this is going to sound insane, like many of the visions that I've had. We've joked about more than a few, you and me. This is different. I know it is. I keep telling myself that it doesn't make sense. I have second guessed myself. But. You know I've always had this sixth sense. This intuition. I have had this feeling about her. About you. I've seen it in my dreams, and I've felt it when I'm wide awake. I know that you are to be together. I know this. I'm sorry if this is too much for you right now. You know that I'm not a very spiritual person. We've not taken you to church regularly. We don't say prayers unless tragedy strikes. Listen to me, my little sparrow. I've prayed about this. I have. She is exquisite. You are remarkable. It's going to happen. I feel it in my bones. You are both so in love. More than even your father and me. It's astounding. The love between you is palpable. It will stop time. I have the sense that I won't be there to see it. I don't know why, but I have this feeling that this is going to happen without me. This is why it's so important that you hear me right now. I've gotten to know her myself. I won't tell you how or why. You'll find out in good time. I love her. I do. You will see her one day and you'll feel it too. She will make you so happy. She will show you what it is to be loved and to love back. You will make her happier than she ever imagined she could be. I know how this sounds. I've told this to your father and he thought it best if you didn't know, but I feel that you should hear this, so I'm writing you this letter in hopes that I will be around when this happens. Should I not be, I hope that your father will give this to you when the time is right. I love you. Always listen to your heart and don't think too much. Go and find your hawk and fly away together.

Henry set the paper on the table and stared at it, like it would disintegrate if he turned away. Hawken squeezed his hand after a minute but remained quiet. She couldn't wrap her head around what she was feeling. How could this be real? How could Anna have written those words years ago and known? Was it true? They had only been together for a few months. Had the full weight of her words already happened?

As she sat there, washed away in thought, she saw Henry move his head slightly to the side. This was such a personal revelation for him, but amazingly, she was so connected as well. She felt like she was fading in and out of a picture. Like in the movie 'Back to the Future' when things started changing and the siblings in the picture started fading. Hawken felt like she was fading, then returning to the scene in full color. At that moment, she tried to hold on to what she was feeling. What the words meant. They meant everything, didn't they? Anna had loved her. That need that she had filled wasn't one sided. Hawken finally felt like she had given Anna something back.

Henry let go of her hand and pushed his chair back, scraping the wooden legs on the tile floor. Hawken cemented herself in place, unable to read his thoughts or movements.

He walked over and pulled out her chair, making the same screeching sound on the floor. She winced but Henry took her by the hands and pulled her up, wrapping his arms around her, burying his face in her neck, his nose resting against her jugular. Hawken returned the embrace, pulling him as close to her as she could.

After a minute, Henry let out a long, slow breath that he'd been holding in. He whispered into her neck, "I love you so much. I can't believe that my mom wrote all of that." He pulled back and looked straight at her. "Are you okay? How are you feeling? This is weird, right?"

Hawken laughed. It felt good. "I don't know. It's a lot to take in." He nodded. "I think it is both amazing and scary."

"Why scary? I don't want this to be scary, sweet girl."

"Scary might be a strong word. Just... a lot of pressure. All of those things that she said." She shook her head and saw the worried expression on Henry's face. "I love you more than anything, Henry Burton Lewis. It's not that. It's just—"

He lifted her face to his and kissed her urgently. He whispered, "I love you more than everything and that's all that matters right now. Okay?" He kissed her again. "There's no pressure. I promise you that right now, this...standing here, holding you like this, this is enough. I just want to be with you. You are everything to me. We are still young, Hawken. I want to finish school and I want you to finish school and do the things that are important to you. This doesn't change anything, okay?" She nodded, cracking a smile. "Part of me feels like this has already happened anyway. You have changed me. You have shown me so much about loving someone and I can honestly say that I'm the happiest that—"

She kissed him. She kissed him to show him what she was feeling, and she kissed him to tell him how happy he made her. And when she pulled away, they were both smiling at each other like full on jack-o-lanterns lit up for the night. "Henry. I just don't want this letter to be the baseline, the reason for us. I want to feel all of it. The good and the bad. Right now. This." She squeezed his body tighter to her own. "We chose each other, even without this and I'm going to keep choosing you."

19

"And the Pleiades burn a bright blue color. You can find the cluster by searching first for Orion's belt, then moving up and over." Henry drew a line in the sky with his laser pointer from Orion to the cluster of bright stars just over and above it. "See, here they are." He turned his head to find Hawken watching him, not the red dot on the ceiling. He smiled. "Did you hear anything that I just said?"

She laughed. "No. Sorry." She was concentrating all her energies on not biting his chin while he spoke. It was more difficult than she would have thought. She was also thinking about the way his chest moved up and down when he took a breath. The way his hands made her feel like she was safe and home. She wanted to feel them in hers.

They had finished their last week of classes for the semester and had the weekend to cram before finals started on Monday. Henry decided that they needed a well-deserved break from the science lounge, and they drove out to the planetarium, accepting the key once again from Fred, and had a picnic on the center of the floor, surrounded by stars. Henry had lit up the night sky and created the illusion of shooting stars when he was in the control room.

Now they were laying on the carpet, Hawken's head in the crook of his arm, Henry animatedly waving around his laser pointer.

"Tell me what you were thinking about then," he asked, kissing the top of her head.

"No way."

"Really?"

"Really."

"Hawken. Please?" He adjusted himself so that he was on his side, looking at her.

"I was thinking of things that I would like to do to you, Henry." A sly smile played on her face.

He raised an eyebrow. "Oh?"

She punched him in the arm, and he fell backwards faking a mortal wound. She was unsure of how she got here, to this place where she felt open and seen. She was sure that it had everything to do with Henry, though.

"Henry." He looked over and smiled.

"Yes, sweet girl?" He picked up her hand in his and started tracing shapes in her palm.

"Will you come home with me over Christmas break? To Phoenix?" She asked, slightly embarrassed, for no good reason.

He grinned at her, then laughed a short laugh. "Finally," he said, sitting up. "If you didn't ask me soon, I was thinking about stowing away in your luggage." He reached over and kissed her, slow and sweet. "Of course, I will come with you. I can't imagine being apart from you for that long anyway."

She smiled, then said, "There's a catch, Henry."

His grin reappeared. "I really do have to stow away in your luggage?"

"No." She picked his hand up again. "I told my parents that

we would leave here next week after finals, but we would be coming back the day after Christmas."

He tilted his head at her, a questioning glance. "Why would you want to come back that early?"

She was looking down at his hand when she said, "Well, I thought we could spend some time with your Dad, Henry." She looked up then, and said, "I'd really like to, if that's okay." She was smiling a wide-open smile at him.

This time, when he pushed her down to the floor and put his weight on top of her, she laughed and pulled his face down, an inch from hers. "I love you, Henry." He kissed her then.

"My dad is going to be so happy, sweet girl. He loves you, you know. This will make his day. You are the nicest, sweetest girl in the world."

"What do you want for Christmas this year, Henry?" She was whispering into his hair, her lips touching the curling strands above his ear.

"I have everything I want right here, right now." He answered as Hawken rolled her eyes and let out a loud groan.

"Henry. Seriously."

"I am serious. When we are together, I want for nothing." He rolled over, back onto the carpet next to her and rested on his arm, his hand propping up his head. "What do you want, Tony Hawk?" He asked, his face a flurry of happiness.

"Hmmmm. I want you to tell me where you see yourself in five years." She had mirrored his pose, face resting on her hand, facing him, all smiles.

"Well, I hope to graduate and get a job using all of my impressive skills as an engineer. I'd really love to be able to don a laser pointer, but that would just be a perk at this point." He smiled and reached his hand over to her face, tracing her lips with his finger. "Every vision of my future, Hawken, has you in it." He swallowed. "Both the immediate and the long-range plans." He gave her a look that bordered on worry and concern. She knew that he worried he might have said too much.

She smiled widely and said, "So, it sounds like we have the same vision in mind then." She pushed him down this time, then put her full body weight on his. "I can't imagine spending any part of my life without you, Henry." She bent down to kiss him, but he stopped her with his hand.

"Don't, then. You don't have to. I love you so much. I want to make a life with you, Hawken." He was searching her face, looking for the panic. There wasn't any. "I know we are young. You are young. I just want you to know how I feel so there isn't any question. I'm in this." He pushed a loose strand of hair behind her ear. "I want to be your family. I want to take care of you. Always."

"How did I get to be the luckiest girl in the world, Henry?" She bent over and kissed him then, shooting stars tracing across the sky above them.

"Have I told you about the Corona Borealis constellation?" he asked, a smirk on his face.

"I don't think so," she responded hesitantly, waiting for a story.

"It's also known as the Northern Crown. The story goes that the king of Crete built a labyrinth to contain a ferocious Minotaur. It was crafted so well that no one could ever find their way out of the maze alive. Every year, the king chose twelve beautiful, young people to be food sacrifices to the beast. The king's daughter Ariadne fell in love with one of the young sacrifices and offered her help if he would take her with him when he escaped, and they could be together forever."

"Wow, that's utterly romantic, Henry. So, did they escape?"

Henry chuckled, sending vibrations along Hawken's entire side before he continued.

"Well, she held a piece of thread that unwound through the maze as he found and slayed the Minotaur, and then followed the line back out."

"So, he slayed the dragon and saved the Princess?"

"WELL, yes, but fate intervened. Turned out the young sacrifice was kind of a jerk and he left her and went back home. Alone, she met Dionysus and *they* fell in love. He commissioned a crown for her with seven of the most beautiful jewels, eventually placed in the sky when she died. And that's why the seven stars are called The Northern Crown."

"I love that." Hawken smiled.

"I THINK we've had our own amazing story, Hawken. Maybe one day there will be scientists looking up at the stars and see a constellation shaped like a bird in a new part of space, never seen before by telescopes or satellites, and we'll be part of an eternal story for generations."

"Any thought about you and me and generations is all I need, Henry."

A NOTE FROM THE AUTHOR

I am so very grateful for each and every person who takes the time out of their busy life to read the words I arrange together. I do it for you. I do it for my characters. Their stories need to be told and I always do my best to ensure I give them the best that I can.

I love hearing from each and every one of you. Please reach out and leave a review on Goodreads, Amazon, Bookbub, etc. You can also find me hanging out on Twitter.com under the handle @forgottenastro2 or on Facebook as Ash Knight.

ACKNOWLEDGMENTS

Creating a new world takes a lot of time and effort and is something that can't be done alone. I am absolutely humbled by the people who have offered me support and friendship, as well as guidance and safe passage into the writing community. It's the difference between success and failure, and I'm one of the luckiest space walkers to have been able to tether my suit to such an inviting group.

Ben, Steve, Halo, Gideon, Drew, and **Ethan.** Oh, my heart. You were the first to tell me I had something here that was worth looking into. I'm so grateful for your lifting words, slaps on the back, and ridiculous notes in my drafts.

I'm also desperate to thank so many of my friends who have offered support and promotion of my writing in general, including Rory, Dean, M.E., Mario, TT, Nero, Claire, Migs, Crow, Tai, my fleet of friends in the Nic Cage Street Team and so many more. Thank you for having my back, believing in me, and helping me believe in myself.

www.ingramcontent.com/pod-product-compliance
Lightning Source LLC
Chambersburg PA
CBHW022202170626
46807CB00005B/2307